MR. ROOSEVELT MEETS THE SIOUX —HEAD-ON

Ben Foster and Teddy Roosevelt had been riding along the edge of the prairie north of the Elkhorn Ranch, and Teddy was expounding on the subject of Indians. Ben frowned. Sometimes the young horse wrangler wondered if his boss and former classmate was a bit soft in the head.

"Sure there are good Indians, Teddy, but you haven't met many of them yet."

As they rode up a slight rise and came onto a broad plateau, ten Indians suddenly appeared. The moment they saw the white men, they whipped their rifles out of their slings and kicked their horses into a full run, whooping and screaming, brandishing their weapons in the air.

"Sioux," Ben said, reining up. "Get down."

Roosevelt followed Ben's lead, dismounting and standing with the horse between himself and the onrushing warriors.

Ben had wondered how Roosevelt would handle danger, and now he had the answer.

The bespectacled Eastern dude stood firm, muttering something like, "Bully challenge," as the Indians came within rifle range . . .

The Fol   The Far Islan dus

THE
WRANGLERS

Lee Davis Willoughby

A DELL/JAMES A. BRYANS BOOK

Published by
Dell Publishing Co., Inc.
1 Dag Hammarskjold Plaza
New York, New York 10017

Dell ® TM 681510, Dell Publishing Co., Inc.

ISBN: 0-440-09838-6

Printed in the United States of America

First printing—December 1982

1

BEN Foster rinsed the tin cup and plate, stowed them in the bag and stretched out on top of his bedding roll. Overhead the stars made brilliant pin pricks in the black bowl of sky. A meteor streaked across the sky, and off in the distance a coyote yapped his disapproval.

"You see that, Ben?" said Davey Morton.

"Uh-huh. Pretty, wasn't it? That's something you don't get to see very often in a city. Too much smoke."

"I purely love watchin' them shootin' stars. Course, it ain't much fun when you're workin' beefs. I 'member one night down in Wyoming when we was movin' a trail herd of about five thousand. Them beefs was spooky as all hell. It was in the second night watch when a couple a them things streaked through the sky so close I thought I coulda reached out an' grabbed one. Afore I could blink my eyes,

5

them beefs was up an' runnin' like the devil hisself was after 'em. Took us damn near two hours to get them critters under control."

Ben waited, knowing that Davey Morton wasn't finished. After a pause and a heavy sigh, Davey continued.

"Lost two men in that stampede. One got trampled so's there wasn't nothin' left of him an' his pony but a bloody splotch on the trail. Th' other one was gored bad, an' died afore midday."

Another meteor streaked across the sky, then a third. Both were small and faint, but clear against the moonless night. "Damn glad we ain't movin' beefs," Davey said again.

"Cows, horses, it's all the same to me," Ben Foster said. "None of them let me get enough sleep."

Because he had the second watch, Ben crawled into his sleeping bag, adjusted his hat for a pillow, and was soon asleep.

He'd no more than gotten his eyes closed, it seemed, when he dreamed he heard thunder, and the thought ran through his mind that it couldn't be thunder on a clear night like this. Maybe it was a meteor streaking close by.

Suddenly he was wide awake, pulling on his boots as he realized the sound was pounding hooves. Davey was only a few feet behind him as he reached his picketed horse, swinging into the saddle. They raced to the north, after the scattering herd of horses, and over the thundering hooves on the prairie they heard the sound of two gunshots.

Muttonhead's close to the point and turning them, Ben thought, seeing the herd veer to the left. A moment later he heard another gunshot, but far to the right of where Muttonhead should be, and he knew what it was that had spooked the horses.

"This way!" he heard Davey shouting, and he veered off to the right, his face stinging from the flying dirt kicked up by the stampeding horses.

By the time the herd had slowed and Ben was able to reach the point to keep them turning, Muttonhead was moving the point into a circle while Davey tightened up the rear. In a matter of minutes which seemed like hours, they had the horses under control, and Muttonhead Jenkins told them what had happened.

"Fust I thought it was Injuns again, but when one of 'em started hollerin' and yappin' to spook the herd, I knowed it wasn't."

"Wonder how many they got away with," Davey muttered, his breath coming in short gasps.

"No tellin'," Muttonhead snorted, wiping his face with the sleeve of his jacket. "More'n a couple. Near's I could make out, they was about four riders, mebbe five."

Davey Morton swore under his breath. "I told the boss we needed more than three of us, but he says ain't nobody bothered us on the trail yet."

"And we always had six or seven make the trip," Ben said with disgust. "Did Fowler think there weren't any rustlers this close to Fort Keogh?"

"Reckon he thinks they's all over t' home." Muttonhead Jenkins took a long swallow from his canteen, wiped his face on his sleeve again, and said, "Reckon we done got off lucky. If them thieves'd knowed we was only three 'stead a six, they mighta killed us all and stole the hull damned bunch."

"Yeah," Davey agreed. "Well, this is the last drive, and we'll be finished by tomorrow afternoon."

Finished. Ben considered how final it sounded. Finished with this act. Time to raise the curtain on the next act. What happens in Act Three? Too bad the great Greek dramatist Aeschylus hadn't written the play, although he could have had a grand time with a continuing tragedy called The Life and Times of Ben Foster.

2

THE three dusty riders moved the herd of horses into the holding pens at Fort Keogh and waited while the veterinarian checked them one at a time. As he gave each horse as close an examination as the animal's wild nature would permit, he pronounced, "Sound!" and the chute opened as two enlisted men moved it into the corral.

"Fine looking string, Foster," said the lieutenant keeping the tally book.

"Thank you, Sir," Ben Foster replied. "Sorry it's the last of them."

"We are, too. I understand your boss has sold out, planning to move up to Canada."

Davey Morton nodded. "Gettin' fed up with Injuns, rustlers an' hungry wolves."

"Indians a problem over in Dakota Territory?" the young lieutenant asked, his eyebrows raised in surprise. "I thought things were pretty quiet now."

Ben Foster grimaced. "The Sioux and Cheyenne steal a beef or two because they're hungry. And they're hungry because white hunters have killed off the buffalo herd. I can't say as I blame them for grabbing a few head now and then. But they only take what they need to eat; they're not out to build up a bank account, the way the rustlers are."

The lieutenant nodded. The agent at the Crow Reservation had been badgering the Army constantly to get extra provisions for his charges.

"Wolves are a big problem, too," Davey Morton said. "And for the same reason. They ain't got no more buffalo to work on, so they work on the horses and cattle that've replaced 'em."

The last of the horses was moved into the corral, and the lieutenant said, "One hundred eighty-three. How many did you start with?"

"Two seventeen," Foster replied. There was a faint edge of weariness in his voice. "Lost three of them when they piled over the edge of a coulee in a rainstorm. One got bit by a rattlesnake. Couple of them picked off by Cheyennes, and the others stampeded by rustlers just this side of the border. We don't have any idea how many they got, or how many of them simply got away from us. Thirty four is a mighty big number to lose, though."

It took less than twenty minutes to complete the paperwork in the finance office, and the three wranglers were on their way into Miles City. Each of the three was lost in his own thought on the two-mile ride, and nobody spoke. Suddenly Muttonhead stood up in the stirrups, pointing to the south along Pumpkin Creek.

"That there's a far-size herd."

Ben's blue eyes squinted across the valley. "Must be close to a thousand of them."

They sat their horses and watched for a few min-

utes, then Davey spat in disgust. "Longhorns, mostly.
Orneriest beasts on the face of the earth!"

"Yeah," Ben agreed, "but they're big, and the bigger they are the more they're worth."

"Hell, ain't worth nuthin' iffen they freeze in this
here country," Muttonhead muttered. "I come up
from Arizony pushin' a herd about thet size. Boss
man I worked for thought he was gonna make a
fortune with 'em, what with all this long grass
'stead a sage. We brung eight hunnert head, an' by
the time them warm-country critters felt a Dakota
winter, he lost all but sixty-three."

"Four years ago?" Davey asked. When Muttonhead
nodded, Davey said, "I like to froze my ass off that
year, too. Thank God I been here long enough now
to like cold weather."

"You must like it," Ben said as they turned and
rode on, "since you're thinking of going on up to
Canada with the boss."

"Yeah. Sorry you two ain't comin' with us. We
been through a lot together in the last three years."

"Yeah," Ben laughed, his blue eyes twinkling. "Like
the first time we rode into Miles City. Still called
Milestown. Remember that wild yarn Muttonhead
gave us about the bear in the stockade?"

"Dammit, I done told it true!" Muttonhead ex-
ploded. "Ask anybody. Sheriff Irvine kept a bear
in the stockade with his prisoners. Armed guards at
each a the corners up on watchtowers, an' 'is pet
bear chained t' the gate."

All three turned their heads to where the new
three-story brick courthouse stood. It was a mag-
nificent building that replaced the old log hut which
had served as the first courthouse in Miles City.
Behind it the ground had been cleared of the high
stockade that once surrounded the old log jail. Miles
City had changed drastically in three years. Neat

frame buildings were rapidly replacing the old log structures, and brick stores and homes were to be seen everywhere.

They dismounted at the telegraph office, where Ben sent a telegram ahead to report the delivery of the horses. While he was taking care of that, Davey went to the bank to handle the financial details. Muttonhead, having nothing better to do, crossed the street to the Cottage Saloon to get rid of some of the trail dust. It was a system they had used on each of the five trips they had made to Miles City.

Davey joined Ben and Muttonhead in the saloon, drained a mug of beer and told them he'd changed his mind about staying over for the night.

"Might's well set Montana behind me. It's still early enough I can make it most of the way back if I push it a little." He counted out two stacks of silver and gold coins, pushing them across the table to Ben and Muttonhead. "I guess that's it," he said, rising. "Happy trails, fellers."

Without another glance he strode out of the saloon, and was on his way east to the Dakotas.

Muttonhead nursed another swallow of beer. "You still thinkin' on goin' back to Dakoty?" he asked.

Ben nodded. "You?"

"Nope. I allus had me a notion to see the Pacific. Reckon the best way's t' head west. Fac' is, I found a feller takin' a freighter west tomorrow, an' signed on as a brakeman."

Ben sat lost in his thoughts for a few minutes. It was strange how the three of them could spend more than three years together sharing the same food, the same bunkhouse on the ranch, work side by side in all kinds of weather, save each other's necks in God knows how many scrapes, and then have each of them go off in different directions this casually. It was probably better this way, though, since farewell speeches never did anybody any good.

But it was one of the things he'd learned to live with since his younger brother had been snatched from the family at the age of six, crushed between a wagon and the loading dock of his father's factory. He'd learned how quickly cholera could take a sweetheart from him, leaving nothing but an aching void. He'd learned it again in the year he spent at Harvard, when a classmate who'd had too much to drink fell from a third-story window and died almost at Ben's feet.

The lesson was repeated when he was summoned home shortly after beginning his sophomore year, and he learned that his father and mother had both died in a fire that levelled the family home in Boston.

And no matter how bad things got, he knew that Old Aeschylus had another act written and ready to produce. If nothing else, the old playwright was teaching Ben Foster that it was unwise to attach himself so closely to anything or anybody that it was going to cause him grief to turn around and walk away. Or have it snatched away from him suddenly. Like Nell, who'd died so young. Like his parents. Like Eva, back in Mandan—blonde, passionate Eva, shot dead in her mother's restaurant by a drunken cowhand. Like . . . What the hell, he thought, the old boy's still writing my life story.

Muttonhead left the saloon to camp out with the drover for an early start, and Ben toyed with the idea of spending a night with one of the box rustlers. It had been a long time since he'd enjoyed the company of a dance hall beauty, and then it was only an illusion of pleasure, for most of them were in a hurry to hustle up another customer. That wasn't Ben Foster's style.

He had a third beer, then put his horse in a stable. He walked to the Macqueen House where he luxuriated in the first hot bath he'd had since his last trip to Miles City with a string of horses for the cavalry. After shaving, he put on the clean suit he always carried for his stopover at the Macqueen House, and went into the wood-paneled dining room that was frequented by the cattle barons and railroad officials. Working cowboys seldom went to the Macqueen, since the establishment frowned on working clothes in the public dining room.

After a supper of pan-fried trout and mounds of fresh vegetables, topped off by a slab of Bavarian chocolate torte, he stepped into the bar for one drink, listening to the quiet conversation around him. Many of the faces he recognized, although he didn't know the men personally. There was Granville Stuart, the old coot who'd led a vigilante group through the mine fields to bring some "law and order" to Montana. Big Charlie Bowen and that oily little Frenchman, the Marquis de Mores, were in a heated discussion with Stuart, talking about the ever-growing problem of rustlers. Hell, Ben Foster had felt the effects of rustlers, too, but if any of those three had lost their stock in the same proportions, it would have taken four or five trains to move the animals.

He finished his drink, and was stretched out on the soft bed in his room by the time it was dark. He mildly cursed the thin partitions between the rooms, embarrassed as he heard the happy voices of a cowboy and a pair of giggling girls in the next room.

He was in no hurry to get back to Dakota Territory, and spent some time talking with ranchers in eastern Montana to see if he was going to go back

to Dakota or move a bit farther west. Certainly there
were plenty of opportunities for him to work here,
since the cattle industry was mushrooming here, and
a few of the ranchers were beginning to feel the
need for more experienced horse wranglers.

Three days later he rode through the beginnings
of a new town that was springing up on the west
bank of the Little Missouri. Medora. Another of the
Marquis de Mores' grandiose schemes. He didn't
like the attitude of the people in the settlement across
the river, and decided to build a new town which
he was naming after his wife. Like most of the
things de Mores was pouring money into, Medora
would probably be doomed to failure as a town.

Ben took the ferry across the river to Little Missouri. How the people of Little Missouri made a
living was more than he could tell. There were the
inevitable whorehouses and a couple of saloons, the
general store run by a Swede who could regale his
listeners by the hour with dirty stories told in a
thick dialect, a railroad station, and a ramshackle
edifice with a crude sign telling the world it was
the Pyramid Hotel. His gaze swept the landscape,
as it did every time he rode through Little Missouri,
but there were still only a few houses dotting the
barren landscape.

The railroad station was its only hope for sur-
vival, and even that was debatable, given the senti-
ment of the people of the town, who simply didn't
give a damn for such things as town governments,
law and the necessity of paying a lawman. So many
towns had sprung up along the railroad as potential shipping heads for cattle, and then were almost
ghost towns a year later. Merchants who had followed the tracks were hopeful, and carried a huge
supply of provisions with them, but unless they were

nomadic by nature, they could as easily starve as anyone else while waiting for a town to collect enough residents to catch on.

Miles City had started that way. But Miles City had the advantage of Pumpkin Creek, the Tongue River and Sunday Creek joining the Yellowstone in the valley where Fort Keogh was located. There were also three stage lines converging on the town, and business along Main Street was brisk with travelers. Little Missouri was nothing but a collection of shacks where the Little Missouri River crossed the stage line. Now the Northern Pacific Railroad was bringing more people and business than the stage line, and some of the business it brought was suspect by everyone. There were land promoters enough in the area, but only the hunting guides (most of whom had previously earned a living as hide hunters) seemed to have any semblance of regular employment. Even that was sporadic enough, for it wasn't every train that brought wealthy men from the East or from Europe to hunt the game that was so rapidly disappearing from the country.

Ben led his horse around to the stable behind the hotel, ordered it fed and watered, intending to have a hot supper and then move on before camping for the night.

The Pyramid Hotel was a far cry from the Macqueen House. In Miles City the Macqueen House boasted a menu that was equal to that of the Palmer House in Chicago, with a selection of at least fifteen meat, game, fowl and fish entrees. The Pyramid Hotel's dining room offered a total of four entrees, one of them with a French name that disguised the fact that it was one of the old standby gut-fillers on the roundup—sonuvabitch stew.

He had just ordered a slab of steak when he heard the train puffing into town with a shriek of its whis-

tle. Four men walked into the dining room just as
he began to carve his way into the two pound slab
of meat.

One he would have recognized anywhere. The
Marquis de Mores, the Frenchman who was married to the daughter of a wealthy New York banker,
and who had more schemes to make everybody rich
than a coyote had fleas. Two of them looked like
any other Easterners coming out to have a crack at
hunting in the Bad Lands. While their clothing
wasn't the rough, dirty denim and leather jackets
commonly seen, neither was it the neat dark business suit of a businessman on vacation. Work clothes,
honest work clothes.

The third one had on a getup that almost beg-
gared description. The fringed buckskin jacket and
flashy boots spelled "greenhorn" a mile away, as
though it had posed for half the covers of the dime
novels that were flooding the East. The Stetson hat
with its feathers wouldn't have been worn by most
white men, and by very few Indians. Under the
brim of the hat peered a pair of near-sighted eyes
squinting through iron-rimmed spectacles, looking
something like a trout out of water. The reddish-
brown mustache gave the appearance of a floor
broom, and under that showed a line of heavy
white teeth.

Ben almost choked to keep from laughing, and
then as the men sat down at a table near his and
the dude removed his hat, he knew why the face
was so familiar. He washed down his chunk of steak
with a swallow of coffee, wiped his mouth on his
napkin and walked over to the table.

"Howdy," he said to the costumed man. "It's been
a long time, hasn't it?"

The slender man squinted through his glasses, his
face at first blank, then smiling tentatively.

"I'm sorry, but I don't believe I can place you." The voice was high-pitched, almost squeaky. "You do look familiar, though."

"I should. The last time we met was at Harvard in seventy-six. You managed to knock me out in the semi-finals that year, and rearrange my nose at the same time. I'm Ben Foster. Good to see you again."

"By Jove! Ben Foster! What a pleasant surprise!" The man jumped up, pumping Ben's hand vigorously.

As he introduced Ben to his companions, the man suddenly stopped and said, "I've quite forgotten my manners. I still go by my own name. I've learned already that one doesn't inquire a man's name in these parts."

"Still Teddy Roosevelt? Or what your sister used to call you—Teedie?"

"By Jove, I always thought 'Teedie' was known only to my family."

"Out here," one of the men said, "we call him Four Eyes."

"Quite so," Roosevelt said happily. "Not an unwarranted name I should say. Do join us, won't you, Ben?" He beckoned to the waiter to bring Ben's dinner from the other table, and when they had been seated, he asked, "How long have you been out here?"

"Almost five years. I had to leave Harvard in my sophomore year, and I've been working cattle and horses here since then."

"Marvelous!" Roosevelt boomed. "I've just become a rancher myself. You're familiar with the Maltese Cross at Chimney Butte?"

"I know the brand, yes. Right down the river a ways, isn't it?"

"Righto. Well, I've bought that, and have also acquired the Elkhorn Ranch twenty miles beyond."

Ben grinned. "I always thought you'd wind up a New York lawyer, or maybe even Governor."

There were a couple of polite coughs as Roosevelt said, "I'm thinking of leaving politics altogether. There's a tremendous amount of support for Blaine, and I simply can't imagine myself in the same party with him. I think perhaps I shall become a cowman instead."

Ben tried to imagine how long he would last in the gaudy getup he was wearing, but said nothing.

"Are you working now, Ben?"

"No. Just trying to make up my mind where to go find another job. My boss sold his horse outfit and went up to Canada to start another one."

"We need some good hands at both places, Four Eyes," one of the men suggested. He looked at Ben. "Horses, cows or sheep?"

"Horses, mostly, but I've worked cows plenty, too. Haven't lowered myself to be a woolie yet."

"Splendid!" Roosevelt squeaked. "The Maltese Cross is where we plan to raise horses. The Elkhorn is going to be devoted exclusively to cattle. Would you be interested in working for me?"

Ben grinned, his deep blue eyes sparkling. "Only if you promise not to knock me out and rearrange my nose again. You know, Teddy, you're the only man who ever managed to do that."

The Marquis raised a curious eyebrow, and exchanged an unbelieving glance with the other men. Ben Foster was several inches taller than Roosevelt, and weighed at least 30 pounds more.

The gaudily dressed Roosevelt squinted at Ben's broad shoulders. "We were both lightweights then, but you seem to have filled out quite a bit. Very well, I shan't try it again. Unless you deserve it, of course."

3

A HUNDRED miles to the southwest, near the junction of the Tongue River and Hanging Woman Creek, eight riders moved a herd of a hundred twenty head of cattle into a vast box canyon to join another herd that numbered about six hundred. As the cows, calves and steers filed through the narrow opening in the rocks, a group of men standing on an out-cropping of flat rocks above them counted, and, when finished, agreed on the numbers.

"Sixty-two cows, forty-eight calves and nine steers. One Aberdeen bool," said the Mexican.

"That's my count," Mike Dwyer agreed. "Eight dollars a head, except for the bull. Won't take less than fifty for him."

The Mexican snorted. "Your bool is made of gold, maybe?"

"That bull is going to improve your stock, and you know it. Forty-five dollars. Nothing less."

"That bool is worth maybe—maybe—thirty dollars. His steaks won't taste as good as the ones from the steers."

Dwyer turned to the men next to him. "Go cut the bull out and bring him back. We can get fifty dollars easy."

"For thirty-five you will save yourself the trouble?" the Mexican asked with a gold-rimmed smile.

Dwyer considered it, then said, "No, but forty will make me think about it."

The Mexican shrugged his shoulders, his long mustaches wafting in the breeze.

"Ah, what has happened to Yankee honor? That I should be treated this way is a shame that will rest upon your shoulders to the day you die. Haven't I been honest and fair with you in all my dealings? Haven't I offered you more money than you have received from other buyers? Do you not consider..."

"Forty, Miguel."

The Mexican threw his hands into the air in a theatrical gesture of helplessness. "Two years I have been buying whatever you brought to me. Two years I have paid you more than others. Two years I have never questioned the health of any of your animals, but paid an equal price for anything that was able to stand on its own four legs. Sometimes even three legs. Never once have I asked you to take a lesser price for an animal we both knew was inferior. And now, two years after we formed a friendship that has been equally rewarding to each of us, now, over a paltry five dollars you would insult my honor, make my family starve, bring shame upon my head, cause me to lose the respect of my countrymen. All that for five dollars. Mike Dwyer, how could you do such a thing to me?"

"Easy. We both know what that bull is worth, Miguel. Forty dollars."

Miguel Sanchez drew himself up to his full five

feet three inches, a look of horror on his face. "Even yet you do not wish to meet in the middle?"

"We're in the middle, you old *ladrón*. You've gone up and I've gone down. Forty dollars."

Miguel did his best to force tears to the surface, but only succeeded in breaking out laughing. "Very well, amigo, forty dollars."

There were smiles all around as buyer and seller shook hands. "One thousand sixty-four dollars," Miguel said to nobody in particular.

"Not to mention grub for the crew," Dwyer added.

"Of course, *amigo*, of course. Even though you would rob me, *mi casa es su casa*. I would never think of allowing a bandit like you to go hungry."

Miguel Sanchez led the group down to their horses, and they rode to the fire where a side of antelope was roasting. As they feasted on the succulent antelope, biscuits and coffee, they watched the men on the far side of the canyon cutting calves from the herd and dragging them to the branding fires. Sanchez offered them a drink, which was refused by all, and they mounted and rode to the work area.

The cowboys had decided to take care of the bull while he was still a bit weary from the drive into the canyon. He had been roped by four riders, two around the horns, one on a front leg and one on a hind leg. He snorted and pawed and kicked dirt high over his back with his free front leg, while resisting every effort to pull him over on his side. The ponies leaned into the ropes, threatening to snap them, but still the bull wouldn't budge. Every time one of the riders tried to rush past him to pull his legs out from under him, the bull snorted, and whirled around, stubbornly resisting every effort.

"Somebody get a loop on that other hind leg," one of the riders shouted.

Suddenly Mike Dwyer spurred his roan gelding

ahead, and the horse smashed into the side of the bull, knocking him off his feet. He was soon securely snubbed and lay there bellowing his wrath.

"Old Sheridan knows how to take care of beasts like that," Dwyer said proudly.

"The horse is brave, no doubt," Sanchez agreed, "but the rider is a bit of a fool."

One of Dwyer's men snickered. "He's no fool, Miguel. Just too dumb to be scared of anything."

With all four hooves bound together, the bull was dragged to the fire by the combined efforts of three horses. The branding crew looked at the brand on the bull's left shoulder. "Rafter B. Make it the Diamond B?"

Sanchez nodded, consulting his brand book. "Two notches in left ear, crop tip of right ear."

The men nodded, and in minutes a red-hot running iron had altered the Rafter B by enclosing the B inside a diamond. The ears were given the required notches, while the bull bellowed in rage. Once the work was done, everyone mounted except Mike Dwyer, whose horse was held conveniently nearby.

Satisfied that everyone was prepared to move in a hurry, Mike removed the ropes from the bull's horns, then loosened the plaited rawhide lariat that bound its hooves. He gave the bull a kick on the rump and shouted, "Git up and run, you dumb bastard!" as he leaped into his saddle.

The bull still lay and roared, the pain from his shoulder and ears keeping him from realizing he was free. Mike rode over to him, whipped him with the quirt, and roared with laughter as the bull kicked out, missing Sheridan's flank by inches. The bull was on his feet, roaring and charging at anything that moved.

Most of the riders moved well off, but Mike Dwyer

and Sheridan rode tight circles around the enraged
bull, teasing him. Twice Mike was able to whip
him across his freshly-notched and bleeding ears
before the confused bull finally gave up and trotted
over to the rest of the herd, snorting, and occasionally whirling around to defy anyone to follow him.

"Like I said, Mike's too dumb to be afraid of anything."

Miguel Sanchez shook his head in admiration. "You
should have made a career of fighting bools, not
stealing them."

Mike Dwyer gave a short laugh as he lit a cigar.
"Tell me, Miguel, how much would you have paid
for that bull if I'd really been stubborn about it?"

Again the gold teeth flashed in the sun. "You started too low, *amigo*. If you had said a hundred, I
would have started at fifty and settled at eighty.
Fine bool. And I have just the buyer in mind."

"I'll see if I can't find you another one like him,"
said Dwyer, with a malign grin.

"Sight unseen I will offer you twenty," Sanchez
said, and they all doubled up in laughter.

4

WHILE Mike Dwyer was disposing of his rustled cattle to the south, and Ben Foster was making his first tour of the Maltese Cross to the east, Granville Stuart sat with other members of the Montana Stock Growers Association in the meeting rooms at the Macqueen House. He listened patiently, or as patiently as could be said of a man who had made a fortune in the mines and brought a certain amount of law and order into the mountains by organizing his own teams of "law enforcers." Stuart had established himself as the third wealthiest baron in the burgeoning cattle industry, behind Charlie Goodnight and Conrad Kohrs. On the Northern Ranges, Stuart's word was law. He was the leading figure in the society world as well as the cattle world, and no one was known to have complained about the leadership assumed by his wife Aubony, the full-blooded Shoshone he married at a time when In-

dian-white hostility was at a peak. At least, no one
lived to tell about it.

Charles Bowen, owner of the Rafter B, sat directly across the table from Stuart. He was an imposing figure in his own right, sitting rigid and round
as a barrel. His thick-chested, bull-necked body acted
as a sounding chamber for his deep, resonant voice,
as his ham-like hands pounded on the table.

"I paid two thousand dollars for that bull in Oregon! That's not counting what it cost me to have
him brought over here. God knows it's improved
not only my herd, but a lot of others on this range,
including yours, Granville!"

The crusty old millionaire absently brushed his
full beard as he stared back at Bowen.

"Take it easy, Charlie. Just because he hasn't been
reported yet doesn't mean he's been stolen. And if
rustlers have gotten him, you're not the only one
who's lost good breeding stock to them. Besides,
there are still a few outfits working the fringes, and
he might even have strayed as far as Wyoming or
Canada."

"Damn it, Granville," Bowen said, the top of his
bald head getting redder by the minute, "how many
range bulls have been lost? Then tell me how many
purebreds haven't shown up on the tally books.
Well?"

Stuart glanced from one to another. There was
general assent that most of them had suffered the
same kind of losses.

"You see?" Bowen said. "It isn't just occasional
cows or horses that are picked off, but they're getting selective. They're taking the best of what we
have."

"We all know," Stuart said, "that losses to rustlers
are an accepted part of this business, just the same

as blizzards and drought and wolves. There are some things we have to live with."

"Well, by God, we don't have to live with this! There's not a thing we can do about blizzards except turn our tails and wait it out. But there is something we can do about low-down cattle thieves and horse thieves." Bowen looked around the room. Of the nearly two hundred members of the Association, about forty were present.

"Pierre?" Stuart asked.

Pierre "Frenchy" Wibaux was a dapper little man who had brought a fortune from France and settled on the Montana-Dakota border. He and his wife Nellie moved into a sod-roofed hut that had been vacated by a hide-hunter, and within two years had built a new house with carved woodwork, a billiard room, a wine cellar, and something that was the talk of the Lower Missouri and Yellowstone Basins for years—wallpaper. Frenchy also built up a herd of 65,000 head of cattle and opened two banks to handle his own finances as well as those of his neighbors. Unlike the Marquis de Mores, everything Wibaux did made money.

"There are honorable ways of dealing with honorable men," Wibaux stated solemnly, his neatly-trimmed beard jutting out as if emphasizing each word he spoke. "Thieves, however, are not honorable men. If the situation persists throughout this year, despite our efforts to convince them they are unwelcome in our midst, I would be happy to cooperate with methods which may not be, ah, shall we say, strictly honorable?"

Stuart looked around the room again. "Anybody else have anything to say?"

"I'm with Frenchy. If we can't make any progress between now and next Spring, let's get as rough as they are."

Stuart nodded, then turned to Bowen. "Is that satisfactory with you, Charlie?"

Bowen grunted. "Fine with me, but I'd like to make a suggestion, since this is all off the record."

"We'll hear it."

"In addition to branding mavericks with the Association brand, I think all of us ought to make a contribution proportionate to our sales this year for a special fund."

Dave Mulholland, who ran one of the smaller independent outfits, asked, "What kind of special fund?"

Granville Stuart smiled. "I believe what Charlie has in mind is a legal defense fund. Dave, do you have any idea what it could cost us for lawyers if we take the law into our own hands? Remember, I've been through it up in the mines. Even before we come to any decision, which is off the record as Charlie has pointed out, I'll contribute the first $20,000."

Mulholland's toothless mouth opened into a wide grin. "I sure ain't got much money, but I got me a lot of new rope that needs stretchin'!"

Bowen stood up. "Dave, what you and everybody else in this room has got to remember—and pass it on to every man you've got working for you—is that there's not a man among those rustlers out there who can't ride anything that ever wore horse hair, maybe hair of any kind including grizzly. There isn't a single man among them who can't rope, throw, tie and brand a steer single-handed. We've probably all of us had them working for us at one time or another. They're the best riders, ropers and gunslingers in the cattle business. They're the best cow punchers and cattle handlers in the Territories. It's likely any two of them can alter more brands in a day with a running iron than a crew of four honest men can with our regular irons. None of those rustlers out there ever knew what fear was. And, gentlemen, we've got ourselves to blame for shoving them on the other side of the law."

There was a murmur of dissent, but Granville Stuart pounded on the table for silence. "Go on, Charlie."

"Remember when we started running cattle on this open range? At first we followed the old Texas rule of burning mavericks with our own brand, right? And we even paid our men three dollars or five dollars a head for adding a maverick to our string. You've done it, I've done it. It wasn't a bad system until some of our hands started thinking. They were wondering why they should get three dollars a head for putting my brand on, when if they registered a brand of their own and ran their cows with mine they could put their own brand on a maverick and have an animal worth anywhere from ten to thirty dollars. And that's what made most of us refuse to hire a man who had a brand of his own. We wanted that twenty dollars for ourselves.

"The result is that we drove off some of the best cowmen in these parts. For two or three years it's been fairly easy pickings for them to work on the outside of us. But they've gotten bolder, some of them even working right along with us on the annual roundup. Once they know we've organized to drive them out, they'll get desperate. And, gentlemen, when desperate men are forced to fight—particularly some of the best men in this country—people are going to get hurt."

"Do you think there is a man in this room who fears death, Charles?" Wibaux asked.

"No, but by God I'd rather see more of them killed than us, that's how I feel."

That was greeted with a resounding cheer, and

Stuart called the proceedings to an end. "We'll meet here again on the 21st of March next year. In the meantime, if anybody should happen to find that prize Aberdeen bull with the Rafter B on his shoulder, send the lovesick old brute home, will you?"

As the men began filing out of the room, Stuart laid a hand on Bowen's shoulder. "Come downstairs and let me buy you a drink, Charlie."

"Hell, it's my turn, isn't it?"

"Have it your way. Or we can play one hand of showdown for the drink and a hundred dollars on the side."

Bowen grinned and scratched the thin fringe of reddish-gray hair on his head. "Since you put it that way, Granville, I don't mind letting you buy me a drink after all."

Stuart chose one of the private rooms off the ballroom, and after the waiter had brought them brandy and fine Cuban cigars, he said, "Charlie, you know I agree with you that it's time we take care of this thing."

"You didn't sound any too anxious upstairs."

"Of course not. I don't want to see any of our men killed any more than you do. But we certainly can't let the word get out that we intend to organize a committee of vigilantes. That would be tantamount to putting an ad in the paper saying, 'Any able-bodied gunmen who would like to shoot and hang the thieving bastards plaguing our range apply to the Stockgrowers Association.'"

"All right, I get hot-headed now and then. But . . ."

Stuart held up his hand and sipped his brandy. "You were a cavalryman, weren't you?"

"Yes." Bowen paused, then added, "Union."

"That's immaterial. You were a soldier. A major, I believe."

"Brevet colonel."

"And you know how to train men, how to prepare them for battle. Charlie, this thing is going to be run just like a military campaign, believe me. It'll be on a smaller scale, that's all. You pointed out something I'd overlooked, and that is that the men we're dealing with are the best in this business. You don't tackle an army of good men, desperate men, without being prepared for the campaign unless you want to see your men chopped up like sonuvabitch stew."

Stuart paused to sip his brandy again, and Bowen waited.

"I don't want any man of importance to take part in this, Charlie."

"I'm an officer, and I'll lead my own troops when the time comes."

"Not if you're smart. What you'll do is take care of training the men and be sitting here at an Association meeting when the time comes. That way nobody can point a finger at any member of the Association."

"You know, Granville, there are times I think you've got as much brains as you have money."

"You see, Charlie," Stuart said, ignoring the remark, "when that committee goes out looking for rustlers, they're not only going to string up thieves who have been robbing us blind, they're also likely to run across some innocent grangers or independents who happen to have someone else's brand nosing into the feed lots. Not only are the rustlers going to pay, and a few of the vigilantes, but there will likely be some innocent bystanders lose their lives. When a band of men sets out to enforce the law, God have mercy on anyone who even looks like a lawbreaker. I've seen it, you know that. And when that happens, all hell is going to break loose, and I wouldn't put it past the powers in the East to have the Army down on our necks. But if the Association is holding an early meeting that lasts a couple of weeks, and we invite General Miles and his staff over here for a dance every weekend, who can accuse us of being off stringing up rustlers?"

Bowen smiled broadly. "Granville, you are a genius. What won't you come up with next?"

"Well, for starters, why don't you bring your daughter over for dinner next Saturday? I'll have Aubony fix you something you've never eaten before."

"What's that?"

"Some of your own beef!"

5

When he decided to sell out his holdings in Dakota Territory and move his horse-breeding business up to Canada, George Fowler had given all of his hands a bonus.

"Before we move the last string to Fort Keogh, each of you gets four head for each year you've worked for me."

His system of selection was as fair as he could make it. His prime breeding stock, including all the stallions and the best of the mares, was what he was going to move north. Each of the hands took turns selecting a horse, and when they had completed the job, the balance was to be taken to Fort Keogh.

Ben picked out nothing but mares, and had five mixed breed riding horses and seven sturdy draft animals. Before moving the string to Fort Keogh, he made arrangements with a neighbor to keep them until he returned for them after deciding where he was going to find some work.

Davey Morton decided to keep his with Fowler's, and Muttonhead took his along to Fort Keogh to be sold with the rest. Of the thirty-four head that were lost on the drive to Miles City, six had been Muttonhead's. Ben and Davey could do nothing but offer him their sympathy.

A month after starting to work for Roosevelt, Ben returned to Mandan to claim his mares. He said nothing to old Twice Thompson who had ridden with him from the Maltese as he passed the house where Bertha had died so cruelly, so senselessly. He tried to keep from looking at it, but couldn't keep his eyes from studying the place. Whoever owned it was keeping it up well, even though he had made some changes in the arrangement of the porches that Bertha had wanted. They rode past the house with its gingerbread trim, and he choked back a tear.

When he went to get his mares, he found that his twelve had become thirteen. He knew she was coming close to foaling, but wasn't aware it would be this soon. The foal was a pretty little roan filly, and had come from the best of the riding mares in his string. Twice offered him twenty dollars on the spot for the foal.

"Sure is a pretty thing, Ben."

"Yep, but she'll cost you a lot more than twenty dollars, Twice."

Twice Thompson made a sour face. "Better take the twenty. That little gal's gonna look mighty attractive to them renegade Cheyenne over our way."

"I'll gamble on that," Ben replied with a smile.

Again Twice screwed his face into a sour look. It was the kind of crooked grin that always brought smiles to men who saw him for the first time. Thompson had earned his handle through his less-than-imposing physique. He stood well over six feet tall, and weighed some one hundred and thirty pounds, counting boots and spurs. When he first came into the Dakotas, someone remarked that he was so skinny he would have to stand in the sun twice to cast a shadow. The name stuck, and nobody could recall what his name had been before then; he'd probably forgotten it himself.

"Comes in handy, though," he said once. "I kin hide behind a cottonwood sapling easy as pie, and I 'member once when a couple Blackfeet was trying to send me to the happy hunting grounds. Them buggers was shootin' so close I c'd feel the wind whistlin' as their bullets flew by. Now, if I'da been your size, why, them Injuns woulda had me for sure. But I reckon I don't make much of a target from a distance."

Twice claimed he was really no better than a slave. "I been out in this here country since before the War. Helped carve out some of the wilderness and bring civilization here. Been a mighty good life, all in all. Done been good parts as well as bad parts. But this here Maltese Cross done had three owners since I started workin' it, an' ever' time it changes hands I change along with it. I reckon they consider me part of the place, just like a barn."

"Hardly," Ben said. "A flagpole, maybe, but not a barn."

As they neared the squalid settlement of Little Missouri, Ben asked, "How much longer is this place going to last with Medora on the other side of the river?"

"Little Missouri ain't about t' fold up, long's a man wants t' wet 'is neck without havin' t' worry 'bout bein' tossed in the hoosegow. Medora is what the Marquis thinks a town oughta be like. Reckon since he's puttin' his money into a packing house an' shipping point, nobody's going to argue with him when he wants t' name it fer 'is wife. Shit, them two Frenchies de Mores and Wibaux has got enough money they can put names on just about anything they want."

Twice paused long enough to take a deep breath. "What about this dude Roseyvelt? You think he's doin' anything but playing cowboy?"

"Hard to tell, Twice. I knew him back East, and all I know for sure is that he plays everything to the hilt, like life was one big game to be won. He's got some money, but not like the Marquis or Wibaux, or any of the big cattlemen. I think he's just trying something different to get over a personal problem."

Twice Thompson kept his silence, knowing that it was considered unhealthy to probe very deeply into any man's background, particularly one he worked for.

"Maybe he'll get back into politics some day, who knows?" Ben said absently. "He was starting to make a mark for himself in New York, but last winter both his mother and his wife died within twelve hours of each other. Since then the political winds have shifted a bit, and he came out here to become a rancher. Who knows? He might stay, and he might go back to New York."

Twice shook his head sadly. "Takes some particular breed to get mixed up in politics."

"Yep, and Teddy's one of those."

"Does he wear fantastical getups like that in New York?"

Ben laughed. "Only when he wants to make sure people see him, I guess. I sure as heck wouldn't be seen dead in outfits like he wears. But he's happy dressing that way, I guess."

"Maybe he's happy, but he ain't real! I'd give my right arm to hear him say 'Shit!' instead a 'By Jove!'

when he got bucked off a pony. Maybe we ought to let him try to ride Water Skipper some morning. That'd jar his ass for damned sure."

"Which one is Water Skipper? I haven't been around long enough to try them all, you know."

Twice described the gelding, his hands drawing pictures in the air as he indicated the blaze on the muzzle and the white stockings.

"Water Skipper don't much care to be rode. Takes two men to snub him while you climb on. Then, after he eases the kinks outen his back with two, three minutes of fishtailin' an' buckin', he limbers up with a five mile race. 'Bout that time he's gotta get a second wind, and then anybody kin climb aboard, and he's as tame as a kitten. Got his name from his cussed hab-it of keepin' them white stockings clean. Don't like to walk through a puddle, so he plays like he's one of them English steeplechasers. He'll be walkin' along as easy as kin be, then when some water gets in his way, he rears up and jumps like he's headin' for the moon. Rivers and cricks is all right, but not itsy-bitsy pud-dles."

Twice paused to build a quirly, and Ben said, "He must have something pretty special to keep him around."

"Yep, two things. He don't bite people, and he's 'bout the best cutting horse we got on the place. He kin find a calf in a herd so thick his rider can't see it, and then there ain't a thing gonna keep him from getting to it. He don't mind bitin' any critter that tries to keep him from it."

As they moved Ben's string onto Maltese Cross range, they spotted two riders leaving the house. As the distance decreased, Twice grinned his crooked smile. "That there's Charlie Bowen an' his daughter Cindy. From over to Miles City."

"I've run into him," Ben said. "Runs a big spread. Fifteen, twenty thousand head, isn't it?"

"More like fifty thousand. Bowen was one of the first to move cattle up here when the buffalo started thinnin' out."

The Bowens pulled to a halt as Ben and Twice approached.

"Howdy, Twice."

"Afternoon, Mr. Bowen, Cindy," Twice replied, touching the brim of his hat. "Good to see you again."

He nodded toward Ben and added, "This here's Ben Foster. He started here about a month back."

"So we heard," Bowen said. "Mr. Roosevelt considers himself lucky to find someone here he knew back East."

"We didn't know each other very well, actually," Ben said, finding himself unable to keep his eyes on Bowen rather than his daughter.

"Those your mares?" Cindy asked. "He said you were bringing your own string onto the place."

"Yep. That's what I've got to show for three years' work."

Cindy Bowen's green eyes sparkled. "I wouldn't mind having that foal. How much are you asking for her?"

"Sorry, but she's not for sale," Ben said. "I've already turned down a couple of offers."

"I can see why," Cindy admitted. "She's got good lines to her."

Ben studied the girl sitting opposite him. Except for her freckled face which was about as beautiful as any he had seen anywhere, she seemed no more feminine than any man who lived in the Territory. Her clothes were the same coarse denim her father wore, and her hands showed that she was accustomed to work. From under the wide brim of the dusty, stained hat, a few strands of hair showed that she was red-headed, and Ben's eyes darted to Charles Bowen momentarily. Sure enough, his hair was red, too, or had been before it began turning gray.

"I said, you seem to know good horseflesh," Cindy said with a touch of impatience.

"Sorry," Ben replied, feeling himself blush. "My mind was off somewhere else for a moment. Horses are what I know best, I guess."

"When your boss can spare you, come over to the Rafter B," Bowen said. "We're near the junction of the Powder and Mizpah. I'd like to have your opinion on some of my horses."

Ben's blue eyes shifted from Cindy to her father again. "I think maybe you're overestimating my judgment."

"I doubt it. George Fowler raised the best horses in these parts for years. I'm sorry to see him leave the country. He tried to convince me I should get rid of the beef and stick to horses. Trouble is, I'm just not sure that what I have is even worth thinking about to start any large-scale operations in the horse-raising business. I'd be willing to pay you a fair price to tell me what I should cull out and what I need to get a good head start on anyone who's planning to replace Fowler."

"Mr. Roosevelt told us how Fowler paid his hands a bonus," Cindy said. Again, Ben could hear the soft music of her voice above the whistle of the wind across the rolling plains. "It's evident you chose well, Mr. Foster. I'd still like to buy that colt."

"The man said it isn't for sale, Cindy!" Bowen snapped at her.

"That doesn't mean he won't sell it to me if I keep after him."

From the corner of his eye, Ben could see Twice's

face slide into its crooked grin, enjoying the sight of Bowen trying to keep his daughter in place.

Bowen turned to Ben. "Don't pay any attention to her. She's going to learn she can't have everything she wants. My offer stands. Be pleased to have you come any time you can."

"I'll be over as soon as I can get a couple of days off again, Mr. Bowen."

"Call me Charlie."

"Sure. And I'm uncomfortable when people call me mister instead of Ben."

Cindy seized the opportunity. "Ben, when you do come . . ."

"But I kind of expect it from kids," Ben said, his blue eyes twinkling.

Cindy's face flushed with anger, and she wheeled her mount around, saying, "Come on, Dad, we've got a long ride ahead of us!"

Bowen's hearty laugh split the air. "I guess that told her. See you, Ben," he said as he rode off to join her.

Ben and Twice watched them as they rode over the rise. "Whooee! You sure ruffled her feathers, Ben."

"Yep. Lots of spunk in that kid."

"Well, maybe you think of her as a kid, but I reckon there ain't a man in this country kin put out a better day's work. You might could change your mind when you see her cuttin' an' brandin'."

"Maybe. Well, let's push these the rest of the way down to the corral and shove some feed into them. I could use some chow."

Twice gave a holler, and the horses moved on again, grateful for the short rest to graze. The foal bolted out to the front of the string, kicking her heels into the air and almost falling over as she fought to regain her balance.

Ben suddenly gave a snicker. "You know, Twice, I think maybe Cindy'd be a good name for that little filly. Beautiful lines to her, a pretty face, and lots of get up and go. Yep, Cindy it is."

Twice wisely kept his cockeyed mouth shut.

6

Four Eyes Roosevelt, as he was derisively known in the country, proved himself an excellent game hunter, although Ben wondered how he could tell the difference between a horse and buffalo at a hundred yards. People could laugh at his costumes, his bookish pale face which seemed to be all teeth, mustache and round eyeglasses. They could snicker openly at his habit of never walking—he bounded from one spot to another —and even laughed out loud when they politely greeted him with a "Howdy" and heard his squeaking "Dee-lighted to meet you!" in reply. But hardened frontiersmen and cattlemen alike soon found themselves filled with admiration for the man's boundless energy.

When he asked Ben to serve as a guide on a hunting trip with a visiting New Yorker, Ben expected the worst.

"We shouldn't have any trouble finding some deer or antelope."

"By Jove, perhaps we might also be able to get a buffalo," Roosevelt replied.

"I doubt it. When I first came out here there were still some scattered herds of them, but the hide hunters have cleaned them out. I haven't seen a stray buffalo for two years now. Maybe we ought to stick to deer and antelope. Besides, the larder's still a bit on the empty side."

Four Eyes agreed to confine the hunt to game that would provide meat for the winter months ahead, and the day before they were to start out announced grandly, "We shall need at least three pack animals to carry the game home, Ben."

"At least," Ben said, wondering if Roosevelt would be able to recognize a deer at a hundred yards.

The third man in the party was Ferris McLeod, a Scotsman who had met Roosevelt in New York, and was eager to compare Western hunting with the stag hunts he had known as a youth in Scotland. While his dress marked him as a city type, McLeod's horsemanship and skill with a Winchester made him the envy of Roosevelt.

Twice quietly suggested, "Reckon we oughta give Mac a chance to go sailin' on Water Skipper?"

Ben nodded, and with the help of a third hand they saddled Water Skipper and held him while McLeod stood by.

"Spirited animal," McLeod said, viewing the nervous horse with dismay.

"He'll be right nice, once he shakes the dust off," Twice said.

McLeod swung up, and his right leg was scarcely over the saddle when the air was rent by a scream from the horse. He jumped four feet straight into the air, fishtailing for all he was worth. McLeod managed to hold his seat through five successive swings, with

Water Skipper's snarling muzzle whipping around to his right flank and then his left.

"My word!" Roosevelt exclaimed.

Water Skipper stopped for a moment, looked around at his rider with a baleful eye, and then decided that another course of action would be more advantageous in getting rid of the devil on his back.

He bucked. He kicked. He snorted, puffed and bucked some more, his heels flashing out behind him four or five times on each stiff-legged jump into the air.

McLeod was still aboard, a grim look on his face. Water Skipper's look was equally as grim, when he settled down to have another look at his tormentor.

"By Jove! That's beautiful horsemanship, Ferris!"

"How much more dust does he need to shake off?" McLeod asked in the momentary respite.

There was no chance for anyone to reply, for Water Skipper took a notion to stretch his legs, and with a whinnying scream took off for the hills in the distance with McLeod grimly hanging on.

Roosevelt bounded toward his mount, saying, "After him! That horse will kill him!"

Twice shook his head. "Nope. He'll settle down in a few minutes. Only thing kin hurt Mac is if he falls off, but it don't look like he's gonna. He's still hangin' on there."

Roosevelt squinted through his glasses at the disappearing figure. "Are you certain he's still in the saddle? I can't tell."

"He's there," Ben said.

Twenty minutes later McLeod returned to the stable on a sweaty but peaceful horse. He swung down, rubbed Water Skipper's muzzle and said, "Once we became better acquainted, we came to terms with each other. I think it's safe to assume he hasn't been ridden much this year."

Ben couldn't keep up the deception. "Truth is, he's normally used for cutting, not range riding."

"Reckon you're a better rider than we figured, Mac," Twice admitted. "He's a right good critter, but that's his way of gettin' started every morning. We were just giving you the hardest test we got. Reckon if you kin calm Water Skipper in the morning, you kin ride anything."

McLeod bowed grandly. "I accept the compliment. However, if you have another horse more suited to the hunting trail, I would be grateful."

As they packed the provisions for the hunting trip, Ben suggested, "You know, Twice, Water Skipper ought to make you a fortune."

"How?"

"Race him. He'll beat anything I've ever seen."

"You race him. By the time he gets done with them acrobatics, any other horse will be across the finish line. An' Water Skipper might take it into his mind to run off in some other direction. Ain't no controllin' him until he gets that second wind."

The following morning was chilly but clear, and the three started down the Little Missouri with each man trailing a pack horse. Ben estimated they had put close to thirty miles behind them by the time they stopped to eat. The ride had taken them through running streams, timbered hills and country so barren it made him wonder why the Indians didn't want to give it up without a struggle. Since Roosevelt and McLeod didn't seem inclined to mention stopping for a meal, Dan decided that he'd ridden far enough without refueling. They came into a broad canyon where there was a rushing stream and plenty of brush to provide kindling for a fire.

"Looks like a good place to build the biscuits," he announced.

While he built a small but hot fire with twigs and

small branches, he put McLeod to work on grinding the coffee.

"You've no grinder?" McLeod asked as Ben handed him a leather pouch with a handful of coffee beans.

"Sure. Just find a flat rock, put the bag down, then find a rock about the size of your fist. Pound it a while. No sense in carrying a heavy coffee grinder on a hunting trip."

Roosevelt's chore was to prepare the dough for biscuits. "Where are the measuring utensils?" he asked.

Ben's blue eyes twinkled. "Open the flour sack and punch your fist in it to make a bowl. Sprinkle on some baking powder, then pour in some water. Stir the mess around with your hands until you've got a ball about this big."

"But, how much water? How much baking powder?"

"Whatever you put in will be just about right. If the ball's too small, add a little more water and keep working it around."

They watched with puzzled looks as Ben sliced thick slabs of bacon and dropped them into the huge frying pan filled with boiling water.

"Really, Ben!" McLeod said. "Boiled bacon? You don't fry it?"

"Not until after I boil it I don't. This is something a Mexican cook taught me on a roundup over to Mandan a few years ago. I'm not too fond of tasting salt all day while I'm riding, and this is the best way to get rid of the salt."

To Roosevelt's amazement, the coffee, bacon and the biscuits he'd placed in the huge Dutch oven were all ready at the same time, and he announced that it was the finest meal he'd eaten since leaving Chicago.

Before they made camp for the night, Ben estimated they'd covered about 45 miles. It would have been 50 or more if one of the pack horses hadn't gotten bogged down in quicksand. Except for the coffee, it was a cold meal, with biscuits left from the mid-day halt and jerky, supplemented by a tin of peaches. The horses were all footsore, and Ben couldn't remember when he'd been so tired in his life. They pitched a tent, and Ben crawled into his sleeping roll.

He woke with a start long after dark, hearing voices outside the tent. He carefully cocked his revolver and peered around the flap.

Sitting in front of the glowing embers of the fire, Roosevelt and McLeod were deep into a discussion of politics, and Ben shook his head in amazement as he crawled back to his blankets. He fumbled through his trousers, found the old Waterbury watch and struck a match.

"Twelve-thirty," he muttered, and for the first time agreed with Twice that his old boxing partner from Harvard wasn't real.

He woke at six the next morning, and rejoiced as he heard a light drizzle falling on the tent. Nobody was going to go out hunting in weather like this, he told himself. We can get caught up on our rest.

He was wrong. Rain didn't dampen Roosevelt's spirits; he bounded out of his sleeping bag, yanked on his trousers and boots, and rushed out into the rain to get the fire going again.

Ben wasn't bothered as much by the energy Four Eyes possessed, as he was at the man's ability to keep up a constant stream of conversation with McLeod. They discussed everything from the profits to be made with sheep and cattle on the free range to international politics and even spent hours reciting scenes from Shakespeare. By the end of the third day, Ben wondered if they would ever wind down and ride in silence for a few miles.

The only silence came when they were stalking

game. McLeod got his sights on a smallish buck early in the day, and bagged it with the first shot. Roosevelt missed three running, and Ben finally brought down the fourth after Four Eyes missed.

"By Godfrey!" Roosevelt exclaimed happily. "I'd give anything in the world to shoot like that."

"Nothing to it," Ben said. "Think of shooting like boxing. Spend a couple of hours every day in training. You've already got a good weapon in that Winchester. A 300 grain bullet backed by 90 grains of powder is every bit as good as an old Sharps."

"The truth is," McLeod stated flatly, "all modern rifles are efficient weapons. It's the man behind the gun that make the difference. An inch or two in trajectory, or a second or two in rapidity of fire counts as nothing compared to a steady hand and a good eye."

There was an embarrassed silence for a moment, and then Four Eyes beamed.

"Bully! I shall devote myself to a rigorous schedule of practice."

On the fifth day of their hunt, and with the pack horses carrying eight antelope and deer carcasses, Roosevelt's luck came through again. The three were on their way back to the Elkhorn and had stopped for a meal of steaks at noon. Roosevelt suddenly stopped chewing, pointed beyond Ben and said, "Isn't that a buffalo?"

On the far side of the valley, what Ben had earlier thought to be another dark rock at the edge of the timber was now placidly grazing its way toward them.

"Move slowly," Roosevelt whispered as he started for his Winchester.

"Don't worry about that old bull seeing you," Ben said. "We're upwind, so he can't smell us, and it's for sure he can't see us this far away. A buffalo is about the most near-sighted beast on earth."

Roosevelt crawled toward the brute, imitating what he had heard described as the Indians' method of moving in close; crawl a few yards, freeze; crawl a few yards, freeze. Ben and McLeod stayed a good twenty yards behind him, spread well to the sides.

When he was about 80 yards off, the old bull suddenly lifted his head from the ground, gave a roar and charged forward. Ben watched as Four Eyes stood, raised his rifle quickly—and struck his forehead with the butt, knocking his glasses to the ground.

The bull charged on, but Roosevelt got the rifle to his shoulder and fired twice. The second shot struck home in front of the hump, burrowing down between the shoulder blades.

Ben and McLeod rushed forward. Roosevelt was wiping away the blood rushing down his face from the gash on his forehead. Ben reached down to the ground and picked up the glasses for him.

"By Jove, that was a close one! Well, who said the buffalo were all gone? Drat, these glasses are a nuisance."

McLeod looked at the buffalo, lying not fifteen feet away. "Bully," he muttered with no enthusiasm.

When they arrived back at the Elkhorn, Ben could tell by the look on Twice's face there was trouble.

"Rustlers moved off about a hunnert of your cows, Four Eyes. Got two of Ben's mares, too."

"Damn!" Ben swore.

"Something is going to have to be done about lawlessness around here," Roosevelt said.

"Oh, we already done somethin'. Caught up with 'em the next day," Twice said. "In the ruckus what followed, some four, five of 'em got away with most a the cattle. But we took two a them thievin' bastards to town."

"I was not aware there was a jail in Medora or Little Missouri," Roosevelt said.

"There ain't. But there's some mighty handy tele-graph poles. We held a regular court. They was guilty as hell, so we strung 'em up. It was all done fair, square and legal."

7

THE Rafter B headquarters was a cluster of a dozen buildings sprawling along the bank of the Mizpah. It had an orderly appearance about it that told the world its owner cared. The neat two-story frame house provided a refreshing contrast to the ordinary log structures that were so common in the Territory. Most of the outbuildings were of log construction, though, and Ben guessed that Charles Bowen had started in one of those and built up the headquarters as he built up his holdings. And like most of the cattlemen in the Yellowstone Basin, he had provided his hands with quarters almost as good as his own; the bunkhouse was the other frame building. Both of them had fresh coats of whitewash, and sparkled in the early autumn sunshine. A third frame building stood between the main house and the bunkhouse. It looked as though it might be two rooms, possibly three, and its position marked it as the foreman's house.

A pair of hounds roused themselves from their permanent employment to howl a warning, then went back to sleep. Bowen came out onto the porch as Ben rode up.

"Howdy, Ben. Climb down and rest your saddle a while."

"Thanks, Charlie. Right nice place you have here."

"It's not the Macqueen House, but it's comfortable."

Inside, Bowen asked, "Care for a drink?"

"Rather not, if you don't mind."

"Frankly, I'm glad. I prefer to do my drinking after the work's done. I can rustle up a cup of coffee, though. Got a fifty-pound sack of Arbuckle's just last week, so it's good and fresh. I keep the pot going all the time when I'm around the place."

He indicated a deeply-unholstered leather wing chair, and disappeared for a minute. When he returned, he was carrying two heavy mugs, and handed one to Ben.

"How're things going over at the Maltese Cross?"

"Fair. I spent a week taking Four Eyes and one of his New York friends hunting to fill the larder for the winter. I wouldn't have believed it, but we got not only deer and antelope, he even bagged himself an old buffalo bull. I thought they were all gone."

Bower shook his head in admiration. "I haven't seen one in two years, myself. When I first came into this country, they were thick as flies at a Fourth of July picnic. The first time I saw this valley I couldn't believe it. It was like a black carpet moving along. They were horn to horn from the Mizpah clear over to the foothills, and about two miles deep."

"I wonder how many millions of them the hide hunters killed off," Ben said. "I know when I was a kid I heard stories about the great herds, but couldn't believe it. My father had a leather factory in Boston, and the first time I went to Chicago with him to buy

hides, I tried to imagine how much space the buffalo
took up. I never forgot the sight of trainloads of
hides, car after car of hides."

"Well, if Roosevelt got himself an old bull, it's
probably one of the last of them."

Ben sipped at the strong coffee before changing
the conversation.

"We lost some cattle and a couple of horses last
week, Charlie."

Bowen's bushy eyebrows raised a notch. "How
bad?"

"About a hundred head of cattle. Two of my mares.
Twice Thompson told me they strung up a couple
of them in Medora."

"I heard there was some justice handed out, but
I didn't know whose cattle they were stealing. Damn,
this thing is getting worse all the time."

Ben leaned forward in the chair. "For the first time
in my life, it really hits home, you know? Up until
now it's always been somebody else's animals. But
now it gets personal. I know two horses doesn't sound
like much, but to me it represents a half a year's
work."

Bowen studied Ben's face for a moment, as though
weighing something, then said, "The time is coming,
Ben. We're going to clear this country of those
thieves. At least they're going to get the message
that they're unwelcome."

"Funny thing, Charlie, I never thought I'd be
pleased to see rustlers hung or shot, but maybe I'm
thinking differently now."

Bowen stood up. "Bah! the thing'll be cleared up
pretty soon, you see if I'm not right. Come on, let's
go have a look at my horses."

As they walked off the porch, one of the hounds
raised a sleepy eyelid and gave a perfunctory growl
before drifting back to sleep. Ben's eyes darted about,

realizing that he hadn't seen Cindy, and wondering where she might be. When they got to the corral, he didn't have to wonder any longer. She was sitting in the shade, her hair free of the hat that rested on the ground next to her while she repaired some harness traces with waxed thread.

"Howdy, Cindy," he said, his eyes riveted to her pretty face.

To his surprise, she gave him a warm smile. "Good afternoon, Mister Foster." She dropped her work, jumped to her feet and stuck out a hand. "I'm pleased you finally came over."

"Couldn't get away any sooner." Her eyes were a deeper green than he remembered, and her freckles weren't as dark. Now that her hair fell free, it was a deeper, richer red than he had remembered, very much like the roan foal he had given her name to.

"Did you remember to bring my foal, Mister Foster?" she asked with a sweet, beguiling smile.

Ben returned the smile and said, "Plumb forgot. I'll have to remember the next time. And you can drop the mister from now on."

"Then you've decided I'm not just a little kid after all?"

"Didn't say that," he teased. "I just feel more comfortable with Ben."

Charlie Bowen appeared around the corner of the stable on his horse. "You two expect me to bring the herd here? Let's get moving."

Ben felt himself blush again, a feeling that was as uncomfortable as having a burr in his bedroll.

"You go ahead," Cindy said, snatching up her hat. "I'll be right behind."

Charlie and Ben paused to look over the scattering of horses in the corral. They were about what Ben had expected; for the most part, ordinary range mustangs. One of them stood out, though. She was a blue roan filly, about three years old. Her head had a splendid shape, and she carried herself proudly as she milled with the others. Ben could recall seeing only a few horses of that color in the five years he'd been in Dakota and Montana Territories, and every one of them had the same bearing, the same strong lines.

"If she weren't so young, I'd say I knew that mare," Ben said.

"I bought her from Frenchy Wibaux a year ago. Paid a hundred and fifty dollars for that mare." Bowen's voice betrayed his pride in the unusual animal. Even the best of the horses that George Foster sold had never brought more than seventy-five dollars.

"I'd say you got a bargain, Charlie. She wouldn't happen to be a pacer, would she?"

Bowen grinned. "Watch."

He spurred his mount forward toward the milling horses, gave a shout and they were off and running. All except the blue roan. She carried her head high and proud, and slipped into a pace step two or three lengths ahead of the pack, her long, powerful legs covering ground as they moved easily, smoothly. Ben had seen a few pacers among the wild mustangs, but none of them as beautiful as this. And it was the same build, the same color as the other rare blue roans. And all of them had the same lofty, proud air about them.

"I covered a hundred and twenty miles on her one day, and she wasn't even breathing hard," Bowen said proudly.

Cindy rode up alongside of them, her hair once more tucked under her hat.

"What do you think of her?" she asked.

"Fair. Tell you what I'll do. I'll trade you my foal for her. Even throw in a saddle."

Bowen snorted. "Did Hell freeze over last night? If it did, then we'll talk about a trade."

"I think Dad would sooner trade me than that mare."

Ben looked at her, then said, "Show me your teeth."

Cindy's face flushed, and she shot him a fiery look.

"I'll keep my filly," Ben said.

Most of the Rafter B horses were in a valley about ten miles from the headquarters. Bowen had about two hundred head, a normal string for a man with forty or fifty thousand head of beefs. Again, Ben found what he expected. Decent horses, but mostly run-of-the-mill.

"Offhand, I'd say you'd need to find a couple of really good stallions and a string of better mares. Unless you do that, you won't have anything anybody else doesn't have."

"I don't mind paying good money for good stock," Bowen said. "That Aberdeen bull I bought in Oregon cost me a small fortune, and it's paying off."

"Charlie, if you want the truth, I'd say your beefs are a lot better looking than your horses. But if you're thinking of changing from cattle to horses, there's no reason why you couldn't make it pay in three, maybe four years."

Bowen heaved a deep sigh. "Until we drive the rustlers out of this country, nothing's going to pay very well. And we just don't have any law to back us up."

"What was it Mister Roosevelt told you, Dad?" Cindy asked.

"Bah! He's so steamed up on politics he thinks that all the problems of the world can be solved by politicians sitting down and passing laws in the Territorial Legislature. But that's only part of it. Once you have laws, you have to have lawmen to back them up. And when you have lawmen you have to pay them, and that comes out of tax money. There's no way you're going to get the grangers, the miners, the cattlemen, the railroads and all the other groups looking out for their own interests to agree on what's best for everybody."

"The Association is a step in the right direction, isn't it?" Ben asked.

"Sure, for cattlemen. But the nesters around here would be happy to see the range chopped up and fenced off so they can grow their wheat and oats. Now you take a bunch like that, they can elect a man to stymie every effort the Association works for in getting laws passed. No matter how it works out, one group or another isn't going to like the laws they come up with, and there's going to be open warfare concerning who's right and who's wrong. Laws and lawmen are fine back East, but we'll never make it work here. This is a country where we have to make our own laws and enforce them. In our own way."

As they rode back to the ranch they discussed the growing problem of the range. The cattle industry in Montana was young; it had only been two or three years since herds were numbered in the thousands rather than dozens, or even hundreds. With the disappearance of the great herds of buffalo, cattle could now graze freely. It was all open range. Cattlemen from Texas and Arizona had been moving herds north to fatten them on the lush prairie grass, and when the railroad finally came through, shipping to Eastern markets was easy. Because of the lure of an abundance of grass and easy shipping, the Yellowstone and Little Missouri Basins were rapidly becoming crowded and overgrazed.

"I spent a few years in Missouri, then went down to Texas," Bowen told him. "I was one of the first to move up here with my herd. Funny thing, though. I didn't have any idea I was going to stay here. The only thought in my mind then was to fatten up my stock, ship 'em off, and go get more. But I never went back to Texas, once I got here."

"You must have been one of the first members of the Association," Ben said.

"Right. Granville Stuart, Frenchy Wibaux, Charlie Goodnight and I were the four that put it together. It's about the closest thing we have to law and order here. When I heard that Roosevelt bought the Maltese Cross and Elkhorn outfits, I hustled over and explained the workings to him. Didn't take much to have him join up."

Ben nodded. Anybody who wanted to go into the cattle business in Montana or Dakota Territories either joined one of the associations, or worked under a cloud of doubt. The organization maintained the official brand books, and by now there were some two thousand brands registered, many of them for herds that numbered less than a hundred head.

Back at the ranch, Cindy said, "I'll change my clothes and fix us some supper."

She disappeared through the doorway into the kitchen, and Bowen said, "Now, how about that drink?"

Ben agreed, and Bowen brought out a bottle of bourbon. Ben settled back into a chair, thinking how attractive Cindy would be in a gingham dress, but a few minutes later she appeared in clean jeans and chambray shirt. She noticed the look on his face.

"What's wrong with you?"

"Sorry, but I guess I was expecting you to get all frilled up. I've been wondering what you'd look like with spangles and jansies."

Bowen laughed. "She ain't worn female duds since she was twelve. I can't convince her that it wouldn't hurt to look like a lady now and then, just to keep in practice."

"I know," Cindy said sourly, "you want me to look like one of those box rustlers in a dance hall."

"Not exactly. But it would be nice to be reminded every now and then that I've got a daughter, not a son."

"I don't see what difference it makes," she replied. "I'm not about to make myself look cheap. Any woman who doesn't wear anything but skirts sure doesn't know how to put in an honest day's work. I'd rather die than have to wear those things."

Bowen sighed. "I keep hoping, but she's about as headstrong as they come. That's why my sister sent her out to me from Philadelphia."

"Dad, you want me to fix the supper, or do you want to do it? If I'm going to cook, I sure can't be bothered thinking about getting frilly sleeves into the fry pan."

"Hmmpf!" Bowen snorted. "How would you know? You never tried."

Ben was enjoying himself, knowing that it was the type of pleasant banter that father and daughter had engaged in for many years.

"Tell you what I'll do, Cindy," he offered. "Next time I come over here, if you're wearing something pretty and frilly, I'll think about selling you that filly."

Her eyes flared. "Keep her!" she snapped, and stalked into the kitchen.

8

CHARLIE Bowen wasn't the gruff man he appeared to be. Ben found him easy to talk to, easy to know, the kind of man he'd be proud to say was a friend. What Ben found most surprising about him was his concern for the rights of every class of settler moving into Montana.

"I'm always getting myself into trouble with other members of the Association," Charlie confessed. "Most of the cattlemen around here act like they've got burrs under their saddles when it comes to the sheepmen. Hell, I don't like the idea of sheep grazing the prairie grass so short there's nothing left but the roots, either, but who's got the right to tell a sheepman he can't raise woolies here? If the range is free, it's free for them as well as for us."

"Tempers run high here, too?"

"Ben, it's more than temper. A group of ranchers over in the higher reaches of the Yellowstone went so far as to publish notices in the newspapers that they considered sheep worse than wolves or coyotes, and any sheep found on their ranges would be killed. Now, even if I don't have any use for them myself, I can't go along with slaughtering a flock of a couple thousand sheep and putting somebody out of business just because he's using the same free land that I am."

Ben nodded. "I've seen the same thing in Dakota. They're even worse when it comes to farmers. Let a nester settle in to raise some vegetables to feed the townspeople, and they'll run him off by any means they can."

"It doesn't make sense," Charlie said. "If it weren't for the nesters, towns like Miles City couldn't exist. It isn't everybody who can grow enough potatoes and corn to see himself through the winter, and you sure as hell can't ship it all in from the East. We had one come out here from Indiana. Settled in down the Mizpah and busted the sod for wheat and corn. That first crop fed some beefs, and he bought a carload of barbed wire. Strung wire around the place, miles of it, just so he could keep cows out of his wheat and corn. Poke Peterson and some of his boys bought every pair of wire cutters this side of Chicago, and by the time the cattlemen got done with that Hoosier, he had tons of short pieces of wire. Packed it in and went back to Indiana last year."

"I don't care to see barbed wire anywhere," Ben said strongly. "As far as I'm concerned, it's the worst thing ever invented."

Charlie studied Ben's face. The hard look told him there was more to Ben's dislike of barbed wire than cutting the range, and he didn't press the subject.

"Maybe, Ben, but times change. One of these days every cattleman is going to have to fence off his own land. Can't say I like it, but it's going to come. Well, looks like it's about time to eat."

Conversation through supper was aimless, and Ben was grateful. The mention of barbed wire had sent his mind rushing back to the time he turned his back on Mandan and the hide business. He didn't care what anybody said about Glidden and Bates, the inventor and promoter of the wire. They were just two more insidious actors in the continuing drama by Aeschylus.

When Ben left the Rafter B, he turned and waved back to Cindy who was waving to him from the porch. For a brief moment, he imagined he could see Eva waving, and he felt his throat tighten. It had all been so utterly senseless.

When he rode out of Mandan that winter day so long ago, he had no thought about what he was going to do. During the long months of recovering from the wound, he had considered going back to Boston, or even to Chicago. But the brief time he and Eva had spent in Chicago proved to him that he no longer cared for the pace of big cities, and that his future was here on the western frontier. Staying in the leather business had no appeal, either; it had brought him nothing but grief. His second year at Mandan had been profitable, but all the signs pointed to a dead and dying industry. The great herds of buffalo were gone, and he'd only shipped about half the number of hides he had the year before. The shed where he'd bought hides and shipped them East was now used by bone crushers, who bought wagonloads of buffalo bones that littered the prairies, crushed them and shipped carloads of the powder to fertilizer factories.

He rode to Dickinson the first day, and was having supper when Harley Dillan walked into the restaurant.

"Benny! What in tarnation damn you doin' here?"

"What's it look like, Harley? I'm eating."

Harley pulled up a chair and ordered a slab of steak with a pile of potatoes.

"Heard what happened, Ben. I'm sorry."

Ben choked back a lump in his throat and nodded.

"Thanks, Harley. But what are you doing here yourself? Don't tell me you've decided to turn honest after all these years."

"Reckon I might have to. Sure as hell ain't gonna make a livin' huntin' buffalo any more. They're gone. Thought I might move south afore the winter sets in. Dunno for sure."

"Mind if I ride with you? I don't have anything else to do. Besides, I could use someone to teach me how to hunt. I've got a rifle and a pistol, and I've never fired either of them."

"You serious, Benny?"

"Absolutely. So serious I'd even be willing to pay you."

Ben and Harley never left Dickinson that winter. Ben paid for a room at the little hotel, and every day they rode out of town to spend hours teaching Ben the fundamentals of tracking game and how to shoot. There were times when the shoulder wound had him wincing with pain, but constant exercise began to loosen it up, and soon he was hardly aware of it.

Harley took him a step at a time, standing, crouching, kneeling. They spent days as Ben learned to fire from horseback, and it wasn't until March that Harley was satisfied he could teach Ben nothing more about bringing down anything that moved.

"There's some fancy stuff, too, but you ain't gonna need it."

"What do you mean by fancy stuff, Harley?"

"Little tricks only a gunslinger ever uses, like the road agent flip. Once anybody sees you use somethin' like that, you git branded as a professional gun-fighter, an' who needs that? Better you learn how to rope and handle beefs. Man who can punch cows ain't never gonna be outta work."

Two weeks later they signed on with a small ranch-er who needed extra hands for the Spring roundup and Ben found he liked the work. It was better than being cooped up in a smelly hide shed or a city of-fice. He enjoyed the nights in the open, and thought life couldn't be better. The exhausting work of gather-ing cattle and branding them left him with little time to think of Eva.

He and Harley were riding night herd on the third watch when he experienced his first stampede. By the time the crew got the cattle under control, Ben knew Aeschylus was still at work.

"Where's Harley?" someone asked.

"I don't know," Ben replied. "He was on the far side from me. Let's go have a look."

It was shortly after daybreak when they found him. During the wild ride to get ahead of the stampeding cattle, Harley had swung wide and ridden into a fence. He was still alive when they found him ripped to shreds and tangled in the wire. His chest and belly were torn open, and his guts spilled out, droop-ing into the dirt.

"Jesus Christ!" Sam said. "I've seen a lot of men tangled up in wire before, but none like this."

"Take it easy, Harley," Ben said. "We'll get you out."

Harley didn't reply, but stared vacantly as Ben and Sam began cutting his clothing from the sharp-pointed barbs. He died before they finished.

"Damn!" Ben shouted. "I'd like to get my hands on the man who invented this inhuman stuff!"

They buried Harley near the fence, and Ben vented his anger by getting a pair of side-cutting pliers from the tool box and hacking the fence in several places. He was cutting wire when two riders appeared on the other side of the fence.

"What the hell do you think you're doing, mister?"

"Cutting some wire, what does it look like? This wire killed a friend of mine last night."

"That ain't very smart, I'd say," one of the men replied as he reached to pull the rifle from the boot.

Ben's Colt was out and one shot knocked the rider from his horse. Sam had his Winchester aimed at the other by the time Ben realized what he had done.

"Go pick up his carcass and git," Sam said. "I reckon he made a mistake by drawin' on us."

As they rode back to the crew, Ben's stomach was churning. "Damn it, Sam, I killed a man."

"Right nice job, too. Pure self-defense."

Self-defense or not, Ben thought, Aeschylus had a way of turning the tables on him and chuckling. Once more he'd turned around and snatched someone Ben had allowed himself to become attached to. Would it ever stop?

9

CINDY watched from the porch as Ben rode away, and waved at him when he turned in the saddle for a look behind him. What was it about this particular man that bothered her? He could be infuriating, and yet . . .

The horse and rider topped the rise in the distance without looking back again, and Cindy went inside. Her father was sitting at his desk, studying the receipts of the first shipment of cattle for the season. His brow was deeply furrowed, and he had a worried look on his face.

"Something's bothering you, Dad."

He looked up, and his face eased into a smile. "Not really. Just trying to make up my mind whether to stick with cattle or switch the operation to horses, that's all. That and people trying to tell me I ought to get into politics. Any coffee left?"

She nodded and brought two mugs from the kitchen. He had put the papers back into the desk drawer, and was tilted back in his chair.

"Thanks," he said, taking the mug. "Well, now that you've had a chance to meet him, how does he strike you?"

"Ben Foster?"

"I'm not talking about Frenchy Wibaux, gal."

Cindy could feel herself blushing, and then felt the anger rising again.

"He seems to know quite a bit about horses. But he's stubborn."

"So are you."

"Dad, just because I'd like to have that foal doesn't mean . . ."

"What it means is that you're going to make a fool of yourself if you keep pestering him. He feels the same way about her as I do about the blue roan."

Cindy dropped her eyes. "I know."

After a moment of silence, she asked, "Dad, what is it about him that's so different?"

"Different how?"

"Well, he doesn't strike me as being like all the other men in the Territory. He's . . . he's . . ."

"Better looking?" Charlie asked with a smile.

"Well, there's that, but . . . oh, that's not what I meant. It's like somehow he doesn't really belong here, you know what I mean?"

"No."

"He's . . . well, polite, without being toady. He just isn't like most of the men around here."

Charlie shrugged his shoulders. "Is that good or bad?"

"I don't know. But he just doesn't act like a man who . . . well, a saddle tramp. Somehow he seems to be so much better. You know, easier going, more polite, more . . ."

"Stubborn?" Charlie's eyes sparkled.

Cindy flashed him a look of impatience.

"Maybe you find him different because he's got

some polish, education," Charlie said. "Roosevelt told us they went to Harvard together, and you don't find many men riding this range who have been to Harvard."

"That's what I can't figure out about him, Dad. What's somebody like that doing out here?"

"What're any of us doing out here?" he replied. "Why anybody comes out here is a private affair, you know that. It could be that he's just looking for something better than he had before. A man with nothing but brains and ambition can still make a fortune here. Particularly one who can do more than read or write a little."

She nodded, then suddenly stood up. "Well, I don't care about his background. But I'm going to have that foal if it's the last thing I do."

"Keep thinking that way, and maybe it will be. One of these days, gal, you're going to find out that you can't have everything you want."

"Dad, let's not start that again," she said, impatience in her voice. "I've heard it a thousand times."

"And you'll hear it another thousand times until you learn there's both give and take in life. If you think you're going to get that foal of Ben's just because you set your mind to it, you're going to be in for a big disappointment. The only way you're going to get her is to take him with it."

"Hah!" she exclaimed. "The last thing I need is to have a man telling me what to wear, just because he likes to hear the rustle of petticoats, and smell some stinking perfume all the time."

Charlie stood up and walked around the desk to Cindy's chair. He stroked her cheek with the tips of his heavy fingers, and said, "You're so much like your mother. Just as pretty, just as bull-headed. One of these days you're going to make some man a fine wife, Cindy."

"Not me," she said. "Would you want me to wind up like poor Agnes Welch?"

"And what's wrong with Agnes Welch?" Charlie asked with surprise. "Hal's got himself a good woman there. And he takes good care of her, doesn't he?"

"Does he? Just because she's a catalog woman doesn't mean he has to treat her like a slave."

"From what I've seen, Agnes Welch is damned near as independent as you are. And just because he got her to come out here through a lonely hearts magazine doesn't mean she's any less a woman, Cindy."

"Oh, Dad, do you know what he told her the day they got married?"

"Sure, we were there. He promised to love her, honor her and cherish her. That's what he told her in front of everyone in the courthouse. She got off that train, and there were a hundred of us there to meet her. The preacher married them an hour later, and we had a big feast. And they've got two kids now, and Agnes is one of the most respected women in the basin."

"Sure, but she's worked hard for it. And I remember Hal pulling his old watch from his pocket at dinner and saying it was time to go home. 'We got us a working ranch, Agnes, and that alarm clock's going to go off at five. When it does, I want to hear your feet flap the floor.' Those are his exact words."

"So what? They've learned to love each other, haven't they?"

Cindy scowled. "Love! Nothing but weakness. From what everyone tells me, it takes all the energy out of you. I for one don't want to have anything to do with being in love."

Charlie Bowen smiled. "Nobody ever does. But when it happens, gal, there's no stopping it."

"Dad, be sure to tell me when Hell freezes over.

Until then I don't want anything to do with it."

"Not even if it comes with dark blue eyes and yellow hair and a flattened nose, huh?"

"Oh, Dad! Don't be silly!"

10

BEN and Twice Thompson watched with amusement as Roosevelt tried for the third time to drop his loop over Manitou, the black gelding that was his favorite mount.

"Gotta use a bigger noose, Four Eyes," Twice called.

"Or a smaller horse," Ben added.

Roosevelt's large teeth flashed beneath the bushy mustache. "Fear not," he said jovially. "I shall prevail."

The next time the horses circled past at an easy trot, Roosevelt's rope landed flat on the gelding's back, and Twice muttered, "Shit, he's tryin' to snag 'im by the tail. Reckon maybe we oughta give 'im a hand?"

"Hell no. He's got to learn."

It was on the fifth pass that the noose opened and dropped over the gelding's head, and Roosevelt leaned into the rope and eased his mount out of the pack. He walked his way along the rope, rubbed the gelding's nose, and yanked his fingers back just in time to keep from getting bitten. He had no trouble saddling the animal, and even managed to keep his seat while the gelding made a half-hearted attempt to discourage the idea of going to work for the day.

"Reckon he might get the hang of it after a while," Twice commented as Ben climbed aboard his mare. "Sure got a lot of guts, he has."

"Always did," Ben said, rubbing his nose. "I don't think he'd ever back down from anything. He stood up to that charging buffalo like it was a harmless puppy coming to be fed."

Roosevelt and Ben rode to the north and east of the Elkhorn Ranch, along the edge of the prairie. They had come across about twenty scattered head that belonged to the Elkhorn, along with a dozen others that had strayed far from home. Ben showed him how the herding instinct of cattle was used to advantage. He swung wide behind three of the strays, and began to chase them to the south. Before they had gone a mile, they were joined by two that came from a thicket of briers. Before they turned north again, the first three had been joined by nine more.

"By Jove, I didn't know it was that easy," Roosevelt said.

"Sometimes it isn't. Most of them like to stay close to the others, but there are always the bunch of quitters that have minds of their own," Ben said. "They're the ones that make roundup work fun. The minute they spot a dry creek bed, or a brush pile, they head off on their own. You'll find out what I mean when we start the shovedown next month."

"Shovedown?"

"Fall roundup. Shove them down out of the hills before winter sets in. That's when we make the beef cut. The Spring roundup is mostly for branding calves. In the Fall, we cut out the beef steers and get rid of older animals that might not make it through the winter."

They stopped to water the horses and let them graze for an hour, and Roosevelt spent the time talking about one of his favorite topics: the inevitable day when the Territory would become a state. Seldom did a day go by that he didn't find an opportunity to discuss politics. It was almost as though he were still back at Harvard campaigning for free beer.

"It can't take much longer, Ben. Now that the railroad has come through, you're going to see this whole country settle down. Why, the cities are growing so rapidly, I shouldn't be surprised if Bismarck should some day become as large as Chicago. And Miles City may well become the capital of Montana."

"There's a lot of money centered around Miles City," Ben admitted.

"Exactly, and money is power."

"That's true, but a lot of it around here has come out of England, and France. I was talking with Charlie Bowen not too long ago about that, and he doesn't seem to think enough people agree on what they want to settle down and even agree that they want to become a state."

"I assure you, Ben, Charles Bowen is mistaken. I've spent a great deal of time talking with cattlemen, sheepmen, farmers and townsmen alike. I am certain there shall be a great rejoicing when statehood arrives. The people are ready for it, they thirst for it like a dying man on the desert, and it shall be men like Charles Bowen who will become the leaders when the time comes."

"Because he has money?" Ben asked, his mind envisioning Charlie Bowen debating in the Senate at Washington while Cindy sat in the gallery in her dusty jeans and sombrero.

"No, because the man has common sense. He knows that every faction has a right to be heard, and that no one viewpoint alone is correct. He is the only one who will admit that the ranchers have no more rights than the farmers, and that there are good Indians as well as scoundrels. Why, I haven't met an Indian yet who is half as bad as Curly Schaeffer would have them appear."

"You haven't met many Indians, then, Teddy. Sure, there are good ones, but the only ones you've met have been in the towns."

Two hours later they rode up a slight rise and came out onto a plateau that was perhaps half a mile broad. When they neared the middle of it, ten Indians suddenly appeared coming over the edge of the plateau ahead of them. The moment they saw the two white men, they whipped their rifles out of their slings and kicked their horses ahead at a full run, whooping and screaming, brandishing their weapons in the air.

"Sioux," Ben said, reining up. "Get down!"

Roosevelt followed Ben's lead, dismounting from Manitou and standing with the horse between himself and the Indians.

Ben had wondered how Teddy would handle real danger but he was cool and steady, muttering, "Bully challenge," under his breath.

"Lucky we met them here," Ben said. "We've got a better chance on an open plain like this than if it was broken country."

"Even in the open?"

"Especially in the open. They don't have any place to hide and sneak up behind us."

Both horses stood steady as rocks, and when the Sioux were a hundred yards off, Ben and Roosevelt threw their rifles over their saddles and took aim at the leader of the charge.

The effect was like magic. The ten Indians scattered like a flock of wild ducks and doubled back, bending low over their ponies. When they were beyond range, they drew together and spent a few minutes in discussion.

"Here comes the chief," Ben said. "Don't believe a word any Sioux says."

The leader of the band moved slightly away from the others, stopped his pony and with a great show dropped his rifle to the ground. He then waved his blanket over his head as he advanced. When he reached fifty yards, Ben called out.

"Hold it! Stop right there!"

The Sioux pulled out a slip of paper and waved it in the air.

"What is that?" Roosevelt asked.

"His pass, most likely."

"Pass?"

"Any Indian away from his reservation has to carry a pass," Ben explained. "If he gets caught by the Army without it, he's in trouble. Personally, I don't care if it's a pass or if it's a page from the newspaper. There are too many of them over there for me to feel comfortable."

"How!" shouted the young buck. "Me good Indian!"

"I am very pleased to know you are," Roosevelt called back. "What do you want?"

He began to move closer, and Ben cocked his Remington. "That's close enough!"

"We hunt the deer," the Indian called, reining in his pony at Ben's command.

"There aren't any deer up here," Ben said. "No deer."

"Have white men seen tracks?"

"No deer. No sign," Ben said. "Now go on about your business."

The young Sioux sat impassively for a moment, then pushed the paper back into his breech clout. Once more he raised his empty hand, and then cut loose with a string of unintelligible sounds that could never be mistaken for anything but curses."

"Go!" Ben shouted to him.

"We will go," the Sioux called back. "May your worthless white asses feed the coyotes and buzzards until the day your whoring mothers stop sleeping with the yellow men from beyond the great waters!" He turned and rode slowly toward his band, who were whooping with delight.

"My word!" Roosevelt exclaimed. "That was proper, canonical Anglo-Saxon profanity!"

"Yeah," Ben agreed, watching the band move slowly off. "He's one of the better ones. Well-educated."

"Do you think they would really have attacked us?"

"Why not? That's how they usually get their horses, rifles and any other gear they can. Not to mention a couple of scalps to brag about around the campfire."

The Sioux hovered around on the plateau for a while, as though deciding whether to make another charge or not. Ben and Roosevelt walked, leading their horses until the Indians gave up and rode over the edge, disappearing from sight.

"Let's put some ground between us and them," Ben said, swinging up. "I wouldn't put it past them to try to swing around and meet us on the other side."

They rode hard, leaving the plateau in the opposite direction. Once down on open prairie again, Roosevelt admitted, "Surprising, but it's only now that I'm beginning to feel uneasy."

"I think we got off lucky," Ben said, wondering how well Roosevelt could have handled himself if the band of young bucks had decided to risk an attack. "Maybe all they meant to do was throw a scare into us. They'll do that sometimes, you know. But I was with seven men who brought some of the first cattle up here, and we managed to stand off about fifty or sixty Cheyenne. Lost some cows, most of our horses, and one man. We killed six of them, and wounded a couple of others. They can't shoot very well while they're slung over behind their ponies, and we could pretty well pick them off if they showed their heads."

"My word! I thought those days were long behind us."

"That was a couple of years back," Ben admitted. "But I still don't trust them. I like my hair growing on my head, not hanging from some smelly buck's belt."

Toward nightfall they came upon a shack near the Killdeer Mountains, and hailed it.

"Hello the house!" Ben called.

"Come on in," came a shouted reply, and two men appeared through the doorway, their rifles at the ready. When they saw only the two men approaching, they relaxed.

"Rest your saddles," one of them said. "I'm Farley Crandall, and this here's Sticks Wilson."

Ben grinned. "Howdy, Sticks. Thought you'd gone clear out to the Pacific."

"Well, I'll be damned! Didn't expect to see you, neither, Ben Foster. You still out buying hides?"

"Nope, working for Mr. Roosevelt here. He's the new owner of the Elkhorn and Maltese Cross outfits. What're you doing now that the buffalo are gone?"

"Hell, they ain't gone, Ben," Sticks said. "Jist gettin' harder to find, that's all. Mostly doing some trappin', a little huntin'. Gettin' along."

While sharing the rich, bubbling stew of the two trappers, Ben and Roosevelt told them of the encounter with the Indians earlier.

"Ten of 'em? An' their leader could swear like an ol' mule skinner?" Sticks asked.

"Sounds like you know them."

"Them bastids come through here this morning an' made off with two of our horses. I swear to God ol' Sherman was right. Only good Injuns is dead ones!"

"Maybe, Sticks, maybe not. The last time I ran into any who were out stealing horses, it was because a couple of whites had just stolen some from them. All they wanted to do was even things up a bit."

"They can damn well even things up somewheres else," Crandall said. "Next time any of 'em try to make off with my horses, I aim to get me a couple more of those."

He pointed to the wall next to the chimney, and Roosevelt's gasp could be heard in the small cabin as he stared at four dried Indian scalps hanging on nails.

The next morning, as they were riding south toward the Elkhorn, Ben asked, "Well, Teddy, do you still think Dakota Territory has settled down enough to be a state? Now that you've seen how the Indians and whites get along?"

"Of course," Roosevelt boomed. "There will be ruffians in any society, red as well as white. I daresay that man Crandall is atypical, as were the Sioux who threw a scare into us yesterday. No, Ben, you'll see that men like Farley Crandall and Indians like the ones we met are a very small minority."

"Maybe, but they're a dangerous minority."

"That may be true, but they're not as prevalent as writers in the East would have you believe."

"I doubt if very many of those guys ever set foot across the Mississippi."

"By Jove, Ben, I doubt that one in ten has set foot this side of the Alleghenies."

As they rode further south, they found a few more strays that belonged to the Elkhorn, and drove them ahead. By the time they got to one of the larger herds on the home range, they had pulled together forty-three, most of whom bore the Elkhorn brand.

Twice asked how the trip had gone.

"Not bad. I think he's going to make it."

"One thing for sure," Twice said, twisting the ends of a cigarette, "he don't pay no attention to nobody laughin' at him."

Ben grinned. "I know. He doesn't mind us calling him Four Eyes. The only thing he wants is to be able to prove himself one of us."

"Well, I reckon we cotton up to 'im all right."

"Yep, but one of these days someone's going to call him Old Four Eyes. That's how he'll know he's arrived."

"He done practiced with them six-shooters an' rifles till I knowed he was gonna use up a case a bullets ever' week. An' he kin rope a dogie as well as the rest of us. But he still don't seem real. That's gonna take somethin' pretty special."

"What's that?"

"That's the day he kin ride the hurricane deck on old Water Skipper."

11

CURLY Schaeffer, the huge pot-bellied foreman of the Elkhorn, pulled up alongside Ben and Twice while the Maltese Cross crew was moving a bunch of steers up the Little Missouri.

"How's it going?"

"Not bad, Curly. Twice and I have just about got the bottom lands swept clean. Lot of Rafter B stock over this way, though. Almost as many as ours."

Curly took off his grimy hat and wiped the sweat off his bald head. "We even found some up on the Elkhorn. Wish to God Bowen would put on a few extra hands. Ever since he's come into this country it seems like we're tending more of his cattle than our own."

"Seen anything of a big Aberdeen bull?" Ben asked.

"Not since the roundup last May. I hear he hasn't been seen since then. Looks like Bowen's gonna be out a pretty penny. Is it true he's offering a reward for anyone who brings him home?"

"A hundred dollars," Ben replied. "Gold."

"Wouldn't mind having part of it," Curly said. "But I'll probably have to buy a comb and brush before that bull ever shows up anywhere. Why the hell doesn't Bowen hire a few more range riders to keep track of his stock? Every year we find more of his stock over here than our own."

"Maybe them beefs of his just likes our grass better," Twice said, spitting in the dust. "Last year we branded two Rafter B calves for every three Maltese Cross."

Curly extracted a thin stogie from a silver case in his shirt pocket and lit it with a flourish. "Four Eyes says he's going along on the pushdown. Wouldn't want to miss it for anything."

"Shit!" Twice muttered. "He's gonna be about as much help as a burr in a boot."

"So what?" Curly said. "They're his beefs aren't they?"

"He gonna be runnin' the show?"

"Just going along to work. He wants me to teach him everything I can, then if he thinks he's got the feel of it, maybe he'll take over next year."

"He's learned a lot already," Ben said in Roosevelt's defense. "And from what I know of him, he'll either make the grade or die trying."

"Or get us killed in the process."

Curly studied the steers moving along the river. "Hell, you weren't putting me on, were you? There's almost as many Rafter B critters there as ours."

"Yep. Thought I'd ride over there tomorrow and see if Charlie wants to come get 'em. Shame to push 'em across the river and have them scatter again before he can ship them."

"As long as you're going that way, Ben, how about you going into Miles City and see if you can find a couple of extra hands for the shovedown? We'll need about eight men for a month or so."

At noon the next day, Ben pulled up in front of the neat house at the Rafter B, and stepped over the two dogs on the porch to knock on the door. Cindy called from the kitchen.

"Come on in. You're just in time for dinner."

"Can't stay long enough for that, Cindy. I'm on my way to Miles City."

She met him in the huge living room. "Unless you're planning to eat at the Macqueen House to-night, you won't get any better food than I've got ready for the table."

"Your Dad here?"

"You don't think I'd be cooking a big meal if he wasn't, do you? Even got a couple of huckleberry pies."

"Well, since I haven't had any huckleberry pie since I left Bismarck a few years back, I might slow down long enough to see if yours is as good."

"As good as whose?"

"German woman, name of Kleinstaedtler. Had the best food in the Indian Territory. Ran a place called the Prussian Kitchen. Now that woman knew how to cook."

Ben quickly changed the subject. The memory of what he had lost in Mandan still brought a sadness he couldn't get rid of.

"We've got a bunch of your steers penned into a canyon over at the Maltese Cross."

"On the other side of the River? Seems our cattle stray more than anybody else's. Last year they found a couple of them clear up to Fort Peck."

Charlie Bowen came into the kitchen through the back door. "Howdy, Ben." He tossed his hat at the peg on the wall, then picked it up from the floor.

"That's the second time I've missed. Must be getting old."

"You mean it's the second time this week, Dad?"

"Nope, just the second time. There was the first time, and this is the second time. I don't count the ones in between."

As Cindy carved huge slabs of roast venison, Charley asked, "What brings you over this way, Ben?"

"I'm on my way to Miles City to hire some extra hands for the shovedown. Stopped here to tell you we've got about eighty head of your steers ready to ship."

"Right nice of you to save me the work," Bowen said with a chuckle. "Tell Four Eyes I've got some thirty or forty of his mixed in with my bunch down the river a ways. I was planning on going up to town this afternoon for the same purpose. This time of year the town is crawling with men looking for work."

"Usually," Ben said. "Might not be so many this year, though. There aren't any hanging around over our way."

"How come?"

"The Marquis has been hiring anyone who can swing a hammer or a saw. He's putting up that slaughterhouse."

"That Frenchman has got more ways to make everybody rich than you can shake a fist at," Charley said with disgust. "Last year he had crews building ice houses, and must have kept a hundred men at work all winter cutting and hauling ice. Seventy-five dollars a month to cut and haul ice!"

"How many slaughterhouses is he planning to build, Dad?"

"Who can tell? He's got the idea that if he can put up a slaughterhouse and ice house every hundred miles along the railroad, he'll be able to make more money shipping meat than raising cattle. Maybe so, but you mark my words; he's going to lose every cent he's invested."

He looked at Ben and raised an eyebrow. "I've heard rumors that he and Four Eyes are on the outs."

"I doubt it. They have their differences, but it isn't anything serious. It isn't just because de Mores controls so much over that way; most of it is politics."

Cindy had just cut the huckleberry pie when they heard hoofbeats approaching the house in a hurry. Charlie got out onto the front porch just as Dave Mulholland pulled up.

"Charlie, can you get a couple of your boys and give me a hand?"

"What's the trouble, Dave?"

"I just lost two of my mares."

"Rustlers?"

"Not this time. It's a wild stallion. That critter kicked the door off the stable and made off with them. Big blue roan."

Charlie and Ben stared at each other in disbelief. "You want us to help you get that stallion, Dave?"

"I don't want the damned stallion anywhere around! There ain't one wild stallion in a thousand that can be tamed, you know that. Try to keep him penned up, and he'll kick his way through anything, including brick walls. I just want some help getting my mares back."

"Come on, Ben. We'll get his mares, and then go after that blue roan."

"You think we've got a chance of catching him, Charlie?"

"We can sure as hell try, can't we?"

12

THEY found the band of about forty mares belonging to the wild stallion in a wide valley about ten miles below Mulholland's place. They were grazing peacefully, and it was easy to spot Mulholland's two mares, the only ones who had ever been groomed. The stud was a good mile away from the pack, keeping a watchful eye on his harem. When the strange horses appeared with riders, he whinnied a warning, and the wild mares were suddenly alert and ready to run.

Charlie patted the neck of his mount, saying, "That sure looks like your daddy over there, Bluebelle. We'll go get Dave's animals, and then see if we can get your daddy."

Mulholland had brought two men with him, and the six riders went into action, keeping the band of mares in a tight circle. Charlie Bowen got his loop over one of Mulholland's mares and Ben got the other.

While they were working at rescuing Mulholland's mares from the band, the stallion had moved farther off in an ever-widening circle. Charlie and Ben sat and watched him for a few minutes.

"Lordy, that's a beautiful beast, Ben!"

"Sure is. And he's a pacer."

Cindy pulled up. "You going to give it a try, Dad?"

"Gal, if we can snare that stallion, we've got the makings of the best horse herd in the Territory. Dave, you let me have your two men for a while?"

"Sure, Charlie. I'll take my mares home and come back with some grub. If you're set on catchin' that beast, I reckon you're gonna be a spell."

Mulholland started for home with his two mares on lead ropes, and Charlie and Ben plotted their course of action.

"That son of a gun's settled into a five-mile radius, looks like," Charlie said.

"As long as we keep his mares here, he's not going to leave," Ben said. "I think the best way's going to be relaying him. There are five of us. It'll only take two or three to control the mares. We'll have to tire him out. I'll start. Charlie, you're next. Then Ed, then Jase. Cindy, you stick with the mares."

"Like hell I'll stick with the mares! I don't mind going last, but I'm going to do my share of it."

Ben's eyebrows shot up at her profanity, but he didn't comment on it. "It's going to be some hard riding."

"I can keep up with any man out here. Now let's get started, shall we?"

The stud was pacing easily, keeping a distance of four or five miles from his mares, and as Ben moved in to about a half-mile back, the blue roan began lengthening his stride. Ben expected it, and pushed forward.

The distance between the stallion and the horse

behind was never less than a quarter of a mile. By the time Ben had ridden a half circle, Charlie was moving out to take his place. When Charlie had made a half-circle, Ed took his turn.

"It's going to take a lot to tire that animal," Charlie said. "As fast as Bluebelle can move, we still couldn't close the gap. Sooner or later, though, that boy is going to tire out, and then we'll have him."

"Maybe," Ben said. "Let's see how it goes, first."

Dusk was setting in when Dave returned with a bag of biscuits, some jerky and the coffee makings.

"Still runnin', I see."

"No sign of slowing down, either," Ben said wearily.

"I thought we were being a bit merciless in relaying him like this," Cindy said, "but now I'm convinced it's the other way around. We can't keep this up all night."

"You're right," Ben agreed. "But we can hang onto those mares. He won't leave them. But he'll have all night to get rested up."

"I figured you'd do something like that," Mulholland said. "Brought some blankets, too." He pulled a huge roll of blankets off his horse, and said, "I got me a feeling tomorrow's going to be a long day."

It was a moonless night, and there was a cloud cover which obscured even the faint light of the stars. Charlie had to give up the chase when it was too dark to see, and came in to the campsite. He gratefully accepted the coffee and jerky, but fell asleep sitting up before he'd finished half the cup.

Ben and Cindy had the second night watch to ride herd on the mares. Cindy wasn't as tired as Ben thought she would be. Maybe Twice had been right about her when he said she could work as hard as any man in the basin.

"How far do you think we ran that stallion today, Ben?" she asked around a mouthful of jerky.

"Well, it's about a five mile radius, near as I can figure it. That'd put it at about a thirty-mile circumference, and we've made three full circuits. Comes to about ninety miles."

In the light of the fire, he could see the awe in her eyes. "Ninety miles without breaking that beautiful pace. No water, no rest. And he still kept ahead of us. Do you think he'll still be here in the morning, Ben?"

"Yep. It's going to take a lot more than what we gave him today to make him leave his mares."

"I'm beginning to see why Dad wants him."

"He's not the only one. We've already agreed that if we can catch him, that old stud is going to build up herds for both of us. Just think what we'd have if we could count on even one foal in ten to be like Blue-Belle."

They ate in silence, and then turned in to get a few hours sleep. The fall evening was chilly, and Ben was asleep almost before he had pulled himself into his sleeping roll.

At ten o'clock, Dave Mulholland woke Ben and Cindy. They warmed up with a mug of coffee, then went out and relieved Jase and Ed. Hardly a word was spoken between them, even when they passed on their circuits of the band. From far off they could hear the stallion calling to his mares several times, and once had to work hard to keep them from breaking away in response to his demands that they join him.

At daybreak, they began relaying the stallion again. It was a relentless chase, and as he had done the day before, the quarry kept about a quarter of a mile between himself and the rider behind. Through the morning and into the afternoon he paced ahead of them, never stopping to graze, to drink, or to take a second wind.

Ben's admiration for the stud grew by the hour, and while he was running the relay about three o'clock he saw that they were beating a well-worn path on the prairie.

It as almost dusk again when Ben made his next circuit, and he thought he was gaining a bit. The distance was down to about eight hundred yards, and he urged his mare forward, getting every bit of speed she could manage.

When he had closed the gap to about five hundred yards, the stallion screamed his anger into the air, and for the first time all day broke his pace and began to run. He swerved from the worn trail they'd beaten down, and headed off to the southwest, leaving his band of mares and would-be captors far behind.

It was useless to attempt to follow him. Ben turned and rode back to the campsite, where Charlie shook his head sadly.

"I had a feeling about noon that we'd never catch him up," he told Ben. "It was a good try, though."

"We don't have him, but there are several pregnant mares in the bunch, Charlie. Maybe we'll be lucky."

"Ben, do you think he'll come back for them?" Cindy asked.

"If he does, he'll be the first one. He finally realized that we weren't going to give up. It's easier to find some more mares than to get these away from us. He can pick them up on the range, or he can steal them like he did Dave's. One thing's for sure, though. That horse is going to run free as long as he's alive."

"Lordy," Charlie said, "counting the number of times he ran that circle, he covered better than two hundred miles today."

"Yep, and then left us eating his dust."

As they moved the band of mares back to the Rafter B, Ben watched Cindy on the far side, working trail. After two days of relentless work chasing the blue roan stallion, she was still beautiful, despite the grime she had accumulated. But Ben was wary of allowing himself to think about her. Old Aeschylus had a way of writing another act in his play when things seemed to be going too smoothly.

13

TURNER'S Theater was one of the many saloons that lined the streets of Miles City. Three soldiers from Fort Keogh sat on a narrow wooden bench on the porch, smoking and talking with two cowboys about the problem of rustlers, who had even made off with an occasional Army horse despite the size of the US brand. Inside, the small stage was deserted, but the poker tables and faro layouts were as busy in the afternoon as they would be later in the evening. Cowboys who were in town looking for work were lined up two deep at the bar, laughing and trading yarns.

A dozen short-skirted girls worked their way through the crowded room, trying to entice customers to go upstairs to have "a bottle of wine" for five dollars, or into the curtained rooms behind the stage for a fast fling at love for a dollar. At the foot of the stage the piano player kept up a lively string of melodies, giving a carnival air to the saloon, never missing a beat as he systematically drained his beer mug and threatened to "shut down the orchestra" if the mug wasn't refilled before the end of the tune.

Ben and Charlie worked their way through the crowded room to one of the tables near the stage.

"Mornin', Charlie."

"Howdy, Poke," Charlie said as he eased himself into a chair. "Ben Foster, from over at the Maltese Cross. Ben, this is Poke Peterson, runs the Open P outfit up on Beaver Creek."

Peterson shoved a calloused hand forward. "Nice to meet you, Mr. Foster. I hear there's a new owner over there."

"Yep, man from New York. Teddy Roosevelt. Bought the Maltese Cross and the Elkhorn."

"We're both here looking for some extra hands," Charlie said.

Peterson glanced around the room. "I thought I'd put on eight or ten until the snow comes. Plenty of good men around here this week. By next week they'll be broke and ready to go to work again."

Ben knew the pattern well. Probably less than half the men in the Territory had permanent jobs, and worked only through the Spring and Fall roundups. In between they took whatever odd jobs they could find, and many of them simply lived off the land, camping out and hunting game for their meat. There were the hunters, too, who filled the off season killing wolves and coyotes for the bounty offered by the Stock Growers Association. Two of them had come east from the mountains, carrying bags full of ears to be redeemed. There were bricklayers, carpenters, blacksmiths, men with wide varieties of skills who simply preferred the excitement of working roundups to the more mundane daily chores in town.

There were the inevitable greenhorns, who had come from the cities in the East to try the "glamorous" life of the cowboys they had read about in cheap novels, most of them between fifteen and eighteen years old. Some would last a year or two, then return to their homes and spend the rest of their lives bragging about their part in exploits they'd only heard about, and some would remain for the rest of their lives, which could be extremely short.

Ben remembered the cook who worked a ranch near George Fowler's horse outfit near Mandan. He'd come from Peoria, spent one season working cattle, and during the last week of the roundup was gored in the leg by a nasty-tempered steer. The boy had been thrown high in the air, and most of the flesh of his leg had been ripped from the bone in the process. By the time the doctor could halt the spread of gangrene, he had lost the leg. Rather than turn him out on his own, the rancher decided to put him to work helping the cook. When Ben last saw him, he'd taken over the cook shack and was turning out better than average food. The regular hands on the ranch chipped in to help buy him an artificial leg, rather than the wooden peg he'd learned to use, and gave it to him as a birthday present the day he turned seventeen.

But there were also those who would die under their horses or the hooves of stampeding cattle. They were the victims of their own inexperience, occasionally of Indians, or through some other tragic turn of events. Ben had seen two die slow, painful deaths on the plains far from medical help; one of appendicitis, another the victim of his own revolver when he shot himself in the groin while pulling his revolver to shoot a rattlesnake. Neither of them had been more than sixteen years old.

"Any sign of that bull, yet, Charlie?" Peterson asked. "No, I've given him up for lost, Poke. By now he's probably wound up in some miner's stew pot. I hope he tastes good. That stew meat cost me a dollar a pound."

"Hear what Abner Wilcox has done? Offered a bounty of a dollar a pound for anyone caught stealin' his beefs, but he'll only pay five dollars if he's brought in dead. Wants to string him up slow and easy himself."

"Doesn't sound like a bad offer," Ben commented.

They looked up as a husky man approached the table. "Excuse me," he said, "one of you Charlie Bowen?"

"That'd be me," Charlie replied.

"I hear you're looking for some hands, Mr. Bowen. I'm looking for work," he said simply.

Bowen looked him over. His clothes were worn, but kept in good repair. His boots were expensive alligator hide, decorated with silver ornaments, and the spurs had fancy silver jinglebobs. His face bore the weather-beaten, seamy look that spoke of years in the outdoors. The hand he put out was hard with calluses and the scars of numerous cuts. He wore his black beard short, neatly trimmed, and appeared to be about thirty-five years old.

"Have a seat," Charlie offered. "You look like you've had plenty of experience."

"Working cattle is all I've ever done. Started in Oregon, then came over this way a few years back. Tried the mines for a while, but never made enough to make it worth while. Right now I'm looking for some place to settle down working cattle again."

Charlie nodded. "I'm always leary of hiring anyone who's fresh out of Texas or Arizona. Most of 'em freeze to death their first winter up here."

"I'm used to cold, Mr. Bowen. Can't say I like it, but I'm used to it."

"When do you want to start?"

"I'm ready to move. Got all my own gear and two horses."

"My place is down at the Mizpah and Powder.

Rafter B. Come on down any time this week and ask for my foreman, Slim Menough. Now that you're working for me, call me Charlie. And what's your handle?"

"Dwyer. Mike Dwyer."

14

"Somehow, I rather imagined it would be much like the roundups I've read so much about in the South-west," Roosevelt said, "with everyone tending to his own."

"Ain't that way up here, Four Eyes," Twice said. "Down there them waterin' spots is a long ways apart. Beefs don't wander much more'n fifteen, twenty miles from water, an' a man's range is mapped out on a dividin' line atween the water holes."

Roosevelt took another forkful of his stew, and ruminated a minute before asking. "Isn't there any attempt to keep the animals at home?"

"Sure," Curly Schaeffer said, "but do you have any idea how many men you'd have to hire to ride herd on these two places of yours?"

"Hmm, it would take rather a few, wouldn't it?"

"Frenchie Wibaux's got himself one of the largest crews in this country," Twice said. "Course, he's got about the biggest damn bunch a cows around here, too. But it don't matter how many riders you got, you can't go keepin' tabs on every fool cow you got. Now, down to Texas it's different. You know where your water is, you know where your beefs is. Here, all our beefs just kinda run anywhere through the basin they gets a notion to. Ever'body tries to keep'em to home, but it just ain't possible most a the time. That's what got the Association together in the first place. We all just kinda keep track of ever'body else's."

"When we find more than a few of somebody else's stock mixed in with our own," Curly explained, "we either run 'em on home, or we get word to their owner and he'll come pick 'em up."

Ben took another swallow of his coffee and said, "It really works out well. When Spring roundup gets underway, all the basin is divided into districts, and a captain is assigned to each district. He's someone who knows the land well, and he selects his crews from all over the basin. Even if an owner has enough men to provide six crews, every crew is going to have representatives from at least two other outfits working with him. No matter how many different brands are mixed together, the calves are branded according to the brand worn by its mother."

"Regardless of whose it is?" Roosevelt asked, seemingly surprised that such honesty was taken for granted among the cattlemen.

"Sure," Curly said. "Two years ago Twice and I worked a district just on the other side of the river. Six weeks, and I think we branded about ten, twelve Maltese Cross and no more than twice that many Elkhorn."

"Yeah, an' we tallied better than ten thousand head in that one," Twice added. "That's the year Charlie Bowen's Rafter B irons was plumb wore out. I burned more Rafter B's that year than any other, an' he didn't even have a man on the crew."

Roosevelt nodded, apparently satisfied. "I know it's all written in the Association rules, but it is gratifying to know that men live up to the rules."

Curly shook his head.

"Some don't. I know for a fact that there's some members who joined just to keep a thin coating of respectability, but take someone like Hank Brown; he came into this country from somewhere down south with his herd of breeding stock. Today he runs two, three thousand head."

"Yeah," Twice said. "I seen that herd when he come up here. Them three thousand beefs he's got is all descendants of his herd of four. Oh, I reckon he's bought himself a few, but you don't build up a herd of three thousand from four in two years."

"It does strike one as being remarkable," Roosevelt admitted.

"Especially when his original herd of breeding stock was four steers," Curly said. "He claimed he'd just gotten out of Wyoming when he was ambushed by Indians, lost the three men with him and all but those four steers. We all know he's been rustling himself a herd, but we haven't been able to catch him at stealing anybody else's stock. When we do, he's a dead man, mark my words. Every year more beefs show up with his brand, and no matter how many he sells, his cattle keep increasing. It's just like he had men all over the Territory working with running irons."

"Or does a hell of a lot of branding after the fifteenth of November," Ben said.

"November the fifteenth?"

"It's in the Association rules, Four Eyes," Curly reminded him. "No branding between November 15 and the Spring roundup unless there's someone present from another outfit. Fastest way in the world to get run out of this country is to ship a cow in February with a fresh brand on it."

For two weeks the eight men worked cattle out of the hills and down into the bottoms of the Badlands where the Winter would be less severe on them. Roosevelt worked hard at riding and roping, and was becoming adept enough that he didn't miss looping a runaway any oftener than anyone else. Keeping his saddle was more of a problem, though, and he was forced to mount more often in a day than anyone else. Through it all he kept his smile and his tremendous store of energy. By the end of the first week, nobody was surprised to find him sitting up after midnight, reading The Federalist Papers, or writing an article which he intended to mail back East to a journal. They were only grateful he didn't expect them to put in as many hours a day as he did.

There was a flurry of snow in the air as they moved the herd nearer the Elkhorn Ranch, and Curly announced, "We've just got three more days to get some branding done."

"By Jove, yes," Roosevelt said. "Today's the thirteenth."

Late that afternoon, Ben and Twice spotted a huge maverick back in a gully, and immediately gave chase. The cow headed for a thicket, and Twice crashed in behind her, cursing the thorns ripping at his arms and face. Ben gave the thicket a wide swing, and was around the other side as she came out. His mare swung into action, wheeling around and slipping on a patch of ice. She skidded, fell hard on her side, and Ben felt his leg being ground between the mare and the icy rock beneath.

Twice rode hard, and hollered out, "Ben! You okay?"

The mare had regained her footing, and Dan was able to stand on his bruised and bloody leg. He didn't think anything had been broken.

"I'm fine. Go get that cow!"

Twice spurred his horse ahead and Ben gingerly

began checking himself. Aside from losing a lot of
hide and pride, he thought he'd be all right.

The mare was limping a bit, though, and had a
ragged gash on her left flank. Ben saw it was shallow,
and rubbed it with some liniment he carried in his
possibles bag. With some care, she'd probably be all
right, but it was going to be a long way home. He
began walking her in the direction Twice had taken
following the maverick cow, and after a few hundred
yards he noticed the mare's bleeding was subsiding
and she was walking more easily.

Twice was a quarter of a mile ahead of him when
Ben saw him slip his noose over the cow's head, and
then his horse leaned into the rope. Suddenly the cow
disappeared from sight, and a moment later Twice and
his horse disappeared, as though swallowed up by the
earth.

"What the hell?" Ben muttered.

He paid no attention to his own pains or those of
the mare. He jumped into the saddle and dug his spurs
in hard. The mare took off as though in the best of
health, and Ben didn't let her slow down until they
neared the place where Twice had disappeared.

The slight roll of the ground had hidden from his
sight an arroyo cutting through the valley. What had
happened soon became clear, and Ben felt his throat
tighten, knowing that Twice was in a lot worse shape
than himself. When Twice had lassoed the cow, she
had kept right on running, not aware of the arroyo
ahead of her, and had gone right over the side. The
horse had leaned back into the rope, but couldn't set
a solid footing on the frozen ground that was covered
with a coating of light snow. The tracks where the
horse had been pulled over the rim showed he'd tried
every inch of the way, but lost.

Ben dismounted and ran to the edge of the arroyo.
What he saw below him made him double up in laugh-

ter. The drop had been no more than fifteen feet, and
Twice had managed to kick himself clear before hitting the bottom. The cow, still securely roped by the
horns, had fallen past a stout hickory sapling, and
Twice's horse had gone over on the other side of it.

Twice was standing in the bottom of the gully
brushing mud and snow off his jacket and trousers,
looking up in amazement at the sight of his horse and
the maverick cow suspended by the lariat on her horns,
and his horse swinging a few feet lower, the bitter end
of the lariat snubbed around the saddlehorn.

"Damnedest thing I ever seen," Twice said. "Sure
thought I was a goner when we started over."

Ben studied the situation for a minute. "Well, you
want me to cut them loose?"

"Hell no! I paid seven dollars for that rope, and I
ain't about to let you cut it!"

Ben thought for a moment, then worked his loop
down over the cow's horns. He took the other end,
flipped it around the sapling and said, "Hang on,
Twice, I'll be right down."

Twice grinned up at him. "Hell, take your time. I
ain't likely to see nothin' like this again if I live to be
a hunnert years old. I'm gonna soak my eyeballs good."
He fished into his pocket for the sack of makings, and
sat down on a rock to twist himself a cigarette.

Ben had to take his mare several hundred yards up
the arroyo before they found a place to work down to
the bottom and return to Twice, who was calmly sitting and smoking as though it were the grandest show
of the year.

"Well, let's get to work," Ben said. "That cow isn't
going to come down on her own."

"I ain't finished my smoke yet."

Ben dismounted and walked over to the swinging
horse, whose hooves were about three feet off the
ground. The horse watched him with eyes that were

more curious than frightened. He wasn't struggling, but hanging peacefully, swinging slowly. A bit above him the cow was still giving a feeble kick now and then, her eyes reflecting the terror that had all but paralyzed her.

"You must be the first flying horse since Pegasus," Ben said as he retrieved the end of his lasso from the ground. The horse watched every movement with his wide open, brown eyes, his ears showing his curiosity.

Suddenly the horse's head snapped around, his ears pointing to the far side of the gully.

"Someone's coming," Twice said.

"We're in a lousy spot if it's Indians," Ben said as he scrambled across the arroyo and clawed his way up far enough to peer over the top. The two riders were coming fast, and Ben allowed himself to slide back down. Twice had pulled the Winchester from Ben's sheath, ready for any trouble that was in the air.

"We've got help," Ben said. "It's Curly and Four Eyes."

Twice slid the rifle back into the sheath and sat down again. "They ain't gonna believe this."

Curly Schaeffer was the first to arrive, and when he pulled up at the edge of the arroyo, his face was filled with concern. Then when he took in the situation, he began to laugh as Ben had.

Roosevelt came to a halt, and his smile returned when he viewed the scene below him.

"We were up on the ridge and saw you go over," Curly said. "I thought sure you were killed."

"Well, I ain't. Reckon you could say the same if it was you come ass over appetite into this gulch? Shit, Curly, you couldn't never of done it."

Roosevelt had the last word before they went to work winching the animals down from their precarious skyhook.

"Bully!"

15

CINDY and Charlie sat in the sprawling living room with steaming mugs of coffee. Now that the work of the Fall roundup was behind them, Cindy had taken over the cooking while the Rafter B cook took his yearly three months off to winter in New Orleans. The skeleton crew that was left on the ranch had their meals in the big house rather than at the cook shack. Cooking was the only feminine chore Cindy Bowen had allowed herself to become proficient in, and she could put out a meal that was fit for the likes of Aubony Stuart when she put her mind to it.

The Rafter B cook was an Englishman who claimed to be the second son of "Earl, Lord of Howard." While he was undeniably of English descent and schooling, nobody took his claim to peerage seriously, and he was known to most of the men on the range as Earl, or Howard. He answered to either, if he answered at all. He knew his position as cook was even more important than that of foreman, for if the quality of food on a ranch began to deteriorate the cowboys would quit and find other jobs.

Charlie Bowen's first foreman on the Rafter B had come up from Colorado, carrying a letter of recommendation from his former employer, which stated, "Mark Whitman is the best hand who ever worked for me. Feed him well."

Charlie had asked him, "Whitman, you worked for that outfit for twenty-three years. Why'd you quit to come up here?"

Whitman made a sour face. "The cook started cutting the pie in smaller pieces."

Earl Howard was a commanding sight around his cookhouse. He stood six feet one, sported a thick black walrus mustache and a black bow tie that balanced it. He was never seen without his spotless derby hat, which he wore cocked jauntily down over his right eye; no matter how hot and dusty the conditions when he was cooking at his chuck wagon on roundup, Earl's derby was brushed clean. Nobody could ever remember him wearing a dirty apron, and he had a supply of them that would make a cook at the Macqueen House jealous. Rain or shine, snow or sleet, Earl put from three to five aprons on his clothesline to dry every day after bleaching them out with salt water.

"Dad, how well do you know Mike Dwyer?" Cindy asked.

"No better than any of the others, why?"

"Well, Earl doesn't like him."

"Hmmpf! Earl doesn't particularly have a liking for anybody who doesn't tell him three times a day he puts out the best food in Montana. There isn't any trouble between them, is there?"

"I don't think there's any trouble, but Earl has a way of knowing who's all right and who isn't. How come you picked Mike to stay on for the winter?"

"He's a good worker, and he doesn't have to be

broken to winter weather the way a lot of them do."

"Earl said he's seen Mike somewhere before. He can't remember where, but he knows that Mike Dwyer was up to no good. Frankly, Dad, I don't feel easy around him myself."

Charlie put his mug down on the coffee table and shrugged his shoulders.

"Earl probably worked a roundup crew with him someplace, gal. You know how many different faces you see at roundup time. What I can't understand is why Earl doesn't come to me, rather than you. Like the time he caught one of the hands stealing a five dollar bill from that kid out of Chicago."

"We've always been able to talk with each other, Dad. Earl still thinks of me as a little kid, I guess, and never complains when I ask him for a recipe for something."

"Hah! Don't let anybody else set foot inside that cook shack! He won't even let me in there when he's on the place. Maybe he's starting to think of you as more than a kid, gal. You know, you aren't any more. You're a woman now. And in case you aren't aware of it, every man on the range has his eye on you."

"Oh, Dad," she replied wearily, "you're not going to start that all over again, are you?"

"Why not? We've got the whole winter to discuss it, haven't we?"

"Maybe you have," she said with a twinkle in her green eyes, "but I've got some cleaning up to do in the kitchen. And I've got to start thinking about the Christmas dinner. Rum."

"Rum?"

"I need some more rum. Earl fixed twenty fruit cakes last summer, and I'm going to need more rum to soak them with pretty soon."

"Sometimes I think you and Earl drink as much rum as you use in the cooking."

"Dad! You know Earl doesn't drink."

"Then why do I buy a keg of rum every year, and still run out before the fruit cakes are ready?"

"Well, could it be that every year you want to take another cake to someone else? It started with Aubony Stuart, then you added Nellie Wibaux, then Augusta Kohrs, Mary Ann Goodnight, Medora de Mores, and now you want Four Eyes Roosevelt added to the list of lucky winners in the Earl of Howard's Christmas Fruitcake Bonanza. That's six out of the twenty right there. At first I thought you were courting all the married women in the business, but now you've added a widower."

"You forgot John Clay."

"And you wonder where the rum goes. And what about the punch for the Christmas dinner?"

Charlie Bowen heaved a mocking sigh. "Remind me to buy another keg of rum when I go to town."

16

MIKE Dwyer tied his horse at the hitching rail in front of the Miles Saloon, looked up and down the street, then walked inside. There was little activity in the huge room, and most of that was centered around the pair of hot, pot-bellied stoves. He scanned the row lining the bar, hoping Jack Sully would be here as he promised. It might be another couple of weeks before he could leave the Rafter B again, and winter was setting in with a vengeance.

He stopped, then smiled. Sully was there, all right. There was no mistaking him.

He stepped up to a tall, muscular individual with a black mustache and touched him on the shoulder.

"I still owe you a beer, Jack."

The man turned his head and smiled.

"Wrong, Mike. You owe me three. But I'll settle for one right now."

Dwyer paid the bartender for two mugs of beer, and they carried them to a table far from the stoves.

It was also well removed from anyone who might be close enough to overhear a low conversation.

"How're things going, Mike?"

"Can't complain. I don't mind telling you, though, it sure is different working for someone else again."

"Trust me," Sully said. "There won't be a chance in hell of getting a job after Stuart gets done."

Dwyer shook his head. "I still think somebody jobbed you with a dry sell, Jack. What makes you think he's going to get away with it? That is, if he's serious about it in the first place."

Sully took a long pull at his beer, wiped his heavy mustache with the sleeve of his jacket and said, "He did it before. Up in the mountains. Got damned near a hundred men together and cleaned out the camps. Take my word for it; he's going to do the same thing here on the range."

Dwyer's eyes narrowed. "How does he set himself up as judge, jury and executioner? Does the old bastard think he's God himself?"

"He might," Sully said. "Anybody who's got as much money as Granville Stuart can set himself up as anybody he wants to be. You're one of the few in our old crew who've paid me any attention at all, and you're one of the few who's going to be alive when Stuart gets done. To be honest with you, I'll be glad to see some of those stupid fools swing. They don't have enough brains to alter a brand so it looks natural."

Dwyer remembered watching the branding crew changing the Rafter B on Bowen's Aberdeen bull to a Diamond B. Two straight lines changed the rafter to a diamond, but the resulting fresh burns added to the old brand would be obvious to anyone who took a good look even two years later. Another two minutes' work would have put on a completely new brand. Mike Dwyer took pride in being able to change a brand so skillfully that even a brand inspector couldn't tell it had been altered.

And it hadn't been until after he'd gone to work for Bowen that he had any idea what the fool bull had really been worth. Until Slim Menough told him that Bowen had paid two thousand for the registered stud, he had estimated its value at a hundred dollars, maybe a hundred fifty. But what the hell. Miguel Sanchez didn't care what kind of pedigree it had; all he wanted was to buy stolen cattle at a fair price, and take the risks of getting caught with them before he could sell them to someone else.

"What about Miguel?"

"Don't worry about that slick greaser, Mike. He'll be around to buy anything we can move into Wyoming. In the meantime, I'm leaving it up to you to scout out some men in every outfit. The more we have working on the inside, the better it's going to be. Sam Groot's at the L Bar L, Frank Pendleton's at the Rocking 7."

Before Sully left, he handed Dwyer a leather pouch, heavy with gold coins, and Dwyer dropped it into his pocket. It made no difference to him how much money it contained. Jack Sully would never shortchange him, or anybody else. He might be short on principles when it came to helping himself to a few head, or a few hundred head, of someone else's cattle, but he was otherwise as honest as the next man.

Jack Sully had been in the Territory since before Custer and his men died at the Little Big Horn. Nobody quite knew where he had come from, but most thought it was Canada, or possibly even New York City. He spoke French fluently, and both de Mores and Wibaux thought highly of him. Somewhere along the line, Jack Sully married a Sioux woman and was initiated into the tribe. He lived on the reservation, and was held in high regard by the Sioux, even if he did bring some of his white customs with him. Sully lived in a teepee with his bride just long enough to build a two-story frame house, but was raising his children more Sioux than white.

Because of his marriage to an Indian, he had long been known as a squawman, although he was never referred to as such by anyone after Granville Stuart made that kind of union respectable. He had registered two brands when the Association was formed, although as a "Sioux" he was not allowed to become a member. It had been rumored for years that Indian Jack had been as guilty as anyone when it came to rustling, but nobody had been able to get the goods on him. One of the suspicious things about him was his 'choice of brands—the Dollar, and the Three Slashes Crossed. He had frequently been seen in company with Hank Brown, the legendary figure who built up a decent-sized herd from his four Texas steers. Brown used the Dollar Fifty brand, and both of them claimed their choice of brands reflected an optimistic hope they could make that much profit when they sold a cow.

But it was widely known that a good many brands could be altered into a dollar sign, and that the heavy brand of three slashes crossed by a bar could cover up any others. Brown never owned a proper iron, but did all his branding with running irons. He was asked point blank if he'd altered anybody's brand.

"Hell yes," he said. "Down to Texas, T.J. Walker lost so much money on his first herd he built up another one and used the brand F O O L, since he said anyone who tried to make money with cattle was a fool. I'm not the only one who's roped a bull of his and changed the F to a B just so's a greenhorn could tell the difference."

Jack Sully stood up for Brown. "Now let me tell you something, mister. If you ever accuse either of us of changin' your brand to a Dollar or a Three Slashes Crossed, you'd damned well better have your hog leg in your hand when you do."

Brown soon proved he was fast and accurate with a Colt, and killed a cowboy who let slip a remark that Sully and Brown were rustling themselves a herd. It was the last time anybody was careless enough to mention it to their faces, but there were several hundred who were waiting for the opportunity to catch either of them in the act, or even find an altered brand.

Dwyer finished his beer, then went to the bank across the street and deposited six hundred dollars. The remaining two hundred ought to take care of buying himself a new pair of boots and a supply of cigars to see him through the winter, with some gambling money to boot.

He got the boots as well as two new shirts at the Orschel Brothers, decided against buying a new hat, and was on his way out of the store when a display in the front window caught his eye.

He called back to the clerk, "How much are these music boxes?"

"The lacquered ones are four dollars. The silver ones are eight fifty."

Dwyer wound up one of the silver boxes and opened the lid. It played a catchy little tune, and he grinned as he said, "I'll take it. Even give you another fifty cents if you can do a good job of wrapping it for me."

17

MIKE Dwyer was leaning on the corral gate, the collar of his heavy sheepskin-lined jacket wide open in spite of the cold. He bit the tip off a cigar and spit it over the top rail, then scratched a match on the post as Cindy walked from the house.

"Morning, Miss Cindy. Like me to catch out a mount for you?"

"Thanks, Mr. Dwyer, but there's no need. Watch."

She opened the gate and called, "Bluebelle!"

The blue roan filly's ears perked up, and she paced from the pack to the gate, where Cindy rubbed her nose. "Come on, Bluebelle, time for some oats."

Dwyer shook his head in amazement. "No wonder you and your father think so much of her. Sure is pretty. Almost as pretty as you are."

Cindy hesitated, then smiled. "Thank you, Mr. Dwyer, but I don't really think of myself as anything pretty."

Dwyer laid his hand on hers, and gave it a slight

squeeze. "You are, though. In fact, I don't think I've ever run into a woman half as pretty as you."

Cindy's eyes flashed him a look that plainly said she didn't appreciate his compliment, even though she said, "Thank you, Mr. Dwyer. Would you harness Bluebelle to the buggy, please?"

Her voice was as cold as the winter air, and Dwyer simply shrugged it off. "You use her in harness, too?"

"Of course. Now, if you don't want to give me a hand, would you mind finding something else to do?"

Dwyer bit his tongue, nodded and went into the tack room for the buggy harness. He had the rig ready in a few minutes, and Cindy gave him a curt nod as she climbed into the seat.

Charlie came out onto the porch when she pulled the buggy around the house.

"I'd feel better if the sky didn't look like snow," he said, handing her a large box.

She put the box under the seat and leaned over to give him a kiss on the cheek.

"It's too early to have anything but a few flurries, Dad. Bluebelle and I can handle anything. Of course, this fruit cake might be frozen solid by the time I get there."

"Hell, gal, rum doesn't freeze, and that thing's more rum than anything else."

"So if we get caught in a blizzard, Bluebelle and I can eat the cake. Then we won't freeze."

"Get going," he said with a laugh, and watched the young mare pace her way to the ford.

During the drive to Medora, the leaden skies continued to darken, and as she crossed the Little Missouri light snow began blowing. By the time she neared the headquarters of the Maltese Cross the wind had picked up and was coming directly out of the north, and the tiny flakes had turned into dollar-sized ones, sticking to Bluebelle's mane and tail. Cindy was ready to admit it was fixing to snow a good one. If it didn't let up soon, she was going to have some trouble getting back to the Rafter B, and all indications were that the snow was going to get a lot worse before it was going to get any better.

"Damn!" she said aloud. "I'll probably have to spend a day or two in that rat hole they call the Pyramid."

She drove Bluebelle up to the rail and hailed the house. Ben's head poked through the door, then he swung it wide open.

"What in tarnation are you doing here in weather like this?" Before she could answer, he said, "Get inside and warm yourself. I'll put Bluebelle in the stable."

"I can't stay. I want to take a present up to Four Eyes."

"He's not there, Cindy; he went back to New York three weeks ago. I don't expect to see him again before March."

Cindy's shoulders sagged, then she took a deep breath and made a fast decision. She pulled the box out from under the seat and jumped down. "I guess I could use some coffee, Ben."

"Coffee's ready," Ben said, taking the reins. "Be back in a minute."

Cindy walked inside and put the box on the table, then pulled off her gloves and warmed them in front of the fireplace. A quick glance around the room showed it was clean, well-scrubbed and comfortable. Knowing there were no women on the place, and that there hadn't been an owner living here for several years, she was sure the house would be no better kept than an average bunkhouse.

The small building was typical of ranch houses in the Territory. It had been built of large logs; the outsides were coarse and round, with the joining edges squared and laid close. Inside, the small cracks be-

tween the logs had been chinked with gypsum plaster
and squared off with an adze. Unlike most, these walls
had been painstakingly smoothed, and looked as
though they had been gone over with fine sandpaper
before being whitewashed. The three windows admitted plenty of light, and the white walls made the place
cheery by comparison with almost any other ranch
house in the basin.

A rack of rifles near the fireplace were clean and
freshly-oiled. Cindy's eyes took in the shelves near
the cookstove; provisions were stacked neatly, and
she doubted that Earl Howard ever kept his kitchen
any cleaner. Except for the coffee pot on the stove
and the mug on the low table next to one of the horn
and hide chairs near a window, there weren't any
dirty dishes or pans.

The only thing that would look out of place to a
visitor from the East was the pile of harness next to
one of the chairs, with spools of waxed thread, needles,
awls and a riveting tool. Cindy had spent many long
winter evenings repairing harness and saddles in the
house, and the jumbled pile of leather and brass with
its smell of neatsfoot oil and brass polish was just
as much a part of the room as the home made furni-
ture and the cozy fireplace.

She took a mug from the row hanging under a shelf
and was pouring herself some coffee from the huge
blue enamel pot when Ben returned.

"You keep a clean cabin, Ben," she said.

"I try to. Sometimes it's a job for two men and a
boy to keep up with Twice. He lives in here about the
same way he does on roundup."

"I know the kind," she said with a knowing smile.
"Finish a steak and toss the bone over your shoulder.
Slop the dregs of the coffee onto the floor. Where is
Twice, by the way?"

"Over at the stable. Right now he's giving Bluebelle

a good rubbing down. He was working on harness until the coffee gave out, then got ticked off at me because I let it go dry. He makes coffee just about like everyone else, I guess."

Cindy laughed. "You mean when it gets too strong he adds water, and if it's too weak he throws in another handful of coffee? Pretty ghastly that way, isn't it?"

Ben took off his jacket and hung it on a peg by the door. "We take turns doing the cooking. This is my week. When Sunday comes around, it'll be his turn again. I can take his coffee for about three days, and then I have to give up. Last Sunday when I started, there wasn't room in that pot for more than three or four cups of coffee. I must have dumped out two pounds of coffee grounds before I could make a fresh pot."

The coffee and the fire had taken away Cindy's chill, and she took off her sheepskin jacket, too. Ben took it from her and placed it on the peg next to his. For a brief instant, Cindy thought how good it looked to see their jackets hanging side by side, as though they belonged together. Then she realized it was a foolish thing to be thinking and forced herself to talk about anything else.

"Four Eyes is going to be gone all winter?"

"Yep. I don't know if he really had a lot of things to take care of in New York, or if the idea of spending a winter here was too much for him. It's a drastic change to make, you know, going from the bright lights of city society to a cabin like this, miles away from your neighbors."

"I know," she admitted. "I can remember when I was a little girl back in Philadelphia with my aunt. What I liked about winter was the constant round of parties with a lot of friends."

Ben's eyebrows raised, and Cindy caught it, feeling her face redden slightly.

"It was fine then, but I don't miss it. I'm really much happier out here."

Ben studied her eyes, and she had a strange feeling of light-headedness, as though she hadn't eaten for two days. That was the aggravating thing about Ben Foster—he didn't have to say a word, and she had strange feelings she couldn't identify. Could it be that her father had been right? That she was falling in love with Ben Foster?

No, she told herself. Falling in love was silly, and she didn't want to have any part of it. There wasn't a woman she knew in the basin who hadn't turned into a bony, dried-out wreck after marrying a cowboy and giving birth to half a dozen children. The exceptions, of course, were the few like Augusta Kohrs, Nellie Wibaux and Medora de Mores; they were the ones with money, more money than they really knew what to do with, and had large houses filled with servants to take care of the work while they could remain beautiful. None of them were slackards, but they spent almost as much time keeping themselves beautiful as they did taking care of a family. The others, those who married the common working man, even those who lived in towns like Miles City, were worn out by the time they were thirty. No, let them think they were better off married; it just wasn't going to be part of the life of Cindy Bowen.

"But it isn't all loneliness, Ben," she said after what seemed like an hour's silence. "We all get together for parties around Christmas time and before we get snowed in. Say, why don't you and Twice come over for Christmas dinner with us? I'm planning on a really big feast."

"Well, I'd like that, but I don't know. I'd have to check with Twice."

"Bring him with you," she said hurriedly, and wanted to bite her tongue. She was beginning to sound like she was begging him.

Ben looked out the window. "You can ask him yourself, Cindy. He's coming in now."

The door opened, letting in a swirl of snow along with the lanky figure of Twice. He pulled the door shut, stomped the snow off his boots and gave Cindy a brief nod as he walked to the fireplace, shivering as though he would fall apart.

"You could use some of this, Twice," Cindy said, pouring him a mug of coffee. "I never knew you to be bothered by cold weather before."

"Thanks kindly, Miss Cindy. Reckon I'm gettin' old; it ain't hardly winter yet."

He took the coffee in three deep swallows, then put down the mug while he stripped off his outer jacket. Under the sheepskin jacket he wore a sheepskin vest, and two different colors of shirts were showing above the red woolies.

"I can't remember seeing this much snow come down this hard so early," Cindy said, beginning to wonder how she was going to make it home, and tried to ignore the nagging little thought that she wouldn't mind if she couldn't.

"Does seem more like February, doesn't it?" Ben said. "Well, if it doesn't let up, we've got plenty of food here."

"Oh, but I couldn't . . ."

"Reckon you ain't got much choice," Twice said. "It's pilin' up pretty good out there. Driftin', too."

Ben's blue eyes smiled at her. "If it doesn't let up, maybe you'll have to fix the Christmas dinner for us here. Twice, you know what she did? She rode all the way over here to invite us to Christmas dinner at the Rafter B."

"Don't go jobbin' me no dry sell, Ben."

"It's true, Twice," she replied. "I came to bring a present for Four Eyes and to invite you and Ben to come over with him for dinner on Christmas day."

Twice looked out the window. "That'd be Tuesday, an' this here's what? Friday? Saturday? Might could be it'll stop snowin' by then."

"Oh, of course it will," she said, hoping the little fear she felt about being snowed in so far from home wouldn't come true. "I'm going to fix smoked tongues, pork roast . . ."

"I told her I wasn't sure, Twice. It'd leave the place short-handed."

"Wheeoo!" Twice snorted. "Reckon since I'm the foreman around here, I got a right to decide when we're gonna be short-handed. Miss Cindy, I'd purely be honored to accept your invite. I guess maybe me an' Ben'd better get out our snowshoes an' get started."

"Better still," Ben suggested, "I ought to start some vittles, else we're going to be hungry before dark."

"I've a better idea. Why don't you two work on that harness while I get something started? Or you might open the present I brought over for you."

Ben took the box off the table and unwrapped it, while Twice stood by, his eyes as bright as a ten-year-old's on his birthday. When he undid the paper wrapping on the box, he got the first whiff of the aroma that unmistakably said fruit cake. Inside the box was a tin, and when the cover was removed, the cabin was filled with the odor of rum and preserved fruits.

Twice took a deep breath.

"We gonna eat it or drink it?" he asked, licking his lips.

"This your work, Cindy?" Ben asked. "Sure does look good."

"Sorry, but Earl's responsible for that. Says the

recipe came over from England with him. All I did was pour on a half cup of rum every two weeks for the last month." She handed him a knife. "Go ahead, Ben, do the honors."

Ben cut a couple of healthy wedges from the cake and passed one to Twice as Cindy refreshed the coffee mugs. She took a furtive look out the window, and her heart rose. The skies were lighter, and the snow was getting thinner. She could see clear to the stable. And almost at the same instant she cursed under her breath, knowing that she was beginning to look forward to being snowbound with Ben Foster.

And while she cut up the vegetables for the stew, she argued with herself. How can someone like Ben Foster, a wrangler with a ridiculous-hooked nose, make you tingle when you think about him? Damn! Was she beginning to soften? Certainly there was no reason to. After all, she told herself, you've lived and worked all these nineteen years without feeling any need for a man. Especially after what happened with Uncle Henry. Why should Ben Foster march into your life and change everything? Damn!

18

THE wind died late in the afternoon, and for a brief few minutes the sun poked through the gray skies, bathing the Maltese Cross with brilliant white light. Twice pulled on his jacket and gloves and made his way through the snow to the stable. When he came back to the house twenty minutes later, the sun had disappeared again, but most of the clouds were lighter and didn't look so threatening.

"Reckon maybe it ain't gonna be so bad after all," he said. "Gets a bit warmer, this here snow's gonna start meltin'."

Ben stepped out onto the porch, then came back in. "Sure, the snow's going to melt, all right. Thermometer's up to seventeen. We're in the middle of a heat wave, Twice."

"Maybe I ought to get back to the Rafter B," Cindy said doubtfully.

"I think it'd be a mistake to try it," Ben said.

"There are some pretty deep drifts out there. Blue-belle's going to have some mighty hard work pulling that buggy through belly-deep snow."

"Let me borrow a saddle. After all, it's possible there's more snow here than closer to home."

Ben gave her a disgusted look.

"What happens if you find it's worse before you get to Medora? Or if it's blowing worse on the other side of the river?"

"You're all full of cheer, aren't you?"

"Just being practical. I've learned to expect the worst in life, that's all. 'Course, if you want to go, there's nothing to stop you."

"Sure there is," Twice said. "I don't reckon Miss Cindy's the kind who'd get the supper started an' then walk out on us."

Cindy gave him a smile of gratitude, but it froze on her face when Ben said, "I'll finish the supper if she wants to leave."

"Can't," Twice argued. "That's our agreement, 'member? Whoever starts the grub is the one who's gotta finish it."

Cindy laughed. "You two sound like a couple of little boys fighting over who does the chores. I suppose you'd choose to go hungry if I didn't stay to finish it for you."

"Might," Twice said. "Since this here's Ben's week to cook, he'd try to finish it and botch it up somethin' terrible. Eatin' his cookin's almost like goin' hungry anyways."

"At least the coffee's good," Ben said.

"When there is any," Twice said with disgust. "Least when it's my week, the pot don't go dry when you want some."

"If you didn't drink coffee like a fish drinks water, you wouldn't have fits waiting for a fresh pot to boil."

"Yep, you got it right. Drinkin' your coffee's about like drinkin' water, but I ain't no fish."

Cindy held up a hand. "I'll stay, but not because I'm worried about getting home. I don't want you two to kill each other before Christmas."

Twice's face slipped into its crooked smile. "I promise, I won't kill 'im afore then. Maybe after."

The sun made another brief appearance, its last of the day. During supper Twice said, "Talked to Curly this morning. Said he found some XIT stock over near Sheep Butte couple of days ago."

"Doesn't surprise me," Cindy said. "Ever since they brought that herd up from Texas about two years ago, the XIT can be found anywhere along the Yellowstone or Missouri. Dad says there's some thirty or forty thousand of them through here now."

"Curly done some snoopin' around," Twice went on, "and found a campsite that'd been used by rustlers. Figures there was about six or seven of 'em."

"Why does he think it was rustlers?" Ben asked.

"Who else is gonna butcher some meat from steers wearin' two brands? J Bar N and Circle Dot. They didn't even have the decency to get rid of the hides."

Cindy banged her fist on the table. "The next thing they'll be doing is riding right into our corrals and helping themselves."

Twice and Ben exchanged a quick glance. Cindy noticed it and said, "You know about plans for the Spring, don't you?"

"What plans are you talking about, Cindy?" Ben asked.

"You know very well what I'm talking about. Dad's been picking some men already. They'll be ready to ride as soon as the snow's gone. Hasn't Four Eyes talked to you about it?"

"Yep," Twice admitted, "but he don't want his men getting involved."

"Namby-pamby, that's what he is," Cindy snorted.

"Maybe just careful," Ben said.

"How about you?"

"Something's going to have to be done, Cindy, and I expect to do whatever I have to."

"Just don't let Four Eyes catch you at it," Twice said around a chunk of biscuit.

After supper, Twice worked on the harness for a while, then went into the other room and built a fire in the pot-bellied stove. He carried an armload of blankets into the kitchen so Cindy could make a pallet in front of the fireplace, and returned to the bedroom without saying more than good night.

Ben and Cindy had more coffee and a piece of the fruitcake while they talked at the kitchen table. Within minutes, Twice's snores could be heard from the other side of the curtain. Only then did she bring up the subject of the vigilantes again.

"Dad said he thought you'd be willing to ride with them, Ben. Something you said to him the first time you went over to the Rafter B."

"Yeah. My mares are involved. I've lost a couple, and I don't want to lose the rest of them."

"Then I can tell him you'll go?"

"Cindy, I'm still working for Four Eyes. If they decide to take some action before he comes back, yes. If they wait until after, I don't know."

"What's the worst thing he could do to you? Fire you?"

"Maybe. But if he decides against doing it, he could ruin the whole plan. I don't think he would, but he could."

"He hasn't been here long enough to know how bad the problem really is, Ben. How many head has he lost to rustlers in one year?"

"There's no way of knowing until after the Spring round-up. I think what your father needs to do is get some of the other Association members to pay him a little visit when he gets back. Sort of explain to him how things really are."

"I'd like to go myself, but Dad threatened to lock me up if I tried."

"It's not going to be any place for a lady, Cindy."

"Damn it, I'm not a lady!" she retorted. "You think I've never watched men being hung?"

"The hangings are going to be the easy part. You're dead wrong if you think anybody's going to walk up to a vigilante group, tilt his head forward and say, 'Howdy, fellers. If you got the rope, I got the neck.' There's going to be people killed on both sides."

"I'm not afraid of that, either."

Ben shook his head. "Didn't say you were. All I said was it's not going to be the place for a lady. And even if you aren't a lady, I'd like to think of you as one."

She felt herself blush.

"Why should you really care if I got hurt?"

"Because I've got a history of . . ." He caught himself, and Cindy saw the look on his face.

"Ben, you really would care if I got hurt, wouldn't you?"

"Yeah, I would, Cindy. I'd care a lot."

Impulsively she said, "You've been married, haven't you? And lost her?"

Ben stared into his empty coffee cup, and after a long moment nodded.

"Would it help to talk about it? Ben, whatever happened, I can see it's hurting you."

"Now it's my turn. Do you really care, Cindy? Do you really want to know why I won't let anything take over my life again, whether it's horses or cattle or women? Do you really want to know what I've been living with for years?"

She laid her hand on his, for the first time knowing that she truly did care about him, and that sooner or later she was going to have to have Ben Foster. "Yes, Ben, I do."

He took the pot from the stove, filled both mugs and walked to one of the leather chairs. She followed him, taking a blanket to wrap around her legs, and sat on the floor next to him while he told her about Nell Adams, about his family, about Bertha Kleinstaedtler and the two drunken outlaws who had changed his life completely. By the time he had finished, it was well past midnight.

"You loved her very much, didn't you? And you still do."

He stared vacantly into the fire and nodded. "I thought maybe time would take care of it, but it hasn't. And I'm afraid Aeschylus is still writing."

"Ben, you don't really think some old Greek playwright could have anything to do with your life, do you? That's nonsense."

"Maybe, but Aeschylus knew a lot about people. Some are born lucky, some aren't. Take Frenchy Wibaux, for example. No matter what he does, he's going to make money, and he's going to be happy; de Mores loses money, and he's never happy about anything. It's all a matter of fate. And every time I think everything's going along just fine and I'm happy with life, Fate comes along and gives me a comeuppance."

"Maybe your fate will change."

"Nothing can change fate, Cindy. Nothing." He looked up at the clock over the fireplace and gulped. "Good Lord! Look at the time. We've got to get some sleep."

"Just a few more minutes, Ben, please." Her heart was racing, and she knew she was blushing.

"Ben, isn't it possible that fate has saved you for me?"

There, she'd come out and said it. It wasn't anything she'd planned to say, and she regretted it immediately.

"Nope," he said simply. "I'm destined to find a frilly little gal some day with spangles and jansies and smelling of perfume while she twirls a parasol."

She leaned back and stared at him.

"You're serious about that, aren't you?"

"Sure I am. What's wrong with wanting a woman who dresses like a lady? Maybe if you'd give it a try, I could think about it."

"Ben Foster, you're impossible!"

"Yep. Now get some sleep. It's going to be a long ride home tomorrow with all this snow."

19

THERE was one gray gelding tied to the Rafter B hitching rail, and Ben's experienced eye told him it was a well cared for animal with plenty of stamina and power to his long legs and solid body. The saddle wasn't that of a common cowboy, though, but was expensively made and inlaid with silver conchas.

Cindy walked onto the porch, narrowly missing stepping on the ear of one of the dogs.

"Merry Christmas! I wasn't expecting you for a couple of hours yet."

"We can go fishing," Ben said with a smile, hoping his disappointment didn't show on his face. Somehow he'd conjured up a picture of Cindy in a dress for Christmas Day, but she was in jeans and a checkered shirt with a huge white apron wrapped around her.

"Try it! I'll set Hercules on you." She indicated the dog at her feet."

Ben scratched his head. "Does that old hound ever move off the porch?"

"Only when he's being fed. Go put your horses in the corral. Coffee's hot."

As they turned toward the stable she said, almost as an afterthought, "Oh, Twice, would you go down to the bunkhouse and tell Slim Dad wants to see him, please?"

"Go on in," Twice said. "I'll take care of the horses and Slim in one trip."

Cindy led Ben inside, where the huge living room was festooned with branches of pine. Charley Bowen was standing at the fireplace with Granville Stuart, and boomed him a greeting.

"Howdy, Ben. Like you to meet Granville Stuart. Granville, this is Ben Foster, from over at the Maltese Cross."

"How do you do, sir?" Ben said, feeling the strength in the elderly man's slender hands.

"I've heard quite a bit about you, Mr. Foster. Even have a few horses I bought from George Fowler over the years. Good stock."

"I agree, Mr. Stuart. It's too bad he decided to move up to Canada. Good man to work for."

"Good man to deal with, too. I've been talking with Charlie about some business we need to take care of in the Spring, and he tells me Roosevelt has already talked to you about it."

"He doesn't want us to get involved with it, though, Mr. Stuart."

"I think he'll change his mind. How do you stand?"

"I've lost some of my own mares, so I'm willing."

"Good," Stuart said. "Most of the Association members have agreed to keep any man out of it who hasn't worked for us for at least three years, but we're willing to take you with us because we know what kind of men George Fowler had working for him. Besides, Charlie and Cindy both think pretty highly of you."

"And don't get that humble look on your face, Ben," Charlie said. "You're okay in my book."

Before Ben could reply, Twice and Slim came in, and Charlie said, "I believe you all know each other?"

"Sure," Twice said. "Howdy, Mr. Stuart."

"Howdy, Twice. How do things stand over your way? Still losing stock?"

"Yep. Bad as it ever was, maybe worse."

"That's how it is all through the basin," Stuart said, absently combing his gray beard with his long, thin fingers. "Come March 14 when the Association has its next meeting, things will change. It's long over-due, and there's a lot of support for the idea of cleaning up the mess ourselves. I must caution you, though, keep it quiet. I don't want anybody we don't know like our own families to hear how we're going to pull it off."

Slim Menough shook his head. "The word is al-ready out, Mr. Stuart. You can't go into a saloon in Miles City without someone bringing it up."

"Of course, and that's part of the plan. We wanted it rumored that we were getting fed up with it. I don't like the idea of killing people any more than anybody else does, and I hope we can scare them off without a lot of bloodshed."

"Their kind don't scare, Granville," Charlie said flatly. "Poke Peterson said a couple of his boys caught four of them up on Beaver Creek a couple of weeks ago blurring brands on about twenty head. They put up a hell of a fight, and it's lucky Poke's boys weren't killed. One of them had his horse shot out from under him. You just don't scare men like that. That's what I tried to tell everyone. We're deal-ing with desperate men, good men when it comes to cattle, and they can fight like hell when the chips are down."

"They're going to find that we can, too. How many

of your men here are going with us?" Stuart looked
from Charlie to his foreman.

"Two," Charlie replied. "Slim and myself. I've got
eight hands out here this winter, and three of them
just hired on. Fred McCoy, my Cherokee blacksmith,
still thinks he's pretty sharp, but he can't see very
well any more. Hell, he was one of the best marks-
men Andrew Jackson had in the war against the
Creeks at Horseshoe Bend, but that was more than
fifty years ago. Jim Cooper couldn't hit the wall of
the outhouse if he was sitting inside with the door
closed. Willie Wooten's a real Bible pounder, and
wouldn't kill anyone if his life depended on it. That
leaves Cal Bradley, and he simply chooses not to.
Nothing wrong with his courage, he just doesn't
want it."

Stuart nodded. "No matter. I think we've got almost enough men to handle it."

He reached for his hat, and said, "If I don't get
home, Aubony'll have my scalp. Merry Christmas to
all of you."

"Same to you, Granville."

Stuart looked around the corner into the kitchen.
"Merry Christmas, Cindy. Don't forget to bring your
pa over for dinner on Saturday. The girls always look
forward to seeing you."

"We'll be there," she promised.

After Stuart had left, Charlie asked Slim, "The new
men haven't gotten word of it, have they?"

"Only what they've picked up in town. Mike Dwyer
asked me what I'd heard, but I told him I thought
it was just more saloon windies. Kenny Reynolds
hasn't said anything, and neither has Clark Terry. Of
course, those two birds keep pretty much to themselves, and don't hardly ever speak unless they're
spoken to."

"Best we just let the matter ride, Slim. Tell the

boys to come over about noon. We won't be having dinner until a while later, but I think Cindy's left enough rum that we can each have a bit to melt the snow off our ribs."

Cindy came from the kitchen with a tray of coffee mugs. "You stay out of the rum until right before we eat. When old Fred gets a couple of drinks into him, he'd rather finish the night drinking than eating."

Slim let out a dry cackle. "For an Indian, though, he can hold a pretty good snootful of firewater. Come on, Twice, I'd like you to meet the new hands. We'll be back in time to wet the neck before dinner, Charlie."

Ben followed Cindy into the kitchen to refill his coffee mug, and helped himself to a chair.

"Sure smells good in here," he commented, savoring the aromas that permeated the room. Mingled with the fresh bread was the spicy smell of sage dressing, and a pork roast.

"If you go home hungry, it won't be because I didn't try." She opened the oven door, pulled the rack part way out and basted the huge roast with its own juices. "Another hour and the pies go in."

He watched her graceful movements around the kitchen, noting that there was nothing unladylike about the way she moved. If only she'd unbend and wear a dress like any other woman!

She wiped her hands on a towel, hung the apron over the back of a chair and sat down with her coffee.

"Once a year I put on a feast like this."

"How long have you been at it?"

"This is my fourth year. The first one was pretty awful, I guess. Earl's taught me a lot since then."

"Like it?" he asked, hoping he wasn't going to rub the raw nerve again.

"Sure, but I'd never take a job cooking as a regular thing."

"Don't like it all that much, then?"

She grimaced. "It means spending most of the time indoors. I was born for the outdoors, Ben. I couldn't stand to be cooped up in a hot kitchen all the time. I don't know how married women take it, I swear I don't."

Ben regretted steering the subject in that direction, but decided he might as well go on a bit.

"Cindy, what's really behind your attitude? You're every inch a lady, but somehow you just don't want to admit it. I've got a hunch there's more involved than not liking dresses and wearing perfume and jewelry.

Suddenly her face dropped, and for a moment he thought she was going to break into tears, but then her head snapped up, and her eyes had that defiant look again.

"Ben," she said softly, "we're friends. Let's keep it that way."

"Cindy, I was just teasing. I didn't mean to say anything to hurt you."

"I know. Maybe it isn't fair that you've told me all about yourself and you still don't know anything about me, but that's the way it's going to have to be, at least for now, all right? Some day you'll know why I'm the way I am."

He nodded. The tone of her voice told him she was filled with something she needed to unburden herself of, and that she wasn't angry, wasn't hurt. Just that she wasn't ready to talk about it. It was something he knew well, having carried his own sorrows for so long without being able to share them with anyone.

"Fair enough." He grinned, then said, "One of these days, you're going to show me how pretty you really are, though, and wear a dress with some earrings and a necklace."

She grinned back at him, wrinkling her freckled nose. "Sure. That'll be the day you decide to give me that filly."

He feigned a look of horror. "Mercy, madame, you do drive a hard bargain!"

"Hard enough to assure myself of something worthwhile for the unaccustomed effort. I suppose you'd expect me to keep on wearing the fool things forever."

"Nope."

"Then I might consider it in the Spring."

"You understand, of course, that she goes back home with me when you revert to your old ways?"

She stood up, still smiling. "Go keep Dad company. I've got too much to do in here to have you underfoot, you . . . you evil-minded man."

"Yep, that's what I am, all right. But I promise I'll behave."

"For how long?"

"All day."

"Git!" she said, giving him a quick kiss on the forehead.

He was so flustered he wasn't able to keep his mind on much of anything he and Charlie talked about, and it seemed only minutes until the hands came in from the bunkhouse. Charlie introduced them to Ben, and then brought out a crystal decanter filled with rum. There was also an iced bowl of the rum punch on a table.

"Here's to a good year," he said, raising his glass. "Bumper crop of calves, mild winter, good rains in the summer."

"And all the bunch quitters in someone else's district," Slim added.

They all drank, and Charlie said, "Some of the boys are new here this year. We have something of a tradition at the Rafter B on Christmas Day. To get the festivities started off on a warm note, everyone has to tell us one thing that happened to him during the last season. You know, something uncomfortable, something you'd just as soon not have to live through again. Like the two days Ben and Cindy and I tried to catch a wild pacing stallion."

They listened as Charlie told of the fruitless chase, and made appropriate sounds when he finished. Twice volunteered next, and told about sailing over the side of the arroyo, expecting to die, then sitting and watching the horse and cow dangle in the air.

"Ain't never in my life seen nothin' like it. My pony looked like he was gettin' swung aboard a steamboat with a sling 'round 'is belly, and lookin' at the scen'ry jist as calm as you please. An' that old maverick cow hangin' bug-eyed, the wind knocked outen her. Lemme tell you, she didn't much care for that experience."

"You should have seen her after we got them down," Ben said. "She acted like it was all Twice's fault, and took after him like the Devil himself. It was all we could do to rope her again."

"Tell us what happened to you at the roundup last year, Fred," Slim said.

The old Cherokee shrugged his shoulders. "I caught a buffalo."

"Whose brand was it wearin'?"

"Cheyenne," he said simply.

Willie Wooten laughed. "First time I ever heard of an Indian running away from a buffalo."

Fred McCoy looked at Wooten coldly. "If you'd been on my pony, you would have run, too." He took a sip of his rum, then turned toward the group. "I was after an old Texas longhorn bunch-quitter. He cut out of the herd and raced into a dry gulch, and I went after him. That gulch got deeper and narrower. Walls up to the sky, and just about room enough for my pony. When I started scraping my knees on both sides, I was ready to find a place to turn around and let the old steer run. I was backing up when I heard rocks clattering down, and that old steer bellering his head off. And he was coming my way, fast. My pony didn't need any encouragement from me, he almost climbed the walls turning around, and then poured on the steam. Right behind us, so close I could feel his breath, came that longhorn, and about that close behind him was a big old buffalo bull, horns like this."

He held out his arms in a wide, sweeping gesture, then brought them together again.

"And this far behind buffalo come two Cheyenne bucks!"

"You should have seen that," Wooten said with a laugh. "I heard it half a mile away. Fred's pony shriekin', Fred whoopin' and hollerin' it up in Cherokee, the longhorn bellerin' and them two Cheyennes screamin' at the tops of their voices. I saw them come out of that gulch like they was all bein' fired out of a Gatlin' gun. Boom, boom, boom! First Fred, then the longhorn, then the buffalo, an' then the Cheyenne. Fred cut around let the old steer go, then slipped his rope over the buffalo. Those Cheyenne pulled up short when they saw five of us waitin' for Fred. You know, you never did tell me what you told them, Fred."

McCoy shrugged his shoulders again. "I told them if they didn't come kill their buffalo, I'd do it for them, then kill them, too. Game belongs to the man who kills it. A Cheyenne don't mind stealing a buffalo someone else has killed, but it don't add to his standing as a hunter. Besides, I was getting paid to hunt cattle, not buffalo."

They passed an hour swapping yarns, and then sat down to gorge themselves on the feast that Cindy looked forward to once a year. After the dishes were cleared away, some of the hands returned to the bunkhouse, and Ben sought an opportunity to talk with Cindy before he and Twice had to start back to the Maltese Cross.

"Cindy, I . . ." He cut himself short as Mike Dwyer stepped up with a brightly-wrapped package.

"Excuse me, Ben. Yes, Mr. Dwyer?"

"I don't mean to intrude, Miss Bowen," he said, "but I've got some work to do, and I wanted to give you this before I left. Just a little something I thought you'd like." He handed her the package.

Ben could feel the blood rising as he watched Cindy blush while she opened the package.

"Isn't it beautiful!" she exclaimed when she saw the silver music box. "And listen!" She opened the lid, and the tinkly music brought a wide smile to her face.

"Why, thank you. It's lovely."

"Thought you might like it to remember the day," Dwyer said. "Now, if you'll excuse me, I've got some work to do before it gets dark. Merry Christmas, Miss Bowen."

Ben seethed as he watched Dwyer leave the house. Cindy's attention was no longer on the man who had a colt she wanted. She was engrossed with the present one of her hired hands had given her.

20

SHERIFF Tom Irvine and livestock inspector Gus Adams sat on the porch of the Miles City Civic Association and Roller Skating Rink, greeting the Association members as they convened in March, 1884. This meeting was the first of two held before the big blowout in May. The main order of business was to establish preliminary districts for the roundups which would get under way in May. Another meeting would be held in April, when the boundaries of the districts would be firmly established and crew captains assigned. Neither meeting would draw as many people to Miles City as the one in May, which signalled the opening of the Spring roundup, but attendance this month seemed heavier than normal.

"Morning, Tom," Dave Mulholland said as he stepped up from the street. "Looks like an early Spring."

"Sure does, Dave. Feels right good."

"Your bullfrog get through the winter all right?"

Irvine grinned and pulled a huge frog from his pocket. "Yep. He'll be up to his old tricks pretty soon."

Irvine's pet frog had been the talk of Miles City for two years. It was one of the largest frogs anyone could remember seeing, and had been trained to ride in Irvine's coat pocket when he wanted to take it for a ride. He enjoyed a swallow or two of beer whenever the sheriff stopped at a saloon for a cold one. Betting on how many flies the frog could catch in a fifteen-minute period was common, and Irvine aided the frog by painting his nose with molasses to entice flies from behind the bar.

Mulholland moved inside, and Adams said, "I hear Dave gave you a bit of trouble couple of months back."

"What would you expect? I spent three weeks tracking down a horse thief. Caught him just inside Wyoming, which is a mite outside my jurisdiction. Tom Newhouse, that's who it was, had made off with a horse and saddle belonging to Matt Burack. When I caught up with him, he was riding that stolen property just as though he'd bought it all legal and proper. Well, I didn't have any papers to take him, and I didn't really have any right to arrest him in Wyoming, but I said to hell with formalities, I wasn't going to let him go. When I was passing Dave's place, he and a couple of grangers over his way met me, and Newhouse started bitching about his rights. I didn't have any business catching him out of this county, I should have gotten a warrant in Wyoming, and he was going to raise hell if I didn't turn him loose.

"Well, for a while, I thought Dave and those boys were on Newhouse's side. Dave stood right in front of me and told me he wasn't going to see Newhouse's rights violated, and that I wasn't going to bring him into Miles City."

Adams shook his head in disbelief. "Dave Mulholland sticking up for a horse thief?"

"That's what I thought," Irvine replied. "Not for long, though. One of the grangers said, 'Hell, Sheriff, takin' him to your jail'd be a crime since you didn't have no call to bring him here without no papers. We don't want you committin' no crime, so we'll just take him off your hands.' Then Dave says, 'Yeah, we've got some good cottonwoods right up the creek a ways. Save yourself some trouble, Tom, we'll take care of his rights.' "

Adams laughed. "What did Newhouse think about that?"

"Damned near begged to go to jail. I had to hustle him away from those boys in a hurry. But, hell, you know what happened after that? A week later they extradited him down to Wyoming where he was wanted on other charges of stealing cattle and horses. He spent one week in a hoosegow at Sheridan, then got turned loose on bail of $100. Last anybody heard of him, he was in Colorado."

"Where he's probably stealing cattle again," Adams said disgustedly.

Zeke Oldmar dismounted, and merely gave Irvine and Adams a perfunctory nod.

"There's a slick one, all right," Adams commented.

"About as honest as a sneaking Sioux," Irvine spat. "How many head do you figure he owns?"

As a cattle inspector, Adams had as much knowledge of range business as anyone. "Twenty-five, thirty thousand."

"He declared seven thousand for tax purposes. He has more cattle than that, sure as hell. Maybe they'll show up at roundup time. I'd give my horse—and even my frog—if I could nail him for fraudulent filing."

"I worked for him down in Texas for two years," Adams said. "When the assessor came around to have a count, Zeke had us drive most of his herd into New Mexico for a couple of weeks, then bring them home after the assessor moved on. A month later, one of the big English outfits came through and bought one of his herds. We drove them through a pass so they could get a count. What those Englishmen didn't know was that while the tail end of that herd was moving through the pass, Zeke had us drive about a thousand of them around a hill and bring them through the pass to be counted again."

"Yeah," Irvine said, spitting into the mud of the street. "And he'll holler as loud as anybody when somebody steals a couple of his beefs."

As more riders approached, Adams said, "Winter's over, all right. Four Eyes has come back from the East. Gawd, ain't he a sight?"

Roosevelt's fringed buckskin jacket and decorated boots could be seen two blocks away. In place of the wide sombrero he had worn to Miles City the previous summer, he now sported a warm bearskin hat, of the style the old hide hunters and trappers wore in severe weather. Riding with him were Ben Foster and several of the ranchers from the western Dakota range. The Marquis de Mores and Pierre Wibaux were carrying on a heated conversation in French, which Roosevelt joined as they arrived at the skating rink.

They pulled up as Granville Stuart and John Clay arrived from the other direction in Stuart's carriage. Irvine pulled his heavy gold watch from his vest pocket. "That figures. Old Stuart never gets here until five or ten minutes before the meeting starts."

Once inside the building, Stuart wasted little time in exchanging pleasantries with Association members. He walked straight to the table in the back of the room, took off his overcoat and pounded the gavel to bring the meeting to order.

Four new members were admitted to the Association, and their brands duly registered in the record books. Five professional bounty hunters presented certified papers attesting to the number of wolves, lions and coyotes they had killed during the winter. One of the hunters stated, "Deduct the value of a yearling heifer from that bill, Mr. Stuart. She was wearing your DHS brand."

Stuart looked up from the papers that had been placed in front of him.

"What circumstances?"

"I was short on provisions, and she was alone up in a box canyon off the Powder."

"I wouldn't have missed it," Stuart said. "But if you're honest enough to admit it, I'll say you're welcome to it," he added with a smile. "Most men simply help themselves to supper and bury the hide if they're out of sight."

"Mr. Stuart, I don't give a hoot how far up in the mountains I am. If I've got to eat somebody else's meat, I intend to pay for it. That heifer wasn't mine."

Stuart declared an estimated value of a dollar for the stray in order that the hunter's conscience remain clear, and the secretary made a notation in the record books.

Problems with marketing were discussed for nearly an hour, and then more time was spent on deciding the number of bulls each owner could maintain. The afternoon was growing late when the business got down to the ever-growing problem of rustlers.

"Mr. Chairman," de Mores said after being given the floor, "I would like to read an editorial that appeared this week in the *Yellowstone Journal*. I believe it fairly well states our position."

"Read," Stuart said.

The presence of horse thieves whether white or red is so apparent and their work so proven

*that it calls for some concerted action on the part
of those most interested. Valuable animals, cattle and sheep as well as horses, are constantly
disappearing and the losses incurred at this por-
tion of the season are irremediable. These preda-
tory scoundrels are gathering fast. They have their
organizations and are desperate men. They know
they deserve to be strung up or shot down on short
notice, and that when caught that method of disposing of them is usually resorted to. While we
are positively opposed to mob law except in the
extremest cases, we are fully aware that something must be done for the protection of our
property . . .*

"I have gone through this week's journal, gentlemen," de Mores added, "and there are no less than
seven notices of stolen horses, and six of cattle. These
represent only the ones flagrant in the extreme, and
which catch the fancy of the editor of this journal.
Nobody will ever know how many animals have been
stolen. I will read one more item in the editorials:"

*There appears to be a horse stealing boom
throughout the territory, and if it doesn't collapse
the organization of the old-time necktie festivals
will be in order.*

"Gentlemen," de Mores shouted, "the esteemed
editor is correct: The time has come for action!"

A resounding cheer rose through the huge room,
and Stuart banged on the table with his gavel.

"This meeting will be conducted with decorum, gentlemen. Dave Mulholland, you have the floor."

"I think the Marky is right. We can get up an army
of good cowboys and sweep the basin clean in no
time."

Another round of cheers rose from the men who had come to this particular meeting with just that idea in mind. Again, Stuart pounded for order.

"Such a motion is out of order!" he announced. "This Association will not take any part in mob action."

A stunned silence filled the room, and Roosevelt jumped to his feet.

"By Jove, Stuart! You're back-pedaling!"

"Sit down, Four Eyes, you haven't been given the floor." Granville Stuart's steely gray eyes bored into Roosevelt's.

"Damn it," someone shouted, "Dave made a motion, and I'll second it! Then we can discuss it."

Stuart pounded on the table, and when a semblance of silence had been restored, he said, "Such a motion is contrary to the laws of the Territory in which we operate, and as such cannot be entertained. The motion is out of order, and I'll personally attend to any man who tries to introduce it again, is that clear to everybody?"

A stunned silence fell over the room. Could this really be the man who had advocated such a course of action only last year?

"Do you have any other solution, Granville?" Charlie Bowen thundered.

"Yes. We shall appeal to the governor. He could quite well send troops of the guard to put an end to this business."

A rising murmur of discontent swept through the hall. Stuart rose and announced, "There being no further business to come before this body, I declare an adjournment until tomorrow morning at ten o'clock. At that time we shall take up the matter again. Perhaps cooler heads will prevail. Meeting adjourned!"

The following morning, Roosevelt asked Sheriff Irvine, "I say, have you seen Ben Foster this morning? I can't find him anywhere."

"Foster? Can't say I have, Four Eyes. You seen Gus Adams? He disappeared right about the time the meeting broke up yesterday. Maybe Granville knows where they are."

Thirty minutes after the scheduled time for the meeting, John Clay announced, "Granville Stuart was called home during the night. In his absence, I shall conduct the business for today."

Charlie Bowen sat through the day's arguments with a smug look on his face.

21

Less than an hour after Stuart arrived at the DHS, Gus Adams rode in with six men. Stuart knew all of them well, and he nodded to his foreman. Ten minutes later, a procession of fifteen men and a string of twenty spare horses made their way to a railroad siding where a special train was waiting. Stuart and his men led their horses quietly into the two box cars, then climbed into one of the two coaches that made up the special.

He spread out a large map of the basin, and laid out his plan of action. "We'll get off at Coulson and clean out the nests between the mouths of the Judith and the Musselshell. We'll pick up the train again at Junction City and get off at Porcupine Creek. From there, we'll work our way over to Sunday Creek, go down the Big Dry to the Missouri and then head south along Redwater Creek. If word doesn't get back to that bunch along Cedar Creek, we ought to nab some of them there, too. We'll join up with the Medora crew in five or six days, then we can make a clean sweep of it from Medora clear through to the Missouri."

Slim Menough asked, "How many are there over at Medora?"

"Ben Foster said he's got ten he can count on."

"You can count on Ben," Gus Adams said. "He'll get the best."

"Four Eyes is going to shit his britches when he finds out Ben's going along with us," Slim said.

"Maybe not," Stuart told him. "He and de Mores were ready to hang me this afternoon when I refused to allow a motion to do what we're doing." His grey eyes sparkled. "Did you see how Charlie went along with it?"

"Yeah," Adams said with a smile. "He even had me fooled. But how long do you think they're going to sit on their asses in Miles City?"

"Four or five days at the very least," Stuart said. "Clay will take over the meetings, and we've arranged to have a couple of lawyers from Washington, who just happen to be passing through, come in and interpret the Territorial Statutes for us."

"Oh, shit!" Slim said gleefully. "By the time a lawyer gets done lecturing about all the ramifications of the differences between a bull and a steer, they could be tied up for a month."

"Exactly," Stuart said, stroking his beard absently. "And do you have any idea of how long it will take to explain the difference between first and second degree murder, negligent homicide, homicide in the first degree, homicide . . ."

"Granville," came a voice from a seat in the back of the car, "if I'd wanted to hear all that crap I'd still be in Miles City, not here."

Stuart chuckled. "You're right. I suggest we get all the sleep we can, gentlemen. This is going to be a short but hard roundup."

Five hours later the train slowed to a stop, and Stuart led his men north through the gray early morning toward the Musselshell. About halfway they came upon two punchers moving a herd of about two hundred head through a gentle valley.

Stuart signalled, and the band moved out toward the flanks, while he and Gus Adams rode up to the two men guarding the cattle.

"What the hell is this?" one of them demanded.

"Whose cattle are these?" Stuart asked.

"Ours. If you think you're going to steal them . . ."

A shot rang out, and he pitched backwards off his horse. Slim Menough slipped his revolver back into its holster as he brought his horse to a stop.

"Looks like every one of these beefs is wearing a different brand," he said.

"Now, look," the other rustler said, perspiration dotting his face in spite of the chilly air.

"Mister, you have thirty seconds to tell us how you come to be playin' nursemaid to some of my beefs," one of the vigilantes demanded.

"I bought them," the man said, "from somebody who . . ."

"Get out a bill of sale right quick, you slimy bastard."

"I . . . I got it back at the cabin."

Slim's rope was around him, and he was pulled off his horse. Five minutes later his toes were making their last feeble twitches as his lifeless body swung from a low branch. Pinned to his shirt was a notice that was to become common in the next few days:

"LET THIS BE FAIR WARNING TO ALL THIEFS IN THESE PARTS."

By nightfall twelve more of the crudely printed signs were swaying in the breeze, or on the bloody bodies that lay on the cold ground. Stuart was highly satisfied with the first day of the "roundup."

22

BEN and Twice leaned against the depot wall and listened. They heard nothing but the normal sounds of carousing from across the river at Little Missouri. From the eaves of the depot a barn owl hooted at them.

"Reckon something's happened?" Twice asked.

"I hope not. They should have been here an hour ago."

Another thirty-five minutes passed before they saw the black smoke beyond the hills to the west. Ben wasn't sure whether to breathe easier or not. He felt strange sensations prickling through his insides, and recognized it for fear. It wouldn't be the first time he'd killed a man, but it had never been planned before, and this couldn't be claimed as self-defense. He knew now what the old army veterans talked about when they described how they felt going into battle for the first time.

The train wheezed to a stop, and Granville Stuart

and Gus Adams stepped onto the platform, followed by the rest of the small band. One look at Slim Menough's face told Ben that everything was successful so far.

"Everyone's ready?" Stuart asked.

"Right. They've been camped out on this side of the river since yesterday morning."

Stuart looked at Twice. "Four Eyes know you're going along?"

"Four Eyes don't know nothin' about it. Me and Ben and Curly just made up our minds we was gonna go. He don't like it, he can tell us to go look for new jobs."

Gus Adams said, "Just look around, Twice. There are at least six ranchers here who'll take you on tomorrow."

As they walked back to the box cars, Ben said, "You're late. You run into some kind of trouble?"

Adams laughed. "Not for us."

"I sent a telegram through just as we were ready to leave," Slim said.

"I got it all right, but where'd you get that fancy idea about cookies? 'Have dispatched three dozen cookies. Am coming for more. Love Mother.'"

"As long as you got the message, what difference does it make? We took care of thirty seven of them back there. We were about ten miles down the line when the engineer put on the brakes. Would you believe four stupid fools were going to hold up the train?"

"You're jobbin' me," Twice said, his crooked grin stretched from one side of his face to the other.

Stuart let out a sigh. "Anybody in his right mind would have some kind of idea what cargo a train carries before attempting a holdup. They must have thought that a special train this small meant a shipment of gold or silver."

"If they thought that, were they so stupid they wouldn't think there'd be an armed guard riding with it?"

"We'll never know what they were thinking, Ben," Gus replied.

Stuart waved an impatient hand. "Let's get the horses off and get going. I'd just as soon finish what we started before the word spreads too far."

"It's here already, Mr. Stuart."

"How long?"

"Two days. You know what kind of name we've got?" He was unaware he'd included himself in the group before actually riding with them. "They're calling us The Stranglers."

Twice nodded across the river to Little Missouri. "Some feller in the bar at the Pyramid said he don't give no damn, since it's all over to the Montana side."

"That's what he thinks," Slim said.

Before nightfall, they had joined forces with the Dakota vigilantes and gratefully accepted a hot meal of stew, biscuits and coffee. It was the second time in five days they'd had a proper meal.

"Well, we did have some fresh cornbread and what was left of a roasted calf," Slim said. "But fifteen of us made short work of that, seeing as how they were only cooking for four."

"We've got enough provisions to last us a week," Ben said. "Might not have a chance to stop and cook, but there's plenty of jerky and smoked pork."

"I don't hesitate to pick up food from any rustler's camp," Stuart said. "But nothing else. They're taking the food out of our mouths. Nothing wrong with taking our own food back from them after they don't have any more use for it."

The sun was barely above the eastern hills the next morning when they spread out to surround a shack set back on a ridge overlooking the Little Missouri.

Smoke coming from the chimney indicated the residents were up and starting their day. The shack had been built by a former rancher named Abner Witherspoon, who lost eighty percent of his stock in the bitter winter of 1881–82, and half of what was left to rustlers. He gave up and returned to Illinois.

"Nobody's used that place for two years," Curly Schaeffer said. "Looks like we've got some prime suspects."

They rode slowly toward the shack, but one of the horses in the corral whinnied a greeting to the animals approaching, and a few seconds later a rifle barked from one of the windows.

The air was shattered with gunshots as the vigilantes returned the fire. The door opened a crack, and a hand waved a flour sack.

"Come out with your hands grabbin' for clouds," demanded Adams.

The door opened far enough to let the man out, and he began walking toward the string of riders. Suddenly he broke into a zig-zag run as two rifles inside began barking. While the others poured lead into the little cabin, Ben snaked his rope out and caught the running man, then spurred his horse for cover behind a rise, dragging the captive behind him.

Stuart and Adams rode up. "How many are inside that cabin?"

"Three. One's dead."

"Two more are going to be in a few minutes," Stuart said matter-of-factly.

"Who the hell are you to set yourself up as judge, jury and executioner, Stuart?"

"A property owner, my friend, a property owner who's been watching scum like you erode my profits."

"You stinking cattle barons think just because you've got so goddamned much money you can get away with anything. And you, I know who you are.

You're Gus Adams. High and mighty cattle inspector, carry the money of the Association behind you, and the power of the law on your shirt. I notice you're not wearing your tin badge now, Adams."

"I'm not working in any official capacity, either. Just my private bit to keep the range free."

"You talk like a bunch of damned pollyannas. Free range, shit! You want it free for the likes of Stuart and his money-hungry friends."

"The range may be free, but the cattle aren't," Stuart reminded him.

"And where'd you get all your stock? I'll tell you where. A few of you like Goodnight and Kohrs and Clay just rode around gettin' a few here, a few there. And don't try to give me any shit about mavericks, damn it. Hell, you stole most of those cows down in Texas, and you know it."

"You're beginning to try my patience, friend."

"You talk big, don't you? I suppose you think murder's less a crime than a little rustling?"

"My friend," Stuart said, "there is no more such a thing as a little rustling as there is a little pregnancy. Gus, go tell those two to surrender and get out here, or we're going to come in after them."

"Sure, you old bastard," the man on the ground spat, "when the high and mighty Granville Stuart speaks, everybody in the world is supposed to listen. You want to make a bet they'll come out of there?"

"Makes no difference," Stuart said. "They'll be dead in a few minutes one way or another."

"So what the hell are you keeping me for? Go ahead and hang me, damn your soul!"

"I'm a gentleman, friend. I'd like you to have the pleasure of hanging with your friends. I'm not one to break up long friendships."

Slim Menough rode up. "Looks like they're going

to have to be convinced, Mr. Stuart. May I do the honors this time?"

"It's all yours," Stuart said with an icy smile.

Ben watched as Slim gathered a few bunches of grass and twigs, holding it together with stout binder twine. One of the men unlashed a gallon can of kerosene from his saddle and soaked the bundle. Slim nodded, and Stuart waved to Gus Adams, who shouted an order to the men.

Eighteen of them started forward at a gallop firing as fast as they could at the door and windows of the shack while Slim slipped around behind and struck a match just before throwing the blazing torch on the roof. He was back on his horse and racing out of the angle of fire in a matter of seconds.

The men outside held their fire long enough for the ones in the shack to realize what was happening. When the flames had spread from the roof down two walls, the door burst open and both of them ran out, their clothes afire and their Winchesters being levered as fast as their arms would move. Neither of them got off more than three shots before being cut down by a rain of lead.

Stuart looked at the burning bodies in front of the cabin, and said, "Let's use this tree over here. That way he can have a last look at his friends before he dies."

Ben had to admit his captive was no coward. He didn't offer any resistance, but spat his defiance every step of the way as he was half-dragged, half-led to the tree where the rope was waiting.

"Anything to say, friend?"

"Go to hell, Stuart! You lynched men this way over at the mines, too. You don't know what the law is all about, do you?"

"You're mistaken." Gus Adams pulled the noose

tight around his neck. "This here is a legal court-room. Mr. Stuart is the judge, I'm the bailiff, and these are the jury."

"What is the charge?" Stuart intoned.

"Stealing livestock," replied Slim Menough.

"What say the jury? Guilty or not guilty?"

"Guilty as hell, your honor!"

"Hang him."

Ben spurred his horse forward, feeling the rope snap taut across his thigh, then pulled to a stop. He looked back over his shoulder, and got a glimpse of the thief's eyes bulging far out of their sockets while his tongue stuck grotesquely from his mouth. His legs kicked convulsively, twisting his head a few more inches to the right. A widening stain on his trousers showed that he had relaxed in death, and his bladder had emptied itself of the night's urine.

Two men grabbed the rope as Ben backed, then loosened the bitter end from the saddle horn. They tied the rope around the trunk of the tree and left the corpse swinging with his boots four feet off the ground.

"That makes forty-one," Stuart said with no trace of emotion. "Let's see if we can get it to fifty by nightfall."

As they regrouped to move farther north along the Little Missouri, Ben hoped no one had seen him duck behind a bush to vomit.

Long after it was over, Teddy Roosevelt wrote, ". . . the stockmen have united to put down all these dangerous characters, often by the most summary exercise of lynch law. Notorious bullies and murderers have been taken out and hung, while the bands of horse and cattle thieves have been regularly hunted down and destroyed in pitched fights by parties of armed cowboys; and as a consequence most of our territory is now perfectly law-abiding. One such fight occurred north of me early last Spring. The horse-thieves were overtaken on the banks of the Missouri; two of their number were slain, and the others were driven on the ice, which broke, and two more were drowned. . . . another gang, whose headquarters were near the Canadian line, were surprised in their hut; two or three were shot down by the cowboys as they tried to come out, while the rest barricaded themselves in and fought until the great log-hut was set on fire, when they broke forth in a body, and nearly all were killed at once, only one or two making their escape. . . . one committee of vigilantes in eastern Montana shot or hung nearly sixty—not, however, with the best judgment in all cases."

Granville Stuart noted in his journal: *"Several of the men who met their fate on the Missouri . . . belonged to wealthy and influential families and there arose a great hue and cry in certain localities over what was termed 'the arrogance of the cattle king.' The cattlemen were accused of hiring 'gunmen' to raid the country and drive small ranchers and sheepmen off the range. There was not a grain of truth in this talk."*

A year later the Medora *Bad Lands Cowboy* summed it up by expressing the feeling of most people in the basin: *"Whatever can be said against the methods adopted by the 'stranglers' who came through here . . . it cannot but be acknowledged that . . . it seems as though a very thorough cleanup has been made."*

The organized bands, for the most part, had been cleaned out, leaving the rustling to the few dishonest ranchers like Zeke Oldmar and the cowboys who occasionally added a bonus to their small pay. Even the Indians took less pleasure in stealing an occasional cow to supplement the meagre rations they were being issued at the agencies.

Jack Sully's business was cut drastically, and he considered taking his Indian wife and children to Wyoming. After giving the matter some thought, he decided to stick around and see how things were going to work out. After all, he still had men like Sam Groot, Frank Pendleton and Mike Dwyer scattered throughout the Yellowstone Basin.

23

THE Northern Cheyenne Reservation was bounded on its eastern side by some thirty miles of the Tongue River. Mike Dwyer and Kenny Reynolds rode south along the east bank, searching with field glasses for cattle that had crossed the river onto Cheyenne land. Bowen had registered the pair with the agent at Lame Deer, and they had permission to cross the river to check "any livestock in sight, but not beyond" and drive them back onto the open range if they belonged to anyone other than the Cheyenne. Twice they'd gone onto the reservation to drive off small bunches that belonged to Bowen, Mulholland or Oldmar, and then continued their search once back on the open range. Kenny didn't like the idea of being on Indian land.

"Suppose a war party finds us?"

"Kid, how long have you been in this country?"

"Almost a year. I've heard lots about what those Cheyenne will do to a white man."

"You've been listening to the wrong people. The reservation is set aside for them, but they don't own any white man's beefs that wander onto it. Bowen registered with the agent at Lame Deer, and got permission for us to search for Association cattle before the roundup. We've stayed within the two-mile limit, haven't we? If anything happens to us while we're here on legal business, the tribe would have the whole damned Cavalry on their necks."

"If they found out. Mike, I don't mind saying I don't give a damn how many head Mr. Bowen and the others lose. I like the idea of keeping my scalp."

Dwyer allowed himself a satisfied grin. This kid was going to be easy to manipulate.

"Okay, let's move east. But if we spot any, we're gonna have a look."

"Fine."

They crossed the Tongue, continued south for another ten or twelve miles without seeing more than an occasional cow or two. Once Mike spotted a dozen animals grazing, and the field glasses showed most of them bore the brand registered to the Cheyenne. They kept riding, and didn't bother themselves if they found less than six head at a time.

By nightfall of the second day they were below the reservation, and ready to double back on their tracks, skirting the edge of the timber to the east until they were in open country again, then cut right and follow the Mizpah back to the Rafter B.

They made camp for the night at the foot of the timber. Mike leaned back on a tree, lit a cigar, and watched Kenny fumble with a sack of Durham. After the boy had torn three papers, Mike laughed and said, "Why not try a cigar?"

"I tried that once, Mike, and thought I was gonna die. Nope, I'll learn how to make a cigarette yet. I've only been smoking since Christmas."

After another attempt, he had a cigarette that resembled a small horseradish, and lit up with satisfaction. Mike waited until he had taken two drags, then asked, "You like this life, kid?"

"It ain't bad, Mike."

"Beats a lot of other ways to make a living, like the mines."

"Yeah, I guess. But sometimes I kinda wish I could have a crack at the mines. Just one good strike, and I could put some money aside. I'll never put any money in the bank this way."

"Kenny, it's damned near impossible to work a claim of your own and make expenses. Hell, the big companies own everything."

"You've worked silver mines, haven't you?"

"Long enough to know that I'd rather make forty dollars a month doing this than seventy-five a month in the mines. Of course, there's a lot more than forty dollars a month in this, if you know how to work it."

Kenny's eyes narrowed, and he looked anxiously at Mike. "How?"

Mike felt his way carefully. "You think I bought boots like these on forty dollars a month? Sheridan cost me a hundred and twenty dollars, and the rig set me back another sixty. The hat I wear when I go to town was twenty dollars. Kid, you can't have stuff like that on forty dollars a month."

Kenny leaned forward and poured himself another cup of coffee. "How, Mike? Tell me."

"Oh, there's lots of ways, Kenny."

"Gambling, I bet."

"Shit, a man's a fool to gamble unless he really knows what he's doing. You'll find about as many honest card dealers in these parts as balls on a steer."

He leaned back, took another drag on his cigar, waiting.

"Mike, you ain't talking about rustling, are you?

Look what happened to all the rustlers couple of weeks ago."

"It wasn't all the rustlers, just the ones who don't have a lot of money. Kid, there isn't a cattleman out here who hasn't done a lot of it at one time or another. And they still do it, even if they don't like to admit it."

"But that's dishonest."

"Is it? You ever hear of Charlie Goodnight?"

"The big baron out of Texas?"

"Himself. How do you think he built up the biggest herds in the country?"

"Well, Slim was telling me how he started out managing a herd for someone else, and got to keep every fourth calf for his pay. Ain't that how it was?"

"Yep, and he rounded up mavericks and put his brand on 'em. Anybody can put his own brand on a maverick."

"I thought it had to be branded for the Association."

"That's only the way they do it here, not the rest of the country. And do you know why the Association makes up rules like that?"

"Why?"

"To keep honest men from having a few head of their own. A few years ago anybody could put his brand on a maverick. Now the rich owners want everything for themselves. Hell, they won't even let anyone work for them if he's got a registered brand. The only exceptions are the ones hired by the big companies like the Mankato, or the XIT, and then it's only the managers who can do it. But do you think those guys who manage the big herds never put their own brands on a calf?"

"Aren't there supposed to be two or three different outfits at each corral when we're branding?"

"Kenny, suppose you and I were building up our own herd. How would you go about it?"

He knew that would stop him, and when the answer finally came, it was what he expected.

"Change some brands?"

"Sure, you could do that, if you wanted to hang. The only way, short of buying beefs, is to put your brand on some mavericks."

"But there ain't all that many runnin' loose, are there, Mike?"

"More than they'd like to think. This range is getting so crowded they don't know if there's half a million or two million beefs around here. They miss almost as many at roundup as they catch up."

Kenny flipped the stub into the fire. Again, Mike waited.

"I don't know. Seems like it would take a long time to find enough to make it worth while. Specially when everyone's thinking the same thing."

He sat and stared into the fire for a few minutes, then said, "I sure wouldn't mind picking up a yearling or two of my own."

"Ever hear of sleepering?"

"What's that?"

"Well, just imagine if you knew where there were some cows that just happened to miss the roundup this year. By the time they weaned their calves and kicked them off on their own, they'd be leavin' some mavericks around, wouldn't they?"

"Yeah."

"And if you happened to know where a thousand, maybe two thousand of 'em spent the winter, you'd be able to pick up some good money branding mavericks, wouldn't you?"

"Yeah, but ain't that against the law, Mike?"

"On the open range the law says a maverick belongs to anybody who brands it. It's just the Association that thinks it can change the way it's been done for fifty years. You think it's any different for one man to claim ownership of a maverick than it is for four hundred to claim it?"

"Gosh, Mike, the way you explain it, it don't seem right for the Association to say it owns everything."

"It ain't right, kid, and all I want to do is get my fair share of what's runnin' around free for the grabbing. You interested in working with me?"

"Well . . ." He stared into the fire again, then said, "Not if it means stealing or changing brands. I think more of Mr. Bowen than that."

"So do I, and I don't intend to take anything that belongs to Bowen or anybody else. That'd be dishonest. All we'd be doing is getting the mavericks that are free for the taking. Play it my way, and you'll have money in the bank by snowfall. You won't steal a cow, and you won't change a brand."

"Mike, if you can promise me that, I'll do it. But I won't steal."

"I'll never ask you to. But you'll help me borrow some cows, won't you?"

Kenny stiffened.

"What do you mean, borrow?"

"We'll borrow some cows and sleeper 'em. We'll see that they're taken care of until the calves are old enough to be weaned. Then we'll return the cows. It's that simple."

"I dunno. It don't hardly seem honest."

"You think Granville Stuart and Charley Goodnight never pulled that stunt? How do you think Zeke Oldmar gets more calves every year than he owns cows? He claims all of his cows have twins."

"Well . . . Mike, won't they hang us if they catch us?"

"You know what Bowen or anybody else is likely to do? When we drive home a herd or two or three hundred cows that we just happened to find back in some box canyon, he'll probably give us a reward."

"A reward? Like the one he's offering for an Aberdeen bull he lost?"

"Yeah, something like that," Mike replied with a grin. "Now let's get some sleep. We got work to do tomorrow."

24

"How many?" Cindy wasn't sure she heard him right.

"Sixty-three," Charlie told her again. "That's what I heard, anyway. Forty-one of them through here, and another twenty-two in the Little Missouri Basin."

"Were you with them, Dad?" Her voice had a wistful quaver, as though she weren't sure herself how she felt about it now that the deed had been carried out.

"No, damn it, they pulled it off while my back was turned. I've been waiting for six months, and then missed out on all the fun."

"Slim went, didn't he?"

Charlie gave her an icy look. "Just what in the name of God's gone wrong with you, gal? Nobody knows who went and who didn't. And the less anybody knows about it, the better off everyone's going to be."

"Dad, I was only—"

"I know, you were only trying to satisfy a morbid curiosity about who could be cold-blooded enough to shoot or hang sixty-three worthless scum who had no concept of right or wrong."

Cindy's anger flared. "It so happens I'd like to thank every one of them! I wish I could have been there myself. It would have given me a hell of a lot of satisfaction knowing that one of them might have been the one who stole our bull."

Charlie took a deep breath of resignation. "There are times I don't think I'll ever understand you, Cindy. Some days I think you know what's right and good, and then you turn around and tell me you'd like to watch men die."

"Didn't you just say yourself you missed out on all the fun? Why should I be different?"

"Because you *are* different! You're not a man, that's why. You're not a man who's been to war and watched other men die, good ones as well as bad. No matter how wrong those rustlers were, no matter how much they've cost us over the last several years, they were still men, and some of them were mighty good men. A few of them had wives and children, and were well respected by their neighbors. They simply had some twisted notions of mine and thine, that's all. And don't ever forget that no matter how you and I and everyone else in this basin feels about them, they were still men who had the right to a trial by jury. No, shut up and listen to me for a minute! How would you feel if a dozen men rode in here right now and dragged me outside to hang me for rustling? Huh? Tell me, what would you think?"

"But . . . that's ridiculous, Dad! Nobody's going to accuse you of rustling."

"How do you know? Look out there! Look! In our corral we've got two of Dave Mulholland's horses, and one of Ben Foster's. Twelve men come up to the door and ask what I'm doing with three horses that don't belong to me. I tell them I'm keeping them for Dave and Ben. So they drag me over to that cottonwood and hang me, because they think I'm lying. Now, what are you going to think?"

"I wouldn't let them get away with it!"

"How are you going to stop them? Tell me that."

"But, Dad, this whole argument is asinine. They couldn't prove it, even if they did suspect it."

"But remember, they didn't give me a chance to prove my side of the story, either. So just suppose it happened. And they kept a good hold on you, and stripped the house of every rifle and pistol in the place so you couldn't shoot them while they strung me up. Now, tell me, what would you do?"

"If I couldn't catch up with them, I'd go get Tom Irvine."

Charlie's face broadened into a wide smile. "And would you, now? And suppose it turned out to be the same bunch that we call The Stranglers, only they happened to make a mistake in my case. Remember, they've killed sixty-three scum who deserved to die, and me, who didn't. Think, gal, think! What are you going to do? You want to drag every one of those men into court because they made one mistake in sixty-four executions? Is that how you'd thank them for getting rid of the rustlers who cut down our profits every year?"

"Dad, you make it sound like, well, like it didn't matter if some innocent men died."

"It does matter, Cindy. I don't know for sure, but I've got a feeling one or two of them might have been innocent as all hell. And their families are already threatening to have every one of The Stranglers taken to trial for murder. And the more people who know anything about who went out in that bunch, the more talk there's going to be, and the more names that are going to be dropped in the wrong places. So I'd suggest you just forget about who did what. It's been done, and we're a lot better off for it. Every man who put his life on the line for all of us deserves more than a medal, and he'll never even get the medal. All he'll ever get out of it is nightmares."

Ben Foster was troubled with only one nightmare from the week he spent with The Stranglers. On the fourth day, when the skies were dark and the wind chill as it can only be in late Spring near the Canadian border, they crossed to the northern side of the Missouri, and came onto a camp of horse rustlers. The broad valley below them had a herd of well over a hundred horses, and there appeared to be three men wrangling them while another three huddled over a campfire.

Stuart dropped his field glasses back into the velvet-lined case after studying the herd. "At least thirty brands. Let's go."

The pounding hooves racing down the slope alerted men and horses below, and in moments the herd was racing north, the three wranglers whipping them with their quirts. Those at the campfire scrambled for their horses, but the panic-stricken animals bolted, broke their tethers and were racing after the others, leaving three men afoot to face the vigilantes racing down on them.

As the herd raced straight north through the valley, the three riders cut off in different directions. Stuart signalled to his men, and pairs peeled off to chase each of them while the main force went for the three men who were taking up defensive positions where they could.

Ben and Gus Adams spurred their mounts toward the rider racing at an angle up a slope to the west. It was a gentle slope, and almost as smooth as the valley floor.

The rider was a quarter of a mile ahead of them,

and Ben had the uneasy feeling that there was something familiar about the way he sat his saddle. It was almost as though it was someone he knew, and he wished for some unknown reason that he had been at the other end of the line to go after a different quarry.

When the rider had reached the crest of the rise, a light rain began falling, and by the time Ben and Gus topped it, the rain was coming down in torrents. He and Gus pulled up to peer through the driving rain.

"Can't see a hundred yards," Gus muttered.

"Looks like we've lost him."

Adams searched the ground, hoping to find sign, but the rain was lashing them so hard any tracks would have been obliterated.

"Let's keep going for a bit," Adams said. "We might get lucky."

Suddenly Ben's mare whinnied, and her head swung around to the left.

"Over this way," he said, letting the mare follow the sound she'd heard.

"There," Adams said, pointing to muddy tracks that were filled with water.

Another five minutes through the driving rain brought them to the edge of a wash where the ground had given way under the weight of a horse. Ben and Gus kept well back, not knowing how deep the undercut might be. Through the roar of the wind-lashed rain came the unmistakable sound of a man groaning. Ben dismounted and walked carefully to the edge.

Below him lay a horse with a grotesquely broken neck, his lifeless body pinning a man beneath him. The water rushing through the wash was pouring over the horse's belly and threatening to drown his rider, who was propped up on his elbows trying to keep his face out of the muddy water.

"For God's sake, git me outta here," the man cried.

Ben shivered, not from the cold rain that had soaked

him to the skin, but from the sound of the voice. It was a voice he had heard almost every day for three years.

"Davey! That you?"

"Ben! Dammit, git me out from under this horse before I drown. I got a busted leg."

"You've got more busted than a leg, mister," Gus shouted.

His Winchester barked, and Ben saw Davey's eyes open wide in unbelieving terror as the slug ripped into his chest. His mouth opened as though to say something, and blood streamed out as he fell back, the rushing, muddy water washing it away as his face disappeared beneath the angry current.

"Friend of yours?" Adams asked as he slid the rifle into its sheath.

"Yeah. Davey Morton. I rode with him for more than three years when we worked for George Fowler."

Adams peered hard at Ben, his face almost obscured by the water pouring off the brim of his hat.

"You're not telling me Fowler ever had anything to do with stolen stock, are you?"

Ben swung up, the seat of his pants soaking up the water that was on his saddle. His stomach felt as cold as his backside.

"If he did, I never knew it. In fact, he once gunned down someone who tried to sell him a couple of brood mares he'd stolen, and eventually got them back to their owner."

"Then what's Morton doing with this bunch?"

"I don't know, Gus. I just don't know," he replied, numb and sick.

As they rode back over the rise to the valley where Stuart and the rest were waiting, Ben Foster felt as cold and alone as he ever had in his life. What could have changed Davey? Certainly Fowler had always treated his men fairly, and paid them top wages. What

kind of weird act was Aeschylus trying to write now?
It didn't make sense. No, Davey Morton couldn't have
been . . .

Maybe he was moving some of Fowler's horses and
had them stolen by the gang just before Stuart's men
had come on them.

Ben fought back a tear, thinking of the high times
he and Davey Morton and Muttonhead had had during
those three years. Suddenly the whole idea of joining
Stuart seemed to be a mistake, and Ben wished he
could be back in Miles City and say, "No, Mr. Stuart.
I just don't care to be a part of it."

But it had seemed such a natural thing to do, the
thing anybody would have done to get rid of the
rustlers. But sometimes the natural—seeming things
wasn't always what it appeared to be. Now Ben could
spend the rest of his life with the vision of his friend
Davey Morton being gunned down by a blood-crazed
band of vigilantes without having a chance to explain how he happened to be in the wrong place
at the wrong time.

Granville Stuart stood in the rain, his sopping wet
beard dripping trickles of water. Slim Menough and
Curly Schaeffer were putting a makeshift bandage on
the leg of one of the ranchers from Powder River.

"We got lucky," Adams said. "Found him pinned
under his horse where they fell into a ravine. Chalk
up one more."

Ben watched as Stuart reached under his overcoat,
using it as a shield while he made a pencilled notation in a small memo book.

"We might have made a mistake," Ben said. "I knew
him."

Stuart stopped. "Who was he?"

"Davey Morton. Worked for George Fowler when
I did."

Stuart cocked his head to one side. "Morton, eh?

Sorry to hear that, Ben, but if you want to go get his body it's worth two thousand dollars. Fowler posted a reward for him last December. Morton made off with about fifty head of Fowler's breeding stock and headed for the United States. Some of those horses, by the way, have been found in Colorado."

Ben couldn't believe what he'd heard, and the look on his face showed it. "I know it's hard to take, but it's the truth," Adams said. "I've seen the poster in Tom's office."

Ben felt drained and weak, and sat his horse dumbly. Stuart reached out and laid a gentle, bony hand on Ben's knee. "I know how you feel. On our first day out we hanged two men who'd worked for me for years."

Before they felt they'd finished their work, The Stranglers had worked their way across the border into Canada, where they hanged the last three. Every mile of the way, Ben could see Davey's frightened face falling beneath the swirling, muddy water.

Not until a month later, when he next went to Miles City, did he fully believe that Davey Morton had turned rustler. He saw the poster on the bulletin board in Tom Irvine's office.

"See anybody there you know?" Irvine asked, his eyes searching Ben's face.

"Only a couple of familiar names," Ben said.

Irvine studied Ben's face. "Morton one of 'em? You worked together. I remember you bringing Fowler's stock over here for the Army."

"Yeah, I know him."

"Seen anything of him lately?"

"Last I saw him was last summer when we brought a string over to the fort."

"Haven't seen him since then?" Irvine studied Ben's face.

"Nope."

25

ROOSEVELT watched in admiration as Curly boarded Water Skipper and kept his seat through the preliminaries, then whooped for joy as they sailed off to let Water Skipper's early morning fire burn down to manageable proportions.

"By Godfrey! Some day I shall do that."

"Sure y' will," Twice said. "An' when y' do, I'm gonna shout, 'Bully fer you, Old Four Eyes!'"

Twice watched while Roosevelt lassoed Manitou and got his saddle on him. Manitou seemed resigned to his owner by now, and didn't bother to buck, but once Roosevelt was on board and nudged with his knees, the gelding took off in imitation of Water Skipper. The race was short, though, and Roosevelt had him back to the corral ten minutes before Curly and Water Skipper arrived.

The four of them rode together as far as Little Missouri, where Curly and Twice headed for the Badlands General Provisions to order their supplies for the roundup. Roosevelt and Ben turned west toward Miles City.

"Now that the general situation concerning outlaws has been improved, I should think Washington will be more favorably inclined toward admitting these territories to statehood," Roosevelt said. "You seem to be very close to Charles Brown, Ben. Perhaps you could influence him to get into politics. I truly believe he'd be a good man in the Legislature."

"I don't know that I have that kind of influence. Right now he's trying to make up his mind whether to stay in the cattle business or switch over to horses. About all I can do is talk horses with him, not politics. We've even talked about the possibility of becoming partners in the horse business."

"I think I'm going to keep the Maltese Cross and Elkhorn ranches primarily for cattle. If you decide to join Charles, I'd miss you, but you know I'll understand. I rather imagine Charles Bowen will make a success of anything he tries. He has the respect of everyone, even the Marquis."

"I heard you and de Mores had a falling out."

"That rascal has a falling out with everybody from time to time. I simply wanted no part of being a business partner in his abbatoir scheme. I foresee it doomed to failure."

"He's putting a lot of money into it, Four Eyes."

"By Jove, he's invested a fortune. But what he's actually attempting to do is circumvent the Chicago packing plants, and no amount of money in the world shall prevail against such powerful people. Why, he has become so carried away with the scheme that he envisions moving on to other areas through the country. Can you imagine places like Omaha or Bismarck as meat-packing centers? That should give you some idea how impractical he is. But I do find a certain pleasure in his company. Such refinement and good taste are so scarce out here, you know."

"Sure. There are times I miss places like Boston and Chicago."

"On the whole, you're pleased with the life, though?"

"I can't complain. In fact, I can't see myself living anywhere else any more. If Charlie and I do go into business together, it'll be right here in the Yellowstone Basin."

The Montana Livestock Association kept an office in the Macqueen House, and Roosevelt stopped there to pick up a copy of the instructions for the roundup. The Maltese Cross was in District 6, and the Elkhorn spread from District 6 up into District 7. Bernard J. "Curly" Schaeffer was named foreman of the District 6 roundup, and there was a list of ranches that were to be represented in the crew of a hundred or so cowboys.

The Rafter B lay in District 4, and this year Charlie Bowen was named foreman. The Maltese Cross was to supply a representative to District 4, and one to District 8. Ben wasn't surprised when Roosevelt announced that he was sending other hands to work with Bowen's crew, since they had spent more years in the country and knew the area better.

Charlie Bowen and Granville Stuart walked through the lobby of the hotel, and hailed them.

"Deelighted to see you!" Roosevelt boomed. "We were just checking the roundup assignments."

"That's why I'm in town today," Charlie said. "You in a hurry, or can you stop by the house and put on the feed bag? Earl's been roasting a hog to try out a new barbeque sauce recipe he got down in New Orleans."

"I've some other matters that need attending to,

but I'm certain Ben would be pleased to accept your gracious invitation."

"If I didn't have to spend so much time with my lawyers," Stuart said with a twinkle in his eye, "I'd go myself. One of these days I'm going to steal that cook from you, Charlie."

"I doubt it. Earl doesn't mind cooking for twenty or thirty, but not the hundred and fifty you keep around the DHS."

"I'll be glad to see how Earl's barbeque compares with the stuff put out by that old Mexican over at Mandan," Ben said.

On their way to the Rafter B, Charlie asked, "Who's Four Eyes going to send to my crew?"

"Danny Langdon."

Charlie nodded. "Good man, Danny. I was hoping maybe he'd send you, but it just might work out better this way. I'm going to send Mike Dwyer and Kenny Reynolds over to Curly's crew. Keep an eye on them, will you?"

"Problems?"

"I don't know," Charlie admitted. "Kenny and Clark Terry hired on about a week after Dwyer, and those two kids kept pretty much to themselves all winter long. They're good workers, but quiet. I don't think either of them has ever taken a drink, and they used to spend most of their spare time sitting around playing checkers or dominoes. Real nice kids. Never give anyone any trouble, except for some of their fool pranks.

"But for the last couple of months, Kenny's been dogging Dwyer's heels day and night. I can't put my finger on it, but I've got a nagging feeling something's wrong. A kid like that normally doesn't turn his back on a buddy his own age and take up with someone like Dwyer."

Ben hadn't liked Mike Dwyer from the first day they'd met, and he knew it was only because of jealousy. That little silver music box Dwyer had given Cindy for Christmas seemed a simple enough thing at the time, but in the months since then it had grown out of all reasonable proportions. Mike Dwyer was no longer just one of the hands at the Rafter B; to Ben he was a threat to Cindy. Like Charlie, he had nothing he could put his finger on, but he couldn't get rid of the suspicions that kept nagging him.

Women on the range were few and far between. Outside of the towns like Miles City, the men outnumbered the women about fifty to one, and nearly all of them were married to ranchers or some of their older help. Ben estimated their average age would be forty, maybe forty-five. Cindy was younger, nineteen, but she was also an exception to what the average ranch woman looked like. Instead of being washed out and tired-looking, she was vibrant, full of life and spirit, and certainly as beautiful a woman as could be found anywhere, despite her disdain for feminine clothes. In a country that was woman-starved, one like Cindy would have an unlimited number of potential suitors lined up waiting for a chance.

Mike Dwyer was older than Ben, but not so much older that it would raise any eyebrows if Cindy ever decided to choose him.

Ben bit his lip, angry with himself. In the first place, Cindy's affairs were her own, not his. In the second place, he'd vowed long ago never to allow anyone or anything to take over his life again. And Cindy was coming dangerously close to it.

"You think Mike and Kenny might be up to something, Charlie?"

"I don't know, Ben. I just have an uneasy feeling about the way those two have been buddying up to each other."

"Be glad to keep my eyes and ears open."

As they descended into the valley that housed the Rafter B spread, they could smell Earl Howard's roast pig a quarter of a mile away. Even before they reached the house, Ben was willing to bet that the Mexican's barbeque was going to have a run for its money. Smoke from the rock-lined pit outside the cook shack where the whole hog was turning on a spit powered by one of the hands lay like a thin fog through the valley.

As they dismounted at the corral, Ben saw Cindy heading for the house from the vegetable garden with a basket under her arm. Mike Dwyer was hoeing a row of cabbages, and she stopped to speak to him.

Ben felt the hair on the back of his neck bristle. It bristled more when he and Charlie went into the house and he was greeted by the tinkly sound of the music box coming from the kitchen.

"Brought some company along for a hunk of Earl's roast pig," Charlie said, tossing his hat at the peg and missing again. Cindy was sitting at the table shelling some early peas. The silver music box was next to the huge wooden bowl.

"Hi, Ben," she said with a bright smile. "I wasn't expecting to see you until after the roundup."

"I wasn't expecting to be here, either, but I was lucky enough to run into your dad in town. That pig sure smells good." He did his best to ignore the sound of the music box sitting on the table.

"We've got something of a tradition here," Charlie said. "Couple of days before we start the roundup, Earl tries out a new recipe on us. It's always something he finds in some exotic place in New Orleans. If we like it, and if he feels like it, we'll have it again later in the year."

Cindy let out a little laugh. "And if we praise him enough for it."

"Earl Howard sounds like he's a bit of a prima donna," Ben said, helping himself to a mug of coffee.

"Why not?" Charlie replied. "He's the best cook in these parts and everybody knows it."

"You should have heard him carry on this morning when he found he didn't have enough peas," Cindy said. "As soon as I get these shelled, he'll pop them in a kettle, then we can eat."

"Don't look at me," Charlie said. "I've got a mountain of paperwork to straighten out before roundup." He took his mug of coffee and headed for his desk.

"Let me give you a hand," Ben offered, and began popping open the fresh-smelling pea pods. "I haven't smelled anything this good in years. Takes me back to the time I was just a kid and helped my mother with it."

Before he'd shelled a dozen pods, the music box ran down, and Cindy paused long enough to wind it up and start it running again.

"You play that thing all the time?"

"Almost. Whenever I'm doing something here in the kitchen, anyway. I like it. It was one of the nicest Christmas presents I ever got. Isn't it pretty?"

Ben felt himself smoldering inside. He'd been hoping that she would consider Dwyer's gift too effeminate, and have it shoved into the back of a dresser drawer.

"Yep, real pretty."

There was very little said until the last of the peas were in the bowl, and Cindy carried it to the cook shack. Ten minutes later Ben heard the wagon tire gong booming its invitation to dinner, and he and Charlie headed for the cook shack.

Earl Howard's mustache bristled with pride as he and three of the hands removed the blackened hog from the spit and carried it to the huge table under the canvas awning stretched between some trees. His bow tie bobbed up and down with his adam's apple as he began disjointing and carving the succulent pork, spearing huge servings onto the plates of the men as they passed by. Before the last of them had been served, the first ones through the line were letting Earl know they approved whole-heartedly of his creation, and he beamed from ear to ear.

"I brought enough of the pepper sauce from New Orleans to last a couple of years," Earl told them. "Cajun recipe. They've a method of fermenting the pepper that gives an unequalled flavor. I'm pleased you enjoy it."

Ben gnawed at a nearly-clean rib bone, and said, "Charlie, if this is the way you eat over here, I just might hire on. Twice can't boil water without burning it."

"Funny, but I don't have any trouble keeping help around here once they taste Earl's food."

"Charlie, if we ever go into the horse breeding business together, that cook's got to be one of the crew."

Charlie let out a guffaw. "No matter what I do, Earl Howard is part of the deal."

Everyone had seconds on the barbequed pork, and some came back for a third helping. They knew it was going to be their last big meal with no pressures for six or eight weeks, and there was no rush to finish. Even the lethargic hound had moved off the porch, and gorged himself on scraps and bones.

As Ben saddled up for the ride home, Mike Dwyer leaned on the corral fence.

"Been seein' a lot of you around here, Foster."

"Maybe it's because I've had a lot of business around here," Ben said.

"Yeah, maybe. And maybe you're finding a lot of business around here because you think you're going to get an inside track with Cindy, huh?"

Ben stopped after pulling the cinch tight.

"How does any of my business here concern you, Dwyer?"

"When it comes to saddlebums trying to make time with her, then it's my business."

"Funny, she didn't tell me that," he replied, trying to ignore the insult.

"Well, I'm tellin' you." He slowly chewed the end off a cigar and lit it. "It doesn't take a genius to see there's been something going on between you two—particularly since you went and got snowbound over there last winter."

Ben tensed, but checked himself.

"Dwyer, I'm a guest here, and I wouldn't consider it right to bust you one on Charlie's place. But don't you ever let me hear you make remarks like that about her again."

"Ooh, touched a raw spot, didn't I? Cheer up, Foster, we'll meet someplace where you won't feel so haired over about offending your host. In the meantime, don't get any designs on that red-headed girl, you understand? I've got my own plans for her."

"I suppose she doesn't have anything to say about it herself? Dwyer, you're looking for trouble."

Dwyer's fist flew forward, and Ben rolled with the punch that glanced off his jaw. He came back with an uppercut that sent Dwyer slamming back into the fence, his cigar smashed against his nose. Ben rushed forward, ready to finish what he'd started, but stopped when he heard Cindy's shout.

"Stop that! What's gotten into you, Ben?"

"Sorry, Cindy, we just didn't see eye to eye over something."

"Well, that doesn't give you any right to act like a bully. If you can't behave any better than this, I'd just as soon you stayed away!"

Ben looked at Dwyer, who was grinning contentedly from where he sat on the ground, then swung aboard his mare.

"Maybe I'll just do that," he said as he rode out of the corral.

26

CURLY Schaeffer talked quietly with Slim Menough, and then put Mike Dwyer and Kenny Reynolds to work on the crew that would be working the land just to the south of the area assigned to Twice's crew.

"Ben, Slim told me that there's some bad blood between you and Mike. I don't know what it's all about, but if you two want to batter each other's skulls around, you'll do it after we finish."

Ben bit his tongue. He couldn't find any reason for wanting to be on the same crew as Dwyer without sounding like a fool, so he let it ride. At least he'd cross trails at the end of every week when they moved to a new part of the district.

Roosevelt had chosen to work with Twice's team, and pitched into the work with his usual boundless energy. He proved adept at rounding up cattle that were in fairly open country, and never knew that Twice made sure he drew the easier sections. Working with Ben and two men from the DHS, Roosevelt spent the first day working cattle out of the hills down toward the central gathering point where the branding crew was waiting.

"You going to keep him gathering, or let him try his hand at cutting?" Ben asked.

"Shit, he ain't good enough in the saddle yet to know how to work a cutting horse. Ain't no sense in makin' 'im look like more of a jackass than he is. Not yet. I'll spell 'im off every two, three days with the irons. Don't wanta tucker 'im out completely."

"Hell, Twice, I don't think anything can wear him down."

Working in the branding circle suited Roosevelt fine, and he marvelled at the skill displayed by the old timers. As a calf was dragged bawling and hollering from the herd, the cutters would announce the brand.

"Maltese Cross."

"Circle U, left hip."

At first, Roosevelt was at a loss to understand how they knew the difference.

"Easy, Four Eyes," said the grizzled keeper of the brand book. "A calf suckin' a Circle U cow gets its momma's brand."

He looked across the open ground to the bewildering mass of cattle and cowboys who all seemed to be moving in different directions at the same time.

"My word! How can anybody tell which calf belongs to which cow if it isn't nursing at the moment?"

"The cow knows. She ain't about to let nothin' happen to her baby if she kin help it." He pointed to the herd. "There, that's what I mean."

Roosevelt watched as one cowboy dragged a calf from the bunch, and two other riders had to move fast to keep the cow from attacking him. She was a rangy old longhorn, and looked as mean as any bull in the bunch.

Clouds of dust began to rise as more cattle were brought into the valley's roundup point. The herding instinct made easy work of it now, for the cattle felt easy in the company of their own kind, and once settled it took few riders to control them. The hot sun beat down mercilessly, and the air was filled with the bawling of the calves, the lowing of the cows, and the angry bellowing of steers and bulls who didn't like the restrictions that were being forced on them.

Once the herd had been assembled at the central point and the cows and calves had a chance to find each other—Roosevelt learned that few calves know their mothers, but a mother can locate its own calf by the sound of its voice—they began to settle down to graze. The herding instinct is so strong that three or four riders can manage a herd of a thousand or more without much difficulty.

They paid little attention to anything but unbranded cattle and calves. Riders moved in to cut cows and calves from the herd, move them to a smaller gathering point at the branding corral, then the calves were removed and branded. Mavericks of all ages and sexes were branded with the Association brand, and to Roosevelt's surprise these were few in number. The occasional cattle that bore brands from outside the Montana Association were cut out and "thrown over" if they weren't too far from home. If they had strayed far, they were simply tallied, and allowed to remain with the herd.

At the beginning of each day's branding, the herding instinct worked in favor of the cowboys again. They sized up the animals, then cut out a couple of tractable old cows who were content to stand quietly apart from the others. Once these "decoys" had been separated, it was easier work to get a cow and calf from the herd.

When he saw how the cowboys worked at cutting,

Roosevelt admitted he couldn't begin to handle it. "My word! That fellow simply drove into a milling sea of horns and hooves. Simply marvelous!"

"Yep," the tally man said laconically. "Simply marveelious, ain't it?"

As the work progressed, the air was filled with the acrid stench of burning hair and flesh, and the pile of testes grew larger next to the men who were castrating bull calves and cutting ear notches.

"Lazy JN Connected," called a rider as he dragged a calf by the heels to the fire.

Roosevelt grabbed it by the hind legs, Twice twisted the ears, and they threw it to the ground while Ben pulled the proper iron from the fire. Roosevelt sat on the ground with his legs wrapped around the calf's, while Twice sat on its head, to hold it still as Ben pressed the hot iron onto the calf's shoulder.

"Lazy JN Connected, heifer," repeated the tally man, and he licked the end of his short, stubby pencil, then marked the book. Before the calf was released bawling and shrieking, he slipped the leather-bound tally book under his arm and sharpened the inch-and-a-half pencil with a huge bowie knife honed to a razor sharpness.

Once the calf was released, it joined its mother, and stood with sprawled legs, sick and dizzy, while the mother licked its wound and murmured her protests at what the men had done to her baby.

On several occasions, the rider dragging a calf to the fire had misread the brand on the cow, and when the mistake was learned later, the tally man simply squared it up by having the next calf from a corresponding cow misbranded. Roosevelt wondered if that wouldn't cause confusion, to see a Maltese Cross calf sucking a Rafter B cow.

"Yep, reckon it might, Four Eyes. But that ain't no worse'n a Rafter B calf suckin' a Maltese cow. Any-

ways, we got it all writ down, an' by the time they's
weaned and growed up, they'll both be worth about
the same."

The herd gradually diminished in size, and the men
looked like they were wearing suits of gray dust.
Roosevelt had given up trying to keep the dust off
his glasses, and it was a wonder he could see his hand
in front of his face. When the last of the calves had
been branded, the men rode over to the creek, washed
most of the dust off their hands and faces, then made
their way across the valley where supper was waiting.

As soon as they had their saddles off the horses,
the men were finished with their work for the day,
and their only thoughts were to fill themselves with
food and see if they could get enough sleep before
morning.

"Well, that's the first week of it, Teddy," Ben said
as they sat down on the ground to a pound or so of
beefsteak and some tinned vegetables. "Still think
you're cut out to be a rancher?"

"By Jove, it's an invigorating life!"

Ben finished a quart of rich Arbuckle's coffee and
a basket of biscuits, then stretched out under his
blankets with his saddle for a pillow. Roosevelt was
sitting by the campfire reading a book of Byron's
poetry.

The next morning started the same as the first one
had a week earlier. The cook was walking through the
sleeping figures banging on a kettle, hollering, "Roll
out, durn yer miserable hides, roll out! Rise an' shine
like the morning star! Roll out afore I burn yer miserable backsides in the trench!"

Blankets were kicked aside, boots pulled on, faces
washed hastily at the stream, and then the campsite
became a scene of organized confusion as the men
ate a hasty breakfast, packed their gear and tossed it
onto the wagon. While they were eating, washing,

packing and cursing, they heard the sound of hooves
as the night wrangler moved the string of horses into
the rope corral. Men began roping their mounts and
saddling up. From the time they were called out until
the time the caravan of riders moved out to the next
gathering area, forty-three minutes had elapsed. The
cooks stayed behind to break camp, stow their gear
into wagons and head out for the next campsite some
twenty miles away.

When the crew moved into the area for the day's
work, they had just gotten started when Twice
Thompson fell off a peaceful horse for the first time
in his life. They were starting into a box canyon when
a rangy old longhorn steer rushed past them, heading
for the safety of some timber.

In his high, squeaky voice, Four Eyes shouted to
Ben, "Hasten forward swiftly there!"

Everyone around him laughed so hard their sides
hurt, and Twice slipped to the ground as he pounded
his legs and roared with laughter.

The longhorn made a clean escape.

27

THE Little Missouri River flowed sluggishly. It had been two weeks since a decent rain, and the winter snows had long since melted and made their rushing run down the river. The two riders moved a bunch of about two hundred cattle down from the foothills, then pushed them hard. They jammed up at the edge of the water, but the pressure of the shoving animals behind finally forced the leaders to enter the water. Most of the distance to the far shore was fordable, and there was only about twenty yards where they were forced to swim. When they reached the eastern banks, they'd lost only one old cow and three calves to the swirling water.

Three riders came down from the hills to the north, and there was a brief exchange of words, then the first two men returned to the west side of the river.

As they climbed back into the foothills, they turned to check the progress of the cattle behind them. The bunch was being pushed hard through a gap in the hills, and would be out of sight in a few more minutes.

"Well, that wasn't so hard, now was it?"

Kenny Reynolds shook his head. "Somehow, it still don't seem right, Mike. You sure they're coming back?"

"You heard what Jack Sully said, didn't you? They're just bein' sleepered."

"Yeah, but the calves . . ."

Mike Dwyer removed his cigar and spat. "Shit, kid, you got any idea how many calves die every year from the cold, and from wolves? They'll never know the difference. Now let's get going and scrape up another bunch before they wonder what's keepin' us."

"And that's all there is to it?"

"That's all, kid. When we meet Jack after the roundup, you're gonna have some big money coming."

Kenny grinned sheepishly. "Maybe I'll get myself some fancy boots. I always kinda wanted boots like yours, Mike."

28

AFTER working the roundup for six weeks, the cowboys flocked into Miles City to cut the dust from their throats. The bars were lined four and five deep, and the crowds around the roulette wheels and faro layouts were impatiently pushing their way up to the tables to make a fortune, or to lose what little they had in their pockets. The girls had to push their way through the packed rooms to deliver drinks to the carefree cowboys at the back tables.

"Get your hand off my ass, Sam, unless you want to pay for the privilege!"

"Your butt's worth it, Ginger." He dropped a silver dollar down the front of her dress, and she smiled with pleasure.

"You want to fish it out, it'll cost you two more."

He gave her a playful slap on the backside, and she moved to the next table.

"Hi, Mike. What'll it be?"

"Whiskey, Ginger. Some good stuff, not the red-eye Dick keeps behind the bar."

"Gotcha. How about you, kid?" She leaned forward, her face close to his, giving him a good look down her low-cut dress.

Kenny gulped. "Beer, please."

"Sure. Where'd you get such a cute little sidekick, Mike?"

"Nice lookin' boy, ain't he? But don't kid yourself, Ginger; this guy's short, but all man."

Kenny blushed as Ginger gave him a quick hug. "Could be we'll just find out about that, huh? Be right back with your drinks."

She pushed her way to the bar, and Kenny said, "She sure is pretty."

"Not bad for a box rustler, Kenny. Tell me, you ever drink beer before?"

"Sure," he lied. "Lots of times. Well, a couple of times."

"Work it slow and easy until after we've finished our business."

"They're going to meet us here? You sure?"

"I'm sure. Just let me do the talking and you listen."

Ginger pushed her way back with the bottle of whiskey and a mug of beer. She put the tray down on the table and picked up the two silver dollars Mike tossed down, then sidled close to Kenny, putting her arm around his shoulder. She pulled his head close, rubbing his cheek against her ample breast.

"Damned if he ain't an innocent one," she said admiringly. "Lookit him blush!"

"Well, gosh, I . . ."

"Well gosh nothin', kid. We'll get you over that real easy. You got a name?"

"Yeah," he said, trying to remove his cheek from her warm breast. "Kenny Reynolds."

"And a real good cowboy, from what I see."

"Yep," he said, his eyes darting around to see if anyone was paying any attention to him squeezed tightly between her breasts.

"Well, Kenny, I just happen to like cowboys, and I used to be a schoolteacher."

"Honest?"

"Honest Injun. When you finish that beer, I'll take you back to my classroom and give you a real lesson. One five dollar lesson is all it'll take to change you from a cowboy to a cowman."

She gave him another tight squeeze, then moved off.

Mike grinned as he relit his cigar. "All kinds of things happening for the first time, eh?"

"Uh huh." Kenny picked up his mug of beer and took a deep swallow. "That tastes good."

"Slow and easy."

"Yeah." He took another mouthful, then said, "I don't want Ginger to think I've forgotten about her, though."

"Take it slow and easy there, too. She's pretty good. She'll teach you how to keep from shooting your wad before you get your britches down. But tell her three bucks is all you've got."

"Oh, I've got more'n that, Mike."

"Why spend any more than you have to? Three bucks is her normal price."

Kenny's face was beginning to lose its beet-red color. "Five still doesn't seem to be a whole lot."

Mike laughed. "Go over to the coon town cribs after dark. Five bucks will buy you two at a time. Hot stuff, too. Hey," he said, looking up. "They're here." He stood and waved.

Miguel Sanchez saw him, and waved back, and he and Jack Sully pushed through to their table. They made a strange pair, with Sully standing almost a foot taller than the little Mexican.

"Howdy, Mike."

"Hi, Jack. *Buenos diaz*, you old robber."

Miguel bowed, his gold teeth flashing. "So long we have not seen each other, Mike. This is your new partner?"

He introduced Kenny, and then caught Ginger's eye. She knew what Sully and Sanchez drank, and was soon at the table with a bottle of tequila, a bottle of Tres Cepas brandy and two glasses. She looked disdainfully at Kenny's mug, still half full, and said, "You're slow, Kenny. But take your time; I'll be around for a while."

Kenny blushed again, and Miguel laughed.

"Aha, so you've designs on the wench, have you?"

"Well, we . . ."

"We've got a little business to take care of first, Ginger," Mike said. "Then you can take him to school."

She nodded, gave Kenny another hug and disappeared.

"Kenny's doing real well, guys. He's learning the sleeper business just fine."

"*Maravilloso!*" Miguel said. "It shows. That was an excellent bunch you sent."

"You're takin' good care of them, aren't you?" Kenny asked, a frown on his face.

"The best," Sully said gravely. "They're in a good pasture over to Dakota. Kenny, you've earned this."

He placed a stack of eight gold coins on the table in front of Kenny, who stared open-mouthed at them.

"A hundred and sixty dollars?"

"Yep," Sully said. "And here's yours, Mike." He counted out a similar stack.

Mike put the money in his pocket, and Kenny followed suit. "That's just the beginning, Kenny. You think you can take care of any more, Jack?"

"Well," Sully said, his square jaw jutting forward,

"maybe another thousand. Don't want to overgraze the range down there."

"When are you going to bring them back?" Kenny asked.

"Just as soon as the calves are weaned. They'll be back in Montana before the snow flies."

"That's good. I sure wouldn't want to be responsible for anything happening to them."

"Tell you what, kid," Mike said. "Finish your beer and go find Ginger. We've got some old times to talk about."

Kenny obediently drained the mug, and started to rise, Mike laid a hand on his arm.

"Want a word of advice?"

"Sure, Mike."

"Let me hold onto that money until you get back. If Ginger finds out how much you've got, her tuition rates might go sky high."

Kenny considered it for a moment, then dutifully handed over the stack of double eagles. "Sure is nice to know I've got you takin' care of me, Mike. I never would have thought about that."

"Oh, Mike is maybe the best friend you have in the world," Miguel said gravely. "He is an honest man who takes care of his friends."

"Yeah," Kenny said, then belched. "Be back after a while." He moved off in search of what he thought was the most beautiful woman in Miles City.

"Real dumb kid, Mike," Sully said with a grin.

"That's the best kind to have. I've got him convinced you're sleeperin' the bunch."

"Oh, we are, we are indeed," Miguel said. "Most of those beefs are sleeping very peacefully. Very peacefully."

"We sold about half of them at the mines," Sully said.

"Herman Hoffman?"

"The veriest," Miguel said with a nod. "The best German butcher in the country who can transform beef into slow elk through the magic of butchering," He produced a leather pouch and handed it to Dwyer. "The rest of the twelve hundred dollars. You might consider giving the boy a bonus."

"Why? He's happy with his hundred and sixty. And if he has too much money in his pocket, he's going to raise some eyebrows. Let me handle him my way."

Twenty minutes later Kenny swaggered back to the table, his face beet red. Ginger followed with another mug of beer.

"Lord amighty, Mike, you didn't tell me he's like a longhorn bull in the springtime! Wheeoo! You just come see your Auntie Ginger anytime, Kenny, anytime." She gave him a kiss on the cheek, and he turned a deeper shade of red while the three men laughed.

"Pretty good boy, eh?" Mike said.

"This ain't a boy, Mike. This here's a man." She held up both hands, indicating the size of Kenny's male equipment. "A real man!"

Miguel beamed. "In my country we celebrate such a momentous occasion with the very best brandy. Kenny, here's to your becoming a man, and such a man as to bring smiles of happiness to a splendid woman like this."

"Gosh, I . . ."

"Drink, amigo! You will never again experience such a day."

Kenny took the glass of Spanish brandy and downed half of it in one gulp, then wheezed and coughed. "Wow, that's good!"

An hour later, they walked out onto the sidewalk, unaware that Ben Foster had been watching them from the end of the bar.

29

CHARLIE Bowen led Gus Adams into the private dining room at the Macqueen House. Ben Foster, Slim Menough and Granville Stuart sat at the table with coffee, and waited until Charlie closed the door.

"Okay, Ben, tell them."

"Well, Charlie asked me to keep an eye on Mike Dwyer during the roundup, but Curly Schaeffer wouldn't let me work on the same crew with him. Three Finger Bill Smith was foreman of that crew, and told me that three times Dwyer and Kenny Reynolds seemed to be gone for longer than normal, and when they came in to the gather, they didn't have all that many cattle. About as many as you'd expect two men to find in the first hour, maybe two hours. But they were gone most of the day. Bill told me he'd seen them with a bunch of maybe eighty or ninety one morning as he moved off into the hills on the other side of the valley. He swears they had that many by nine, but when they came in around noon, they still only had about a hundred."

"Maybe that's all they found," Slim said.

"Maybe. But they're the only two who could bring in three, four hundred a day regular when they worked with anyone else, and only a hundred or so when they rode together. And all of those days they were working along the river. That's when he decided to split them up."

"So you still don't have anything but some funny feelings about them?" Adams asked.

"You tell me," Charlie said, "how come it was only when they worked together they came in empty-handed? Kenny's a good worker, and so is Mike. And why would a kid like that leave his buddy and take up with someone so much older?"

"You never heard of hero worship?" Stuart said dryly.

"Now, what did you see here yesterday afternoon, Ben?"

"Well, I didn't have any ideas about snooping on Dwyer, but I spotted him taking Kenny into a saloon, and just decided to wet my neck there. I couldn't hear anything that was said, since the place was so noisy, but what I saw still makes me think they've been up to no good. They'd only been there about fifteen or twenty minutes when Jack Sully came in with a little Mexican. I never laid eyes on the Mexican before, but I'd seen Sully. Didn't know his handle, but one of the girls told me who he was. Jack Sully. The Mexican's name was Miguel, that's all she knew."

"Short little bastard with a round face?" Adams asked, his eyes narrowing. "Mouth of gold teeth?"

"Yep, that's the one."

"Miguel Sanchez," Stuart said. "I'd like to get my hands on his dirty neck some day."

"Same with Sully," Adams said. "The only thing is we've never caught Sully with anything that didn't belong to him or the tribe. I've heard all kinds of rumors about him, though. Sanchez? Nobody knows anything about him. He drifts in and out of this country like a cloud. He'll be here today, and in Mexico tomorrow."

"What's his business?" Charlie asked.

"Who knows? Sometimes he claims to be a gambler, and he's even been known to buy and sell timber. First time I ever ran into him, he'd bought two boatloads of fish up the Yellowstone and brought them into town to sell at twenty-five cents a pound. Later he was buying wagons of vegetables from the Indians over in the Gallatin Valley, and selling them at every Cavalry post in the Territory. I know for a fact that the only time I saw him with any cattle was last year, and he had a perfectly good bill of sale from Poke Peterson. I held onto Sanchez until I could check it out with Poke."

Stuart nodded. "I sold him two hundred head last year, and we vented the brand before he moved them out. But there was something about him I didn't like, and later I learned he'd sold three hundred ten of them down in Sheridan. I thought it was amazing how they could be sanctified and multiplied between here and Wyoming."

"What about the money, Ben?"

Ben described the transfer of gold coins. "I can't say the leather bag had any money in it. Could have been coyote's eyeballs or rattlesnake horns for all I saw. But Dwyer hefted it like it was gold, and it was pretty heavy."

"Sanchez didn't give the boy more?"

Ben shook his head. "They sent him off with a floozy, then Sanchez gave Dwyer the bag. When

Kenny got back, they proceeded to get him pretty well liquored up."

Charlie grunted. "I thought the kid had his head caught in the buzz saw the next morning the way he was moaning and carrying on. Nothing more serious than crickets chirping. Gawd, what a hangover!"

Stuart shook his head sadly. "It's terrible what some of these men will do to innocent boys. That's why I don't permit any drinking on my outfit."

Nobody commented on that remark. Granville Stuart was known to operate a strict teetotalling ranch, and would fire on the spot any cowboy who brought alcohol, cards, dice, knives, brass knuckles or any other weapons onto the ranch. He permitted one six-shooter and one rifle per man, and had strict rules on when they could be carried. He was equally adamant about cursing, and any hand who swore where he could be heard by Stuart or one of his foremen found himself collecting his pay before the end of the day.

"Why don't we just fire him, Charlie?" Slim asked.

"We'll blackball him, and he won't find a job anywhere around these parts," Stuart said.

Charlie's forehead wrinkled into deep furrows. "Maybe I'm not really sure about him, but I'd hate to run him off without damned good reason. He can put in as good a day's work as anyone I've ever had on my place. No, I'll wait until I've got something other than a gut feeling that he's up to no good."

They all agreed that they'd let Charlie handle it his own way, and that they'd have a little talk with Sheriff Tom Ervine about Sanchez and Sully.

After leaving Ervine's office, Charlie asked Ben, "You hear what I bought?"

"What?"

"John Clay told me about an Englishman who had

some fine Arabian stallions he'd be willing to sell. He was staying in Bismarck with them, so I took the train over as soon as we finished the roundup."

"They're good?"

"Come on down and have a look for yourself."

The two stallions were the finest Ben had seen anywhere. "Damned if they aren't going to improve your herd, Charlie."

"Now if we could find us a few Arabian mares, we might be able to breed some top-notch race horses."

"Well, maybe. I think you'd be better off just building up your line with these. Race horses are something else again."

"I'd still like to go into business with you, Ben. My offer holds. Fifty-fifty. And if you don't have the cash, we'll work out something else."

Ben thought of the Boston and Chicago bank accounts that were drawing five and six percent interest. He hadn't drawn out a penny since leaving Mandan and the hide business.

"It isn't the cash, Charlie. But when I do, it's got to be without cattle. Cattle can bring in some quick cash if you've got a good season, but horses are going to make you more money in the long run. You're not going to lose so many of them in a really rough winter. How'd you make out in the winter of '80?"

Charlie grimaced. "Thought I'd lose my shirt."

"Most of your horses made it through, didn't they?"

"By golly, Ben, I never really thought about that. Sure, you're right."

They sat on the corral pole watching the two stallions trot, and at length Charlie said, "My offer of a job is still open, too. Just say the word."

Ben thought about the difficulty he'd have working with Mike Dwyer and staying out of Cindy's hair, and shook his head.

"Not right now, Charlie, thanks."

"Dwyer bother you all that much?"

"Not really."

"Well, if you think he's getting anywhere with Cindy, you're wrong. She's been wondering if you were ever going to come back here after she gave you the bum's rush when you and Dwyer started polishing knuckles. Just in case you don't know it, she was just as angry at him."

Ben felt a wave of relief surge through him. "I appreciate your telling me, Charlie, but I got the feeling she was getting a bit soft on him."

"Hah! I'll never know what he said to her after you left, but she didn't like it. Busted that goddam music box and threw it at him. Told him to shove it . . ."

"Cindy said that?"

"Hell, don't be surprised. She's learned her best mad cussin' from me. And when she really gets mad, I think she can outdo me any day of the week."

"She's cute when she gets riled up."

Charlie Bowen knew when to plant a seed, and when to give it time to grow. Having planted that seed in Ben's mind, he changed the subject.

"Four Eyes doing all right?"

"Yep. He's something of a celebrity now."

"Yeah. I stopped in one of the bars over at Medora, and old Wooly Jack Jackson was hollering at the barkeep, 'Hasten forward swiftly, my good man.' Hell, Four Eyes'll never live that one down."

"You know he's back into politics, don't you?"

"I figured it would happen. Do you think he'll run for mayor of Medora?"

"Who knows? But he's taken an appointment as deputy sheriff over there."

"A lawman who can't tell the difference between a buffalo and a rock? Hell, that ought to be something."

"He's talked to you about running for the Territorial Legislature, hasn't he?"

"Hell, Ben, he's got the fantastic idea that I could be elected to the United States Senate if I waved my hand at enough people."

Ben looked him straight in the eye. "Why not?"

Charlie frowned. "Ben, I think you're serious."

"I am. You've got a cool head on your shoulders. When we were sitting in the Macqueen earlier today, I would have bet my last pair of socks we would have come out of there agreeing to throw a necktie party for Dwyer, even if we didn't have any solid evidence against him. But you kept calm enough to make sure we didn't rush off like a bunch of wild Sioux. Once on this range is enough."

"I just want to make sure, Ben."

"And you know as much about the laws of the Territory as any lawyer, and you've worked in government jobs since you left the Army."

"Aw, for cryin' out loud, Ben, you make me sound like the answer to everyone's prayers."

"Maybe you are. Just think about it, Charlie."

"Okay, I'll think about it. But while I'm thinking about that, why don't you think about coming to work for me?"

"I have. If Four Eyes decides to spend the winter back East again, I'll stay until spring roundup to watch the place over the winter. I kind of like having the boss around to freeze his socks while I freeze mine."

Charlie fished in his pocket. "You got a dollar?"

"Yeah, why?"

"I'll bet you this to your dollar you'll be working here next year." He flipped a twenty dollar gold piece in the air.

Three months later, Ben was just as sure Charlie would lose the bet. The Elkhorn Ranch owned a boat they used as a ferry across the Little Missouri when it was high. Most of their horses were pastured on the west side of the river where there was good grazing land that hadn't been overrun by cattle or sheep. Ben found it especially welcome when the river was beginning to crust over with ice, and it was necessary to tend to the horses on the far side.

Roosevelt took Ben hunting on the west bank after the fall shovedown, and one morning they returned to find the boat missing.

"Cut loose," Ben said, holding up the end of the rope which had evidently been cut with a sharp knife.

"Drat!" Roosevelt whipped the end of the rope against his thigh. "As ruthless as this Spring's action may have been, I knew they should have included those three scoundrels who've been loitering in Medora. That man named Finnigan, the one with the long red hair."

"You mean the one with the buckskin shirt?"

"Yes, and his two companions, a German fellow and a stout half-breed. I heard in town three days ago that they were ready to leave. By Jove, I simply know it's they who took the boat."

"Well, do you want to swim after them?" Ben indicated the piles of ice jams in the backwaters.

"By Godfrey, we'll build another boat and go after them."

A chilling dash across a waist-deep ford took them back to the Elkhorn, and Curly and Twice were pressed into work to help build another boat. When it was all done, Roosevelt took Twice and Ben with him, and they loaded the boat with provisions to last them a week.

Working their way downstream, they came across signs where the robbers had camped two or three days before, and on the third day they found the Elkhorn boat pulled up on the bank. It was filled with saddles that had been stolen from various ranches in the area.

They moved quietly toward the camp back against a high embankment. The German was the only one there, and Roosevelt crept up on him. He saw that the man's weapons were on the ground, and seemed disappointed that he made the arrest without any more excitement than having the German put his hands high over his head when he saw Roosevelt emerge from behind a rock with his rifle ready. Twice was delegated to guard the prisoner, and Roosevelt and Ben worked up the trail about sixty yards from the campsite, where they took cover under an over-hanging bank.

About an hour later, they saw Finnigan and the half-breed walking down the trail, their rifles slung over their shoulders with the sunlight glancing off them. They waited until their quarry were about twenty yards off.

"Hands in the air!" Roosevelt shouted in his squeaky voice as he stood up, his rifle cocked and ready, as was Ben's.

The half-breed dropped his rifle, and stood with his knees shaking. Finnigan hesitated only a moment. Roosevelt walked up to him calmly, his rifle pointed at Finnigan's chest, and repeated his command. The rawboned Irishman dropped his rifle, and held his hands beside his head.

Taking the prisoners back upstream was out of the question, for the water and ice were becoming impassable. The three men made no attempt at escape, but calmly followed orders as Roosevelt guided the party further down the river, and then moved ashore on the land belonging to the C Diamond Ranch.

There was only one cowpoke holding down the outlying cow camp, and he offered a horse so Roosevelt could get a wagon at a neighboring spread and take his prisoners to Dickinson. Roosevelt nodded his thanks grimly, for the ponies in the corral were all wild-looking. As he fought to mount the wiry bronc, he heard Twice tell the cowpoke. "The boss ain't no bronco-buster."

Before depositing his prisoners in the jail at Dickinson, Roosevelt had several arguments with ranchers in the area. "Dunno what the hell yuh wanta go to all that trouble fer, Four Eyes. Shit, we kin string 'em up fer yuh right here."

As they rode south from Dickinson, Roosevelt said, "By Jove, this is certainly an exciting life, isn't it? I shall enjoy spending the rest of my days here in the West."

30

WHEN Roosevelt returned to the Elkhorn in early March, Ben packed his gear, and was surprised when Roosevelt offered to help him drive the mares to the Rafter B.

"Of course I have no ill feelings, Dan. I'm grateful you stayed the winter. If you should decide against going into business with him, I would be honored, if you were to come back."

"Thanks, Teddy. I appreciate everything you've done for me."

"Oh, bother! Could I do anything less?"

Ben grinned and rubbed his nose. "You could probably do a heck of a lot more, if you put your mind to it."

During the three-hour ride, Roosevelt filled Ben with all the news he'd been able to pick up in New York and Washington on the progress being made in getting the Western Territories admitted to statehood.

"Montana Territory was separated from Dakota only two years ago, when I first came out here. Within two or three years, it'll be a state, and Dakota is to be split into two states. Idaho and Wyoming won't be far behind. With statehood, there will be a burgeoning growth."

"We've had that already," Ben said bitterly, "and it's bringing its own problems with it. The nesters have been moving in to claim their quarter section of land, and they've been bringing barbed wire with them. Before things settle down, you're going to see range wars over that damned wire. I've heard there have been teams of men sent out to cut wire wherever they find it."

"Really? But it's a boon to the farmer, Ben."

"Yeah, but not to the cattlemen, and not to the sheepmen. The more wire gets strung out across the open range, the more cows and sheep get hung up and freeze to death in a blizzard. Nobody likes barbed wire except the nesters."

He let out a sigh and said, "Teddy, there were wars with the Indians, then wars with the rustlers. Right now the biggest war is the cattlemen against the sheepmen, and next . . ."

"The sheepmen? Oh, they have their differences, but certainly it isn't of major proportions."

"It's major when bands of cattlemen ride onto a sheep herder's spread and burn his wagons, beat him to death and club and shoot a few thousand sheep. All because they want the grass for cows, and they've got the crazy damned notion that sheep excrete an oil from a gland between their hooves that kills the grass."

"Balderdash! That old wives' tale was dispelled and proven unfounded long ago."

"Tell that to someone like Granville Stuart, who

wants to keep the range open, and wants it for beef, not wool."

"Do you think Stuart is behind it?"

"Hell, Teddy, half the cattle ranchers in the basin are against allowing sheep through here. And when they get done with the sheepmen, they'll go after the nesters and their wire, and drive them out by the same tactics."

"Where does Charles Bowen stand in this matter?"

"This is one time he doesn't want any part of the shenanigans of the cattle barons. I think this is going to convince him to switch over to the horse business once and for all."

"Bully! And with such an attitude, he'll have a great deal of support, should he decide to enter public life."

Ben snorted derisively. "Sure, he'll have all kinds of support, but not from the cattlemen who control the Territory. How much support do you think anybody'll have who tries to cross them? About as much support as those sixty-three rustlers had. Maybe even the same kind of support: a stout rope and a tree limb!"

Cindy and Charlie greeted them warmly, and Ben thought he'd never seen Cindy look so pretty. Once the horses were in the corral, they started for the house, but stopped when they heard a shout and pounding hooves coming from the valley up the river.

It was Cal Bradley, riding hard on a winded, lathered horse.

"Boss, get up to the south pass, quick!"

"What happened, Cal?"

"It's Slim! He's been shot. Bad. He's dead."

31

Slim Menough had been shot once, the bullet hitting him in the center of the chest. He lay on muddy ground that was chewed up by tracks of cattle and horses near the southern limits of the Rafter B.

"How'd you happen to find him, Cal?"

"He had us scourin' these hills to see if that Aberdeen bull mighta come home. You know how that bull kinda considered this place as his private playground. Me and Willie took the ridge from the line shack up, and Slim said he'd found tracks of a fair-sized bunch what'd come through in the last day or so. He followed them south while me and Willie worked north. We didn't see him again, and when it come time to put on the feed bag, I left Willie readin' his Bible while I set out to look for Slim. This is where I found him."

"Where's Willie?"

"Corinthians, Galatians, I reckon. Oh . . . still readin' up at Twin Tables Butte, I guess. When I found Slim, I reckoned I'd best get back to tell you. I didn't carry him with me on accounta I thought maybe it'd be best to have a good look for sign."

There were more tracks than they could begin to piece together. The muddy ground had been chewed up by hooves, and once they moved away from the immediate area where their horses had been milling around Cal's body, it took no trouble to see that the cattle had been moving south, heading for the pass.

"Looks like two riders," Charlie said, pointing to tracks on the flanks of the cattle tracks.

"Cal, take Slim back to the ranch. We'll see if we can pick up anything on the other side of the pass. Sorry to get you into something like this, Four Eyes."

"Quite understandable. I shall be pleased to render any assistance possible."

"Tell you what you could do," Charlie said. "How about you going into town and getting Tom Ervine out here. Stop off at Dave Mulholland's on the way and tell him what happened. I've got a feeling some rustlers slipped through the net. Dave ought to be the first to know what's going on."

From the pass through the ridge, they saw a herd of about 80 head grazing in the grass on the rolling prairie about three miles south of the ranch, and most of them were Rafter B stock. They could find no signs of riders anywhere. Charlie, Cindy and Ben had no trouble moving them back home. As the last of them were going through the pass, Ben said, "Over here. Look."

Off to the side of the trail beaten through the pass were tracks where two horses had milled about, then moved west.

"Almost looks like they brought our beefs through here, then left them."

"But why, Dad? If rustlers are going to get them

off our range, why just leave them here? It doesn't make any sense. They've had enough time they could have been well on their way to Wyoming by now."

"Maybe Cal changed their minds when he came looking for Slim, gal."

"From the looks of it," Ben said, studying the tracks, "Slim probably came up on them, got himself killed, and then they moved the herd over here, intending to push them farther south." He turned and looked back to the north. "You can see a long way from here, miles down the valley."

"Anyone up here could have seen Cal coming, and had plenty of time to make himself scarce," Charlie admitted.

"Let's follow these tracks," Ben said.

"Dad, you push the bunch up home. I'll go with Ben."

"You head for home. I'll go with Ben. I don't want you to run into anything you can't handle."

Cindy started to say something, then bit her lip, and rode down the north slope without saying a word. Ben and Charlie started west along the rocky hillside, following a trail that became fainter as the ground changed from lush grass to thin, rocky soil on the slope.

"If they keep going this way, we're going to have a hard time following them across that pan."

He pointed ahead, and Ben saw the outcropping of shelf rock. It sloped downwards at an easy angle, and was three hundred yards across, and about a hundred yards wide at its widest point. Charlie had been right. Once the tracks moved onto the smooth rock, they vanished almost as though the riders had taken wings into the air.

They spent two hours skirting the edge of the pan, but were unable to pick up any tracks.

"Damnedest thing I've ever seen," Charlie said. "Not even a scuff mark from a hoof on this rock."

One more circuit around the outcropping, and they were forced to give up and return to the ranch. They were half way back, when Ben suddenly reined up.

"Now I know what it is that's been nagging at me. Something didn't look right, but I couldn't think what. Now I know."

"What is it?"

"Charlie, just put yourself in Slim's position. If you'd been following those tracks, what would you have done? We'll never know if Slim caught up with them before the cows were pushed through the pass or not, but it's certain he had a little chat with whoever it was that was moving them. He wasn't bushwhacked; there's no place for anyone to hide where he was gunned down. And he was shot from close range."

"Yeah, it was a six-shooter, not a rifle. And it was placed just right."

"Okay, tell me what you would do if you were sitting there talking to someone who's making off with a herd of your cows."

"In the first place, I wouldn't be sitting there talking, damn it. I would have shot the shit out of them!"

"Sure, so would anybody. But if it was somebody you knew, somebody who worked for you, would you shoot first, or talk?"

"What are you driving at, Ben?"

"Slim never drew his gun. That means he was shot down by someone he knew."

32

On a knoll under the cottonwoods overlooking the Mizpah, the small assembly stood silently, their hats in their hands. "Now is Christ risen from the dead," Willie Wooten read from the letter to the Corinthians, "and become the first fruits of them that slept. For since by man came death, by man also the resurrection of the dead."

Willie's deep voice droned on, and Ben's eyes searched the faces of those standing around the open grave.

Cindy's cheek was stained with a tear, and she had the same resigned look her father had.

Fred McCoy, the old Cherokee blacksmith, stood with his shoulders hunched, and unlike any Indian Dan ever heard of, had tears running unabashedly down his face.

Kenny Reynolds and Clark Terry stood back a bit from the others, their faces white and grave. Ben thought it was probably the first time since they'd

come out West to try the cowboy life that they'd run
into any violence, and the looks on their faces showed
plainly they didn't like the prospect of dying as Slim
had.

Cal Bradley and Jim Cooper stood close behind
Cindy and Charlie. Neither of them was a stranger
to sudden death, and both had buried many of their
friends before. Their faces were blank, although Cal's
carried a trace of impatience, as though wishing Willie would get it over with.

Dave Mulholland and Teddy Roosevelt stood on
the other side of the grave with Tom Ervine and
Earl Howard. It was the first time Ben had seen Earl
without a white apron, and he was an imposing figure
in his stark black, English-style suit, his impeccable
derby held in his hands.

Ben studied Mike Dwyer's face, but couldn't read
anything that wasn't on everyone else's. He'd hoped
he would be able to detect just a trace of a smile,
a smirk, anything that would bolster his suspicion,
but saw nothing.

Willie paused, bent over to pick up a handful of
dirt from the pile alongside the grave, and Charley
and Cindy followed his lead.

"Forasmuch as it hath pleased Almighty God in his
wise providence, to take out of this world the soul
of our deceased brother, we therefore commit his
body to the ground," he read, tossing the dirt onto
the coffin. "Earth to earth, ashes to ashes . . ." Cindy
and Charlie dropped their dust into the grave.

Willie concluded with, "From henceforth blessed
are the dead who die in the Lord: even so saith the
Spirit; for they rest from their labours."

"Amen," intoned the gathering.

Willie closed the book, put his hat on, and the
assembly began to walk back to the house, leaving
Fred McCoy and Jim Cooper to shovel in the grave.

Cindy looked up at Ben. "Let's take a little ride. I need some air."

She saddled Bluebelle, and Ben took his favorite mare. They rode at an easy pace for fifteen minutes without saying a word, and Cindy led the way up the river to a grove of cottonwoods. They dismounted, hobbled the horses to let them graze, and Cindy climbed onto a rock to sit and stare into the water.

"Slim's been with us ever since Dad came into this country. I was just a little girl when I came out from Philadelphia, and Slim was working for Dad then. It's hard to think what it's going to be like without him around any more."

She pulled her knees up and cradled her chin in her folded arms. I guess maybe I can understand now what you were talking about when you told me about not wanting to get attached to people."

"Slim was a fine man," Ben said lamely. "He meant a lot to you, didn't he?"

"Ben, he was more of a father to me for a long time than Dad was. I came out here scared and lonesome, and Dad was always too busy to pay much attention to me. He never really understood me, and I guess he still doesn't. But Slim did. Slim always had the time to answer the silly questions I'd ask, and I guess I pestered the daylights out of him for years. It was Slim who taught me to ride. I don't know how many hours or days he'd spend with me teaching me how to rope a calf, or break a wild pony. He never lost his patience with me, and he never laughed at me when I did something really stupid.

"Like the time I was driving the chuck wagon on a roundup. Slim had taught me to drive the wagon into the stream every day to soak the fellys and spokes to keep them tight. Oh, I knew that, all right, but he didn't even bawl me out when I backed it into the creek one day and loosened all the hub nuts. Lost two wheels, and spilled the whole rig into the water. Slim just pitched in and helped me get it all together again. I was expecting him to raise hell with me, but all he said was, 'Now you know why you don't back up very far, don't you?'"

Far out in a smooth backwash, a trout jumped clear of the water, flashing its brilliant colors in the sun.

"He taught me how to fish, too. For a little girl who'd never known what a fish looked like unless it was on a platter, that really meant something, you know? And whenever he had the time, he'd take me out with a pistol or a rifle, and teach me how to hunt. I think it was Slim even more than Dad who taught me never to be afraid of anything. Ben, that old man meant so much to me."

She broke down and cried, and didn't resist when Ben cradled her in his arms. He let her cry it out of her system, and when she was finished, she walked to the edge of the water and washed her face.

"There, now maybe you know I'm not as hard as I pretend to be."

"I never really thought you were, Cindy."

"A couple of times since I've come out here, I've come to this very place to have a cry. It was Slim who taught me to do that, too. We were fishing here one day, and I got to thinking about . . . about what had happened to me back in Philadelphia, and Slim just said, 'Go ahead and cry it out, Honey. I'll get us another trout.' When I told him I didn't want to cry, he told me he'd toss me in the river if I didn't, and before I could finish laughing, I broke down and bawled just like you saw me doing a few minutes ago. And when I got done, Slim smiled and said, 'When it builds up, just come down here and cry it out. Nobody's ever gonna know.'"

"Slim was a mighty smart man, Cindy."

"I know. I felt better after that, and since then I've used this as my crying rock the few times I thought I was going to burst."

"He knew you pretty well, didn't he?"

"Slim? Sure," she said, climbing back up on the rock next to Ben. "He knew something about me that Dad has never known, and never will. I always felt I could confide in Slim, but that if I told Dad he might . . ."

She stopped.

"Cindy, don't."

"Ben, yesterday I felt somehow, now that Slim was gone, maybe I could forget it all, and nobody would ever have to know. But now that he's buried, I feel I have to tell someone, and I still can't tell Dad. I used Slim Menough as a crutch for years, and now I need another one. I don't know anybody else I can tell."

Her shoulder heaved as she drew a deep breath.

"Ben, Dad sent me to live with my aunt before he came out here. I was born the year after the war was over, and I never knew my mother. She died about a month after I was born. My mother couldn't have been anything like Aunt Josie. I don't think Dad could have put up with her for a week. She was wishy-washy and mousey, and Uncle Henry treated her like she was nothing more than a piece of fire-wood. I was eight years old when I went to live with them, and I was almost as afraid of Uncle Henry as Aunt Josie was. When I was almost eleven, I made a big fuss about wanting to come out here with Dad, and Uncle Henry gave me holy hell for disturbing him while he was reading the newspaper. That didn't stop me, and I kept after them to let me come to Dad.

"I threw a temper tantrum, I guess, and Uncle Henry turned me over his knee and gave me a good whipping on my bare backside. I was screaming my head off, and Aunt Josie tried to make him stop, but he sent her into the kitchen. He gave me a couple more good whacks, and then suddenly stopped as though he realized how much he was hurting me. He tried to calm me down, and told me he was doing it only because they loved me, and I was going to have to learn how to behave."

She paused and drew a deep breath, as though finding the strength to continue, then said, "I can't remember just how it happened, but I gradually became aware that he was stroking my shoulders with one hand, and the other hand was stroking my bare backside where he'd reddened it. And then he had both hands rubbing me there. I didn't know at the time what he was doing, but I was scared, scared silly that he was trying to find some other way to punish me for misbehaving."

"And you were only eleven?"

"Couple weeks short of it. From that day on he never gave me another whipping, but began to go out of his way to be nice to me. He'd even read stories to me, and I began to think maybe he wasn't so mean after all. But I was aware that he kept sliding his hands all over me while he was reading. Ben, it makes me sick to think I actually liked it. He'd changed from some inhuman monster to someone who made me feel good."

Ben swallowed hard, knowing what she was going through to tell him about it.

"And then one day Aunt Josie was next door at the neighbors, and I was taking a bath to get ready for supper when Uncle Henry opened the door and walked in on me. 'Let me scrub your back for you,' he said. Ben, I was still innocent enough I thought it would be fun to have him treat me like a small child again. I really thought all he was going to do was wash my back. Before I knew it, he was washing me all over, and then his pants were down. By the time all of his clothes were off, my aunt walked in on us, and Uncle Henry said he was just trying to bathe and I'd come in stark naked and wouldn't leave him alone. He even accused me of climbing into the tub with him. Aunt Josie grabbed the razor strap, and I was so happy she'd come to my help, but she didn't whip him. She whipped me with that razor strap so hard I was bleeding for two days. She accused me of all kinds of horrible things, calling me every imaginable dirty name she'd ever heard. That night she packed up my things and put me on a train, and sent Dad a telegram saying she couldn't handle me any more."

"And you've been living with something like that? You've never told your dad?"

"Ben, if I told him, he'd pack up for Philadelphia and kill Uncle Henry without so much as winking an eye."

Ben's anger was slowly subsiding, and he said, "That's something I'd take care of myself, if I were in his boots."

"But can't you see? It wouldn't solve anything. It wouldn't do anybody any good. And it couldn't save me from feeling dirty and ashamed when I think about wearing women's clothes! Ben, can't you understand? It wasn't all Uncle Henry's fault; I could have stopped him. I could have gone to my aunt right away, when he first started it. But I didn't. I liked the feeling of what he was doing to me! That's what the whole trouble was—I liked it. And it was so wrong. When I got out here, I said I was never going to cause anybody any problems like that again, and I've tried to forget that I'm not a man. If only there were some way I could change all that. But I can't. I'm stuck with being what I am."

"Cindy, what you are is a beautiful young woman. A beautiful woman who had a hell of a bad experience. But that's a long time behind you, and it shouldn't make any difference. Can't you see that if your mother had lived, she would have taught you about those things? It wasn't your fault, Cindy; it was your aunt's."

Tears came to her eyes again. "Ben, that's what Slim tried to tell me, but somehow I could never believe him. Do you really feel that way?"

"Of course, Cindy."

She put her head on his shoulder and let the tears flow again. "Oh, Ben, I didn't think anybody but Slim would ever understand what I've had to live with. And I never thought anyone else would feel it wasn't all my fault."

After she'd cried it out fully and washed her face again, she said, "You know, I'm beginning to feel hungry. Let's see what Earl has on the menu today."

Ben nodded, and they walked hand in hand to their horses. He knew that telling him had been one of the most difficult things she had ever had done, and he found himself understanding her for the first time. Yet he knew there was more to her story. When she was ready, he'd be ready to listen.

33

Miles City changed almost overnight from a lusty, brawling frontier town to a hell-raising, rip-snorting cowboy paradise. The saloons and dance halls that were normally crowded with customers letting off a little steam were now jammed tightly, and most of them had set up tables and benches out on the sidewalks to accommodate the droves of cowboys flocking into town before the big roundup. All of the regular hands from throughout the basin were there, along with several hundred who came up from the Southwest every year for the month to six weeks of work. Reunions among old friends were loud and boisterous, and the celebrations went on around the clock.

Most of the cowboys gathered on the sprawling, open land between Miles City and Fort Keogh, and daily the number of small tents and bedrolls scattered about grew. Every outfit in the Association big enough to have one sent a chuck wagon. These were scattered randomly around the huge campsite, and cookfires filled the broad valley with their smoke. Because they never knew how many men would come back from town to eat, the cooks grumbled and complained about too many men for the food they had prepared, or too much food left over. Three of the cooks pulled their wagons together, and pooled their efforts until the roundup began.

Because each working cowboy required from six to ten horses, most of which he could use almost daily during the roundup, the wranglers keeping the cavvy grazing were worked almost as hard as the cooks while the cowboys were off having a fling before the kickoff day arrived. The valley to the north of Miles City was almost as thick with horses as it had been with buffalo only six or eight years earlier. They were kept in four common herds, to be separated when the time came to divide the milling throng of cowboys into teams to scour each district. Until then, most of the men kept one horse tethered at the edge of the sprawling campground for his necessary trips into town. It was not uncommon for a man to walk half a mile to retrieve his horse for a quarter-mile ride into town. No self-respecting cowboy would be caught dead walking.

One disgusted carpenter in Miles City who had no use for cowboys snorted, "Laziest damn bastids on the face a God's earth. Won't even walk across the damn street; gotta climb on a horse and ride! Hell, iffen he didn't have no horse, a cowboy'd never make it to the shithouse."

Ben was sitting on a crate next to the Rafter B chuck wagon talking with Earl when he heard a familiar voice shouting over the campground, "Rafter B! Rafter B! Where's the Rafter B?"

Earl waved a towel in the air. "Here."

A moment later Ben was looking at Muttonhead Jenkins, his face a wide grin.

"Muttonhead! What the hell are you doing here? I thought you went off to Oregon."

"Shore did. Saw me the big damn Pacific. Reckon that's th' onliest reason I done went. Seed it, an' done come back. I heerd you be lookin' fer a couple hands, Ben."

"Well, I'll be damned. You're hired. Earl, how about feeding this scarecrow? He looks like he hasn't eaten in a month."

Earl's mustache bristled, and he ladled a plate full of stew and handed it to Muttonhead. "You'll find a bushel basket of biscuits on the table over there, and the coffee's always ready."

"Thankee. Reloadin' tools . . . yep, I see 'em."

While Muttonhead wrapped himself around the stew, Ben asked, "Didn't like it out there?"

"Didn't say that, did I? I seed the Pacific, and done come back. You done right good fer yerself, Ben. Foreman of an outfit like the Rafter B."

"Just Lady Luck smiling on me for a change, I guess. I started work there the same day the old foreman got himself killed."

"An' Bowen done give yuh the job over old-timer's 'e had on the place?"

"It's a good crew. Only one of them complained about it, a tough nut by the name of Mike Dwyer, but Charlie made his choice and that's the way it's been. I've got a feeling Mike's going to move on after the roundup is over."

"What's chances of permynent work?" Muttonhead asked quietly.

"Offhand, I'd say pretty good. Particularly if Charlie Bowen and I go into raising horses in a big way. If we do, we can use someone who knows horses like you do."

"Shit, I thought I knowed horses till I done went to Orygon. 'Member I got me a job workin' a freighter? Ol' feller name of Wilkins was haulin' five tons of canned victuals an' stuff, an' I hired on as brakeman on the trailer. Fust day out I larned somethin' 'bout horses. We uz goin' up a easy slope, an' them horses stopped. Wilkins calls back, 'Set the brake!' I hauls back on the brake and locks it, an' then I sees a yellow river a pee tricklin' down a rut. We had a eight-horse team pullin' that rig, an' it ain't nothin' special fer wagon horses t' stop and take a pee. I seed lots of 'em afore, with ever' horse in the rig peein' t'gether. But damned iffen Wilkins didn't have a smart team. Ol' John Brown, in the rear off harness, done hisself up proud. I waited an' listened whiles that old boy drained his water tank. From all the splashin', I figured the hull team was taking a leak. 'Bout the time the splashin' dwindled to a little trickle, I uz ready to release the brake, but I didn't figger on them horses wantin' to take a real breathing spell. John Brown finished, then Molly starts up. She peed fer three minutes 'thouten a letup, then Boots lets loose. There wasn't no letup fer twenty minutes. I ain't never seed such control. That team done real good. I hollered up to Wilkins, 'Damn iffen John Brown ain't gonna be able to take another pee by the time they all gets done,' and he sez to me, 'Son, been they mules, they'da bust a gut tryin' it.' That's the way we worked clear to Orygon. Damned horses never hadda pee on a downgrade, neither. Sure wished you and Davey coulda seed that."

Ben swallowed hard. "Davey's dead, Muttonhead."

Muttonhead's fork dropped into his tin plate with a clatter. "Aw hell. How'd it happen?"

"He got caught rustling, and was killed by a vigilante group couple of years back." Ben could still see

Davey Morton's surprised face dropping back into the water.

"Davey? Shit, he allus wanted t' make big money, but I never took him fer no thief."

"I didn't either, but that's how life goes, I guess. Well, you feelin' any better now that you've re-loaded?"

"Shore. An' now that I got me a job, I don't mind goin' inter town t' get me a new hat. Uh, reckon yuh could loan me 'bout twenty 'gainst my earnin's? It ain't I'm bustid, but my gear's mostly wore out, an' I need a few things."

"Here, take this," Ben said, writing a note on a leaf of paper from a notebook he took from his pocket. "Anything you need, just get it at Orschel Brothers and charge it to me. And take this twenty dollars for odds and ends. We'll settle it up later."

Muttonhead gratefully slipped the paper into his pocket, and Ben said, "Just don't get so fancied up in new duds it'll take you two years to work it off."

"Well, I been cornsid'rin' a new set a longies. These here is plumb wore out," he said, pulling a scrap of thin, faded red underwear out of his shirt.

"I'll go in with you. I need to go hunt up a couple of the boys, Muttonhead."

Ben smiled as Muttonhead put his dishes in the scrub pail. Like most of his kind who had been raised out here, Muttonhead never took off his underwear until it was ready to fall off. They wore the same long johns summer and winter, and washed them only on the occasions they were forced to ford a river. Those who swam when they had a chance, swam in their underwear. It wasn't unusual for a man to wear a set of "woolies" for four or five years before taking them off and climbing into new ones.

"Right good grub, Cookie," Muttonhead said appreciatively.

Earl smiled. "You'll find mine is the best anywhere. Glad you like it."

Ben left Muttonhead at Orschel's and rode through the streets looking for Kenny and Clark. He saw Mike Dwyer and Jim Cooper talking with a couple of Dave Mulholland's men in front of the Milestown Hardware Store. He felt some satisfaction knowing that Kenny wasn't with them. Since Charlie had made him foreman, Ben had quietly but successfully managed to keep Kenny and Mike working on different parts of the ranch whenever possible. After Slim was killed, Kenny and Clark became as close as they had been before Mike Dwyer had taken him under his wing.

Ben spent thirty minutes scouting the town looking for Kenny and Clark, and found no sight of them or their horses. Finally he saw Sheriff Tom Irvine standing with a knot of men on a corner.

"Howdy, Tom. Seen anything of Kenny Reynolds and Clark Terry?"

"Those the two kids you got working out there at Charlie's?"

"Yeah. Are they in town?"

"Who isn't? Have you tried the skating rink? A lot of the young kids go over there."

"Thanks, Tom. Just never occurred to me."

The only times Ben had been inside the building before had been for meetings of the Association. He wasn't quite ready for what met him. The huge skating rink was a bedlam of noise. Hundreds of pairs of wheels clattered across the boards while the big Hartford barrel organ in the back of the building boomed out the strains of *The Quilting Party*. It seemed as if hundreds of kids skating and sitting on the benches behind the rails were all hollering and laughing at the same time. Delighted yelps could be heard when someone took a tumble, and now and then the shrill voice of a girl could be heard shrieking.

Ben's first reaction to the noise was that it was like being in a box car full of kids while the train was lumbering through a tunnel in the mountains.

He began walking along the row of benches that lined the walls, and a gruff woman shouted to him from behind the counter, "Mister, I said it costs you five cents to come in here." Behind her was a bold sign proclaiming the five-cent admission price, and skates for rent at ten cents.

"Sorry, I didn't hear you. I'm not skating, just looking for a couple of my boys."

"It costs five cents. Don't make any difference if you want to skate or not, it's still a nickel."

She was a granite block of a woman, reminding him of a stern-faced, mean buffalo. Ben started to say something, then shrugged his shoulders and fished a coin from his pocket.

About halfway down the benches he spotted Kenny's alligator hide boots with the silver trim. Kenny would never tell him how much he paid for the boots, only that he'd learned how to play stud poker well enough to buy the best boots Orschel Brothers had in stock. There probably wasn't another pair of boots or shoes in the place that cost half as much.

He leaned on the rail, searching the faces of the skaters as they rolled by. Most of the kids were town kids, probably between twelve and sixteen years old, although some couldn't have been more than eight or nine. Here and there he could see tall cowboys moving along with the kids, their sombreros clamped tightly onto their heads. Two of them had evidently spent a little time cutting the dust at one of the saloons, and the kids were giving them a wide berth to keep from being flailed by the arms and skidding skates. Ben grinned as both of them lost their footing and hit the floor with a bang. On the far side of the rink he saw a couple of familiar hats. One of them belonged to Willie Wooten.

He laughed watching Kenny and Clark on either side of Willie, supporting him and helping him keep his balance as they pulled him along. When they saw him at the rail, the two boys gave Willie a shove, and he flew straight at Ben, his arms windmilling through the air as his feet shot out from under him. He skidded to a thudding stop at the pole a few feet to Ben's side.

"Lord have mercy!" Willie said. "I thought there wasn't anything these kids could do that I couldn't do better."

"You're not so hot on wheels, huh?"

"Shucks, I got me more bruises on my back porch today then I ever got bustin' wild horses," Willie said, clutching at the rail for support as he tried to regain his feet.

"Heck, you're gettin' the hang of it real good, Willie," Clark said. "Couple more times around, and I'll bet you can do it without our help."

Willie let so of the rail and crawled on his hands and knees off the floor to the bench, and the boys followed him. He gave Ben a pleading look.

"Yeah, he'd probably do all right," Ben said, "but he's all done playing for today."

"You ain't takin' him back to the camp, are you?" Kenny asked.

"Afraid I've got to. We've got some broncs to tame down a bit in the next couple of days."

"Praise the Lord! Broncs I can handle. They don't have wheels." He unlaced the skate shoes and gratefully pulled on his boots.

"You need us, too?" Kenny asked with a disappointed tone.

"No, go ahead and enjoy yourselves today. I'll need you tomorrow, though."

"Okay. Gosh, this is more fun than wrasslin' ponies anyway," Clark said, ducking under the rail and racing to roll up alongside a pretty little blonde girl in a calico dress. Kenny melted into a group of boys.

Willie hobbled outside with Ben, and said, "Sure glad you came along. I mighta been killed. Now what's with the broncs?"

"Little white lie. I saw you needed a way out, that's all. Actually, I was just checking on the boys. Want to make sure they're staying out of trouble."

"That's why I came in with them. I was afraid Kenny'd get himself liquored up, but I think that hangover about cured him of any desire to drink again. Clark still considers strawberry sody pop the best thing that's come along since mother's milk."

"Good. The longer they can stay away from the stuff, the better. Hey, there's Gus Adams. I want to see him about something, Willie."

"Sure," he said, stiffly swinging up into the saddle. "Lordy them boards are hard!"

Ben strode up to the corner where Gus was standing and watching the scene.

"Howdy, Ben. Lettin' off a little steam before you go to work?"

"Nope, just checking on my crew. They seem to be staying out of trouble."

"Good thing. Tom's jail won't hold many more."

"Maybe what he needs is another stockade."

"It'd come in handy right before the roundup, and right after it again. And one of your boys is a prime candidate for a free bunk right now."

"Who?"

"Mike Dwyer. He's got a snootful over at the Red Rose, and pretty soon someone's going to get tired of it."

"Damn! When I saw him thirty minutes ago, he was talking with some of Mulholland's boys at the hardware store."

"Must have been right before Jack Sully took him in for a drink."

"What's Sully doing in town?"

"Same thing everybody else is. Having a good time before going out to work. I've been keeping my eyes open for Sanchez, but that slippery bastard's got more sense than to show his face around here for a while. Poke told me he heard somewhere that Sanchez was selling windmills over in Dakota."

Just then a crowd spilled out onto the street from the Red Rose and two gunshots inside the saloon split the air.

34

BEN and Gus pushed their way through the crowd to the barroom door. Sheriff Tom Irvine was already inside.

Crumpled in a heap on the floor near the far end of the bar lay the body of Heiney Stuber, the back of his head blown off and splattered on the wall. Near his twitching hand lay an old cap and ball pistol. Mike Dwyer still had his revolver in his hand, and the other hand was clutching his ribs. Jack Sully stood a few feet off, his hands on his hips.

"Just what the hell's going on here?" Irvine demanded.

"On the surface," the bartender said, "looks like a case of self-defense. Heiney and Mike got into an argument, and I told them to clear the hell out. I don't like trouble in my place, Tom, you know that."

"Heiney shot first?"

"He sure as hell drew first, Tom. His gun was up

and aimed at Mike's breadbasket before Mike pulled his."

"The Hun shot first," Sully said. "Mike's faster and better, that's all."

"How do you happen to be mixed up in it, Sully?"

"Who's mixed up in it? I was just standing here having a drink with Mike, that's all."

Irvine turned to the crowd beginning to press back inside the little saloon. "Everybody get the hell outside for about five minutes, damn you! I can't hear myself think."

"Ain't much to think about, Tom," Clyde Neff called. "Heiney pulled that old hawgleg afore Mike even put down his glass. You gonna stand there an' drink while someone's got his cannon aimed at yer gut?"

"You got anything to say, Dwyer?"

"Yeah. He was a piss poor shot. Five feet away from me, and he missed."

"You're bleeding," Ben said.

Dwyer pulled his left hand off his ribs. "About as serious as getting nicked by a hunk of nester's wire." The ball had left a crease in the flesh on his rib cage where it glanced off a rib, and made a second hole in the shirt as it exited. Dwyer looked at the bloody shirt.

"See if that German bastard's got enough money on him to buy me a new shirt."

Irvine turned to the bartender. "When you get a couple of minutes, stop by my office and leave a statement. Dwyer, you come with me, and you too, Clyde. Meanwhile, how about a couple of you boys hauling Heiney over to the undertaker's?"

Ben waited outside Irvine's office in the big brick courthouse, and when Dwyer stepped out after signing a statement, Ben stopped him.

"Make sure you're in good shape to tame down some horses in the morning."

"You've been feeling pretty important with yourself since Bowen gave you my job, haven't you?"

"How do you figure I got your job?"

"And how do you rate? You hired on like anybody else, didn't you? How come he gives you the foreman's job the first day you're there?"

"I'd say that's Charlie's business. And it's my business to make sure the crew is ready to move out in a couple of days. Tomorrow we've got some horses to break. Just be ready to go to work in the morning."

"Foster, I'm ready for anything you think you're big enough to hand me. Anything, at any time. And don't forget I've still got a score to settle with you."

Ben grinned at him. "Anything at any time. I've never backed off from anyone."

Without warning, Dwyer ducked his head and charged forward, landing a solid blow on Ben's chin.

Ben spilled backward, tripping over his heels and pinning his left arm under him as Dwyer jumped on top of him, his heavy fists flailing. Ben felt a tooth crack under one of the blows, and struggled to free his arm. He rolled his head as Dwyer slammed another hard fist at him, and felt a cut open under his eye.

He reached for Dwyer's rib cage, dug his fingers in along the bullet crease and twisted. Dwyer let out a grunt, and flinched enough for Ben to raise his body with a heave, tossing him off to one side.

Ben scrambled to his feet and was cocking his arm back to rush into Dwyer before he could get his balance when he felt heavy hands grab his arms.

He spun his head around to find Gus Adams and Cal Bradley holding him, just as Tom Irvine and Dave Mulholland got hold of Dwyer.

"I got a good mind to let you both cool off in jail," Irvine said disgustedly.

"Just put us both in the same cell," Ben said, his breath beginning to return to normal.

"Take it easy, Ben," Cal said. "He ain't worth it."

Charlie Bowen shoved his huge bulk through the crowd. He sized up the situation and asked, "You want him fired, Ben?"

"I can handle him, Charlie. If he doesn't settle down, I'll take care of it myself."

Charlie glared at both of them, his graying red hair bristling under the brim of his hat. "Mike, I'd tell you to take your stuff and get packing, but I'll go along with whatever Ben wants to do. But I'm warning you, the next time you two get into it, you're going to be looking for a new job no matter what Ben says. And as of tomorrow morning, nobody comes into town until after the roundup unless there's some business to tend to."

The campground was taking on a festive air. Reunions among Texans and some of their old friends who had become "Montanified" after eight or ten years in the northern climate were joyous affairs. It wasn't hard to tell the difference between the men who had started out on the southern ranges, for their voices were generally softer than those who had spent most of their lives in the long grass country. Even before listening to a man, it wasn't difficult to tell where he was from. Each group could be recognized by the style of headgear; the four-sided crown coming to a high, pointed peak, marked the Montana cowman. Texas hats had a high rounded crown and wide brim, and most of them had a star cut into the crown for ventilation. The most common hat was the low rounded crown worn by the plainsmen, which was less likely to be blown off by the strong winds encountered on the wide open prairies. The Mexicans, no matter where they worked, usually retained the traditional sugar loaf sombrero with the foot-wide brim that afforded protection from the blistering sun south of the Rio Grande. Instead of the wide bat-wing chaps favored by the Texans, the northern cow-men usually wore slim shotguns in warmer weather, and fur lined "woolies" in the winter. The Mexicans preferred leather leggings that were tied onto the belt rather than buckle-on chaps, and their spurs invariably had long, sharp-spiked rowels.

As he walked through the campground, Ben shook his head in amazement at the number of musical instruments that were in evidence. The standard rule was that each hand could carry his bedding and a bag of personal items on the supply wagon, and if the cook felt there was any room left he determined what a man might take along with him. There were dozens of banjos being strummed around the camp, along with a few guitars. Several of the Mexican hands who worked for the XIT had stringed instruments as well as a cornet and a bass horn. They'd gathered a large crowd as they sang and played folk songs while a trio of black cowboys danced to the music.

"You ain't got no bronc I cain't ride," said one soft-talker. "Got me a system what ain't never failed."

"Hit 'im over the head with a railroad tie, huh?"

"Nope, easier'n that. Gotta think like a bronc. When he gits a rider up on his back, he's thinkin', well I gotta discourage this here son of a bitch, right fast, an' he don't never give up until he either gits rid of his rider, or comes to unnerstand he's been hornswaggled. So long's he sees a man's strugglin' an' kickin' an' hangin' on, he's gonna put on a acry-batic show. I discourages 'em in a hurry, I does. I climbs into the seat and rolls me a smoke with one hand while I'm holdin' my noosepaper with the other. When that ol' bronc sees I don't give no damn, 'e gives up."

"Hell, that ain't nothin'," replied one Arizona cowpoke. "We got us a foreman down t' Yuma what even shaves while bustin' broncs. Holds 'is mirror with one hand, carries a little pail of water slung over 'is arm, an' lets the bronc supply the movement to strop 'is razor on the horse's backside, then takes off a three, four day beard with that straight edge jist as slick as a whistle."

"You think that's something, let me tell you . . ."

One of the most popular diversions in the campground, along with exhibitions of roping and riding skills while the crowds furiously laid bets on their favorites, was the game of chicken which had originated with the Apaches. A rooster was buried in the ground with only his head sticking out. Riders would race along a predetermined course, then see who could be the first to reach the rooster and yank it from the ground by its head. Four riders was the maximum number that could race at any one time, and as they neared the rooster they were nudging and pushing each other to get into position to lean down from the saddle while galloping full tilt and grab the rooster's head. If the first of the racers missed because of interference from another rider, the slower ones usually managed to snatch the prize, and the money that went with it. Not a few of the cowboys wound up battered and bruised as they fell from their mounts in this game, and the damage to the roosters was even worse. Generally, the head came off in a rider's hand if the ground had been packed too solidly on top of the bird, who was destined to go into a stew kettle before the day was over anyway.

"Hey, Ben!"

He turned to see Twice Thompson and Curly Schaeffer riding up to watch the fun.

"Howdy, guys. Big turnout this year."

"Yep," Twice agreed. "Ol' Four Eyes says they's gonna scour ever' hidin' place in the basin this year."

Curly grunted. "Some of those critters've been so well holed up they haven't seen a man in two or three years. Old Four Eyes considers it just another challenge. Gonna be fun catching up those beefs."

"Since when's he been called *Old* Four Eyes? I didn't know anyone thought that much of him."

"Done earned it, sure 'nuff," Twice said, "We was down t' Scotts Bluff couple months ago. Hotel where we stayed two nights, y' hadda go through the bar t' get to the room. Jake Williams, one a the toughs from Medora, was there, an' was kinda liquored up, an' makin' a real pest of himself. He spotted us headin' fer our room, and stood up, barrin' our way. He sez, 'Well, if it ain't Four Eyes come down t' buy drinks fer the house.' The boss, he don't like t' make no trouble fer no one, but he ain't takin' that from the likes a Jake. He tried to walk around Jake, but Jake plants hisself in the way an' sez, 'Belly up to the bar! Four Eyes is buyin'.' Well, I was ready fer all hell t' bust loose, but Four Eyes just sez, 'Well, if I must, I must,' and damned iffen he don't haul back an' flatten Jake. The marshal done hauled Jake off t' the pokey quicker'n a weasel gits a chicken out of a coop. Ever since then, ever'one's done called 'im *Old* Four Eyes."

"Well, bully for him," Ben said, genuinely pleased.

"Yep," Curly said, "he's happy now. Just another one of the boys."

The shouting behind them rose, and another four riders were getting ready for a race at the rooster.

"Want to make some money? Get your bet down on Muttonhead Jenkins, on the sorrel."

"Pretty good, huh?"

"The best. I used to ride with him, and hired him yesterday."

Twice and Curly looked at each other, their faces brightening.

"Bet he can't ride old Water Skipper."

"How much?" Ben asked.

"Ten dollars."

"From each of you?"

Another look was exchanged, and both heads nodded. "Nothing wrong with taking some of your money," Curly said, rubbing his bald head.

"Your money's as good as in my pocket," Ben said confidently. "Muttonhead can ride anything. He used to bust horses with me for George Fowler."

"No shit?" Twice replied calmly. "I stick with my bet. Ol' Water Skipper ain't been rode since last October."

"Damn," Ben muttered under his breath, seeing twenty dollars slipping through his fingers. Suddenly an inspiration struck him.

"You want to get him in condition, huh? Maybe I've got a better idea. Add my twenty to yours, and offer the bet to Mike Dwyer."

"Why, you devious son of a bitch," Curly said, his face widening into a pleased smile. "Think he can manage it?"

"He might. Dwyer's no slouch; but even if he wins, I'll enjoy watching the show."

Miles City the next morning was the scene of the biggest parade of the year. At the head of the column marched the band from Fort Keogh, followed by columns of four Cavalrymen abreast, their guidons flying gaily in the breeze. They were followed by the carriages bearing the officers of the Montana Stock Growers Association, and this year there was an exceptionally large attendance. More than two hundred members were in town, most of them in the parade, but the out-of-towners made a noteworthy group.

There were all the cattle barons who had turned the basin into an industry, some of them with interests as far-flung as the XIT which began in Texas on land just west of Charlie Goodnight's JA ranch, and with Montana land at the other end of the well-worn trail through seven states. John Clay, the doughty old Scot who was the economic genius behind the Association, rode with Granville Stuart and Conrad Kohrs in Stuart's handsomely decorated carriage with the gilt coat of arms on the door. Pierre Wibaux and the Marquis de Mores rode in a cherry-wood surrey with the Association's secretary and parliamentarian, Theodore Roosevelt.

Other dignitaries were representatives of the Northern Pacific Railroad, and officials from the stockyards in St. Paul, Chicago and Kansas City. Tobacco merchants Liggett and Myers, who owned the LO spread near Charlie Bowen's on the Mizpah and had beef contracts with three army posts, rode an open carriage with two Englishmen who had established themselves in the Basin. J. H. Price of the Crown W Ranch was a member of the Association, but had turned his efforts to the raising of fine polo ponies, and was never seen without his monacle. Next to him sat a former Oxford professor, E.S. Cameron, who was a miserable failure in the cattle business, but was destined to become the foremost authority on birds of Eastern Montana.

Some of the Association members came from as far east as the Atlantic, and others from as far west as the Pacific. Most of the herds were managed by absentee investors, who made only one or two trips a year to inspect their holdings.

Behind the long string of carriages came the procession of cowboys dressed in their finest outfits, showing off for the girls who were waving to them from upstairs windows along the parade route. The very end of the parade was comprised of urchins from town, some on high-wheeled bicycles, some riding pony carts, and some on foot.

The Association held its formal meeting at the roller rink, and by four in the afternoon adjourned to get ready for the serious work of the evening. Every saloon in town was loaded to capacity, although the owners knew that this night the crowds would thin out early as the cowboys needed as much sleep as they could get before moving out in the morning. It was only the formal ball in the Macqueen House that would keep going until midnight.

Officers from Fort Keogh and several other posts in the Territory were in attendance, their full-dress uniforms immaculate as they danced with the wives and daughters of the cattle barons. Always in demand at the dances were the half-breed daughters of Granville and Aubony Stuart, who had the dark-eyed charm of their Shoshone mothers, and the proud bearing of their aristocratic fathers. Two bands, one from Fort Keogh, the other made up of members of the Miles City Civic Association, kept the ballrooms filled with music until midnight, when the gathering broke up and began retiring for the night.

Ben had turned in shortly after dark, knowing that it would be the last time in weeks he'd have a chance to get a full night's sleep. It took a while to get to sleep with the murmured conversations through the camp.

"Andy's gettin' up a stud game," came a soft voice a dozen yards away.

"Shit, don't he know Old Leather Face don't allow no gamblin' on a roundup?"

"Hell, Leather Face ain't here. He done took the night train back to Chicago."

"In that case, I reckon I kin stay a couple of hands. I might could use me some extry cash."

"Knock it off, Leaky Mouth. I gotta ride herd on the cavvy later."

"Shove it."

Gradually the camp settled down for the night, with only a few lanterns showing here and there. In no time, the gongs were ringing with cooks walking through the jumbled mass of sleeping men.

"Rise and shine like the morning star. Git them miserable asses outa your bedrolls."

Even Earl Howard's customary polite invitations to chow were tempered by the massive mob at the campground. Ben was pulling on his boots when Earl joined the other cooks in rousting out their men.

"Come and get it before I throw it out! If you don't want it, I'll give it to the other pigs! Get up, damn you, this isn't a picnic, you know! Let's go!"

The big roundup was under way.

35

CHARLIE Bowen had been named captain of District Four again, which was the second largest in the basin. It stretched southward from the Yellowstone almost to Wyoming, and at Powderville it snaked southeast to Dakota Territory. He split District Four into four smaller areas, and divided the manpower among his lieutenants. Ben was his lieutenant for the area from Powderville across the headwaters of Box Elder Creek and into the forested area south of Medicine Rock. It was the smallest of the areas in District Four, but as large as all of District Twelve. Charlie snorted, "Hell, it's only about the size of Rhode Island, if you include the water."

Ben rode southeast from Miles City with Dave Mulholland, who was in charge of the crew that would be working just to the west of him. Ben's crew numbered twenty four men who represented eight different outfits, and Mulholland's was thirty two. For the first thirty miles both crews traveled together, then split off into their own areas. Ben sat atop a grassy knoll watching his men and the cavvy of over a hundred and sixty horses as they progressed. Muttonhead was happy to have a job as day wrangler, even though a wrangler was paid ten dollars a month less than a cowboy. He was in his glory working horses again. Riding with him was Clark Terry.

Just ahead of the cavvy went Earl Howard and the chuck wagon at a brisk trot, followed by Fred McCoy with the supply wagon. They arrived at their first roundup point by mid-morning. Kenny Reynolds and Willie Wooten dragged a good load of firewood to the campsite, and by the time Earl's wagon rolled up, they had a fire ready and waiting for him. They dragged more wood across the valley to the branding pit, where it would be ready to heat branding irons when the herd was brought in. Almost before the wagon rolled to a stop, Earl had the team unhitched and was beginning to prepare the main meal of the day. When the riders came in with the herd, they would be famished from the hard work of the morning after a breakfast that usually consisted of bacon and biscuits with jam or preserves. The dinner consisted of barbequed beef or veal, along with coffee, tinned vegetables, more biscuits and jam. While preparing the breakfast, which was ready to eat when the men were dragged from their short night's sleep, Earl usually baked pies or made other pastries. From dinner time until the afternoon's work of branding was finished a quarter of a mile away on the other side of the valley, he'd have one or two dashing over to grab a quick biscuit or hunk of cold roast as they changed to fresh horses and went back to the chore of branding.

Some of the larger outfits hired boys or men who weren't adept at cutting for the job of chopping firewood and keeping the cook supplied. Most, though, sent their firewood crew ahead, and after dinner they then worked at cutting and branding as the herd was brought in. Usually, the chore was rotated on a daily basis. Because of his age and failing eyesight, Fred McCoy would spend the morning helping Earl pack the camp and move the wagon to the next site, then work the rest of the day at his favorite job of castrating the bull calves. Fred was also the most experienced hand at the Rafter B when it came to dehorning, treating lump jaw, open sores or wounds. He gleefully took all the joking about being a Cherokee medicine man, even though he referred to himself as the Rafter B surgeon.

Ben halted the crew on the trail and drew a sketchy map in the dust, describing the main features of the terrain in the area where they would begin their work. The boundaries for each were defined by streams of ridge lines. When they saddled up again, he gave a signal as they came to each small sector, and two riders cut off from the crew, one to the right, one to the left. After four men had been sent out to the limits of the day's sector, the rest split into two groups, each one veering off and riding to the farthest limits of his area. From one of the higher hills to the west, Ben saw the smoke of the campfire, and settled into his work.

In theory, every day the crew worked a piece of land that was shaped like a pie, and each man had one small wedge of land to work, searching every nook and cranny for cattle. One by one, he would work his cattle into a small bunch, then a larger bunch as he moved them toward the center of the pie across the valley from the campsite. As they converged toward the center the bunches would grow, then be consolidated into larger bunches. The theory stated further that as riders converged toward the center, they could zig-zag back and forth across their wedge of the pie and create a net no cow could slip through.

A neat, round pie is a beautiful theory that seldom matches the configuration of the land upon which it is drawn. More often, the pie was so large it would take two or three days to scour the land and gather the herd into the valley, and the camp would remain in one place for a while. Where it is open and fairly level, land can be worked like that pie. Most of the land that borders the Great Plains takes on the configuration of the crust around the outside of the pie, and even the smooth crust topping is broken by cracks. These cracks are the creeks, the arroyos, the gullies and canyons, the seemingly endless piles of rocks, all put there for no purpose other than to provide cover for cattle who avoided man if possible. In practice, the pie was crumbled into myriad pieces, and the ridges, mountains and streams defining the uneven wedges of the pie provided nothing more than a rough estimate of where a man would have to work to find the cattle in his sector. Often he found himself bullying recalcitrant beasts out of inaccessible locations to run head-on into a man working his in the opposite direction.

Within an hour of the time the first men had moved to the outside of the sector, Ben noticed little puffs of dust up on the hillsides, and knew the first of the cattle were being pushed from their hiding places to join others who had been grazing in open country. By noon, most of the men would have their bunches together in the valley, then eat and change horses for the work of branding through the long afternoon.

The men who drew the far side of the pie ahead of the campsite where the wedges all came together put in a heavy day of riding to reach their area and work back to the central point. It was not unusual for a man to ride twenty-five or thirty miles in the morning, and as far in the afternoon, and still work for hours at cutting and branding. Most foremen rotated the posi-

tions every day, spreading out the harder riding
among all the men.

Muttonhead tied one end of a rope to the wheel of
the chuck wagon, looped it through the spokes of the
supply wagon, and then paid it out to a couple of
thin, three-foot forked sticks Clark had stuck in the
ground. While Fred McCoy held open the rope gate,
Muttonhead and Clark moved the cavvy into the
makeshift corral, where they would be waiting for
the men to rope their cutting ponies for the afternoon.

Once the cavvy was corraled, Fred and Muttonhead
checked the bundle of branding irons and the box of
veterinary supplies. Among the dozen irons were the
marks of most of the outfits in this corner of District
Four, and an assortment of straights and curves would
be used to shape any others.

Gradually the cattle began coming into the gathering area, with Cal Bradley bringing in the first bunch
of fifty. No matter how many he had gathered, even
though he brought in the largest number of the day
and from the easiest terrain, nobody liked to be the
first one in, for he would be the butt of good-natured
insults until they started out the next morning.

"Reckon you woulda found two, three times that
many iffen yuh hadn't got the hungries."

"Shit, I brung in twenty more'n you did, but what
the hell. Easier t' park yore ass here than work."

Almost as bad would be the hazing a man took if
he was the last one in.

"You got the slowest goddam pony on the face a the
earth!"

"Sneakin' in some beddy-bye time up there?"

"Hell, maybe ol' Cowboy Annie's done pitched a tent
out here somewheres. Man's gotta lubricate his pistons
afore his engine's gonna run. Annie say where she's

gonna camp t'morry? I might could take a leetle time fer that muhself."

By the time Ben came in with a bunch from the southeast, about half of the men had returned, and there were some seven hundred cattle grazing in the broad valley.

"Doesn't look like a bad day, so far," he commented to Cal.

"Fair. Wonder what happened to Mike? He was south of me, and I thought he'd beat me in, but he hasn't showed yet."

"You had pretty easy ground, didn't you?"

"Smooth as the middle of Kansas, most of it."

Ben finished his dinner and roped himself a cutting horse for the afternoon. At the branding site, Twice Thompson and Fred McCoy were just starting the fire. It would be another half hour before the cattle that were already in had milled around enough to settle down and the cows to find their calves. As a normal rule, they waited until the last of the riders had brought in their bunches, for a new herd added to the gather would only create confusion when it came time to separate the unbranded calves from the herd.

"Mike's not in yet?" Ben asked.

Fred shook his head. "Only one, I think."

Ben waited another half hour, then said, "Go ahead and get started. I'm going to look for Mike."

Two miles from the roundup site, he saw a cloud of dust rising beyond the hills, and found Dwyer driving a small bunch ahead. He circled wide, moved in to the flank, and helped guide them over the last of the hills where they were content to join their own kind in the milling herd on the valley floor.

"What kept you?"

Dwyer clamped down on his cigar. "Just got stuck

with about a dozen bunch quitters who wanted to go every which damned way and scattered the rest of 'em. I lost a dozen back in the high ground."

For a brief moment, Ben considered riding out to see for himself, but knew that part of Dwyer's area was rugged and broken. It could be a total waste of time. Still, he couldn't shake the feeling that Dwyer wasn't being honest about it.

He couldn't complain about Dwyer's work during the afternoon, though, nor could he fault the big gelding, Sheridan. Sheridan had worked the morning searching out beefs, then taken a brief rest while Dwyer ate and took another pony from the cavvy to start cutting out the calves. After two hours, Sheridan was picked out again, and proved as adept as any at cutting. Dwyer seldom had to use the reins; Sheridan seemed to know exactly which calf his rider was after, and bulled his way into the herd, nipping, biting, kicking and taking Dwyer to his quarry.

It was near sundown when they finished for the day, and Ben was going over the tally book with the big blonde Swede from the J Lazy J, when Muttonhead said to him, "Rider comin' in."

At this time of day, any cowboy working the round-up would be thinking of getting some sleep, and if he wasn't working the roundup, he'd be busy with chores on the home spread. Someone coming in on their camp at this hour could only mean trouble.

It was trouble, but of a different kind than he had expected.

"Cindy, what are you doing down here?"

"I just couldn't stay cooped up at the ranch. I'm going to join your crew."

36

"But, damn it all, I can't let you work with this crew!"

"Why not? You think I can't handle the work?" Her face flushed, and he could see her temples pounding.

"I know you can do the work, but it just isn't right having a woman out here. We don't have any private bedrooms, for one thing, and you show me where there's an outhouse where you've got some privacy. It isn't right, that's all."

She smiled sweetly at him as she took off her hat. "You're cute when you're mad, do you know that?"

Ben could hear a couple of snickers from the men, but he fought to keep himself under control.

As he spluttered, she walked to the chuck wagon. "I'm hungry."

He followed at her heels, protesting. "I thought your dad told you to stay home."

"He did," she replied disinterestedly. "But I didn't. Now if you'll let me get something to eat, maybe we can finish our little chat later, okay?"

He let her go, cursing under his breath. He'd never be able to understand women.

Fred McCoy ambled over to him.

"That girl's got a mind of her own, ain't she?"

"Damn stubborn. She always been like this, Fred?"

"Ever since she come out here. Drives Charlie loco. She gonna stick around long?"

"Says she's going to work with us. Damn it, a round-up is no place for a woman."

Fred grunted. "Let her chop wood and take the night watch. Maybe the rest of us will get more sleep."

Ben nodded his thanks, and then walked over to where Cindy was wolfing down a plate of beans and roast beef.

"What am I going to tell your dad?"

"Tell him exactly what happened."

"We could rope you and take you back, you know."

"Wouldn't be very smart, Ben. I can get ornery when I'm mad."

"So can I," he replied, feeling his temper rising again. "If you're determined to stay, you can have the second night watch with the cavvy. Then you can take the firewood job, and kind of stick around giving Earl a hand when he needs something."

She glared at him in the fading light. "You're trying to tell me I'm not worth much, is that it?"

"Damn it, I'm trying to tell you I don't want the responsibility of taking care of you out here. I don't want anything to happen to you."

Earl tilted his derby forward and said, "If she's going to stay on, put her to work catching beefs. I don't need help with the cooking."

"Firewood, then. And you can take the second night watch with the cavvy so Muttonhead and Clark can get some extra sleep."

"Fine with me," she said, then turned her back on him.

He stomped off to his sleeping roll, and pulled off his boots. Muttonhead and Twice were both snoring loudly, and Ben wondered if they were having a contest. At least they were asleep, and he wouldn't have to explain what was going on.

That was good, because he couldn't find a way to explain it.

He woke, studied the stars, and slipped out of his blankets. The position of the Big Dipper's alpha and beta indicated it was time to begin the third watch, which lasted until morning. He was pulling on his boots even before she came to wake him. The years had trained him to wake when it was time for him to take the second or third night watch, and it was seldom anyone had to pull him from his blankets.

"It's quiet out here tonight," Cindy said softly.

"Be different when we pull in a bunch big enough to keep us in one place for a few days."

She rode alongside as he walked to the corral and picked out a night horse.

"Mind if I ride with you a while, Ben?"

"You need to get some sleep."

"I'm doing fine."

"Suit yourself," he said. "You going to switch horses? Midnight there's done his trick."

"Two hours of easy walking and standing? You don't know much about horses if you think that's going to tire him out."

"Suit yourself," he repeated, and they walked their horses slowly out to the cavvy dozing and grazing along the bank of the creek.

"Sorry I snapped at you, Cindy, but it's going to be hard having you along."

"I still say I can pull my weight."

"I know that. But . . ."

"Ben, I really came out because I had to talk to you again."

"Something wrong?"

"Just . . . Ben, I want to thank you for what you did. You know, the day we buried Slim."

"If it's worth anything, that was the first day I really thought of you as a woman."

"Because I was weak enough to break down and cry?"

"Everybody cries. Even I do when I'm trying to keep something bottled up too long. And you'd been bottling up your troubles a lot longer than you should have, even if you had Slim to talk to. Up until that day, you were a girl. A beautiful girl, but one I thought was hard as nails and enough to vex a man to death."

"And that made you change your mind?"

"Partly."

There was a pause, and she said, "What do you mean, partly?"

"You changed from a hard, quick-tempered girl to a warm, wonderful woman. But you can still vex me nigh unto death. You come out here telling me you're going to work the roundup with us, and don't even stop to think how it's going to affect the crew."

"Ben, most of them are from the Rafter B."

"Oh, they know you all right. But what about the horses?"

"Well, what about them?"

"You came out on Bluebelle. Where's the rest of your string?"

"Well, I . . ."

"See what I mean? You can't do it all on Bluebelle. Unless you're content to handle the firewood detail."

"I'll do anything," she said, and he noticed a strange tone in her voice he'd heard only once before. "Ben, I had to be near you. I couldn't bear the thought of not seeing you again for more than a month. That day changed me, I know it did. Oh, I've known for a long time that you're the man I want, but I've been afraid to admit it to myself. Like the way I talked to you when I rode in. I was just trying to keep the men from seeing how I felt, I think. Ben . . ."

Midnight stopped dead in his tracks, and stood with his ears laid back. Ben chuckled out loud.

"Come on, damn you, git!" she said, nudging her spurs into the animal's ribs.

"You don't know Midnight?"

"What's the matter with this horse?" she said, her voice betraying her impatience.

"Guess you don't know much about horses, do you? Not even the ones you've had at the Rafter B for years. Midnight's one of the best night horses on the place. He's got eyes like a cat, and he can keep his footing on a narrow ledge like a goat. But when he's herding and there's no real activity, he knows how long a two hour watch lasts. When his two hours is up, he quits."

"That's ridiculous!"

"And you said I don't know much about horses, huh? Cindy, right now, I'd say you have just about two choices. Take the saddle off and carry it back to the corral, or sit here until he decides he wants to get a drink. Either way, he's done working for the night."

"You can't be serious."

"Oh, there's a third choice, but I don't think you'd want to try it. You could spook the cavvy, and he'll be ready to go again as soon as you mount up. But you do that, and I'll be the first one to break your pretty little neck for waking up the crew."

She kicked, she urged Midnight to get moving, she whipped him on the flank with her quirt. The black horse sat and flinched, but didn't budge.

"Ben, aren't you going to do anything?"

"Yep. I'm going to keep patrolling. See you when I make my next swing."

"Damn you, Ben Foster!"

"Yep, damn me, all right. But I've got work to do."

"And here I thought you were some kind of man I could put up with for the rest of my life."

"Funny, but I was thinking the same thing about you. But that was before I found out you really don't understand the psychology of horses."

He started off to circle the far side of the cavvy, smiling as he listened to her swearing in the darkness.

37

THE next morning, shortly before the sun rose above the horizon, Ben was working his way along a high ridge. He saw three riders on the crest of a hill about two miles ahead, outlined by the pearly sky behind them. It might have been four, but he saw three without any question. That sector of the pie had been assigned to Mike Dwyer, and there shouldn't have been anyone with him. He eased his mare back into the trees and watched.

After about ten minutes, the riders split up, and two of them disappeared to the southeast over the crest that marked the boundary line of District Four. A single rider started down the hill on his side, and while he couldn't be certain because of the distance, he was willing to swear it was Dwyer astride his big roan, Sheridan. It was something to keep in mind, and he resolved to keep a closer eye on Dwyer.

They brought in more cattle that day than he would have expected, and he knew they'd be there for one more day, if not two. The bawling and wailing from the herd of over two thousand beefs was deafening, and men working in the branding circle had to shout to make themselves heard by a man next to him. Fred McCoy had four pails of testes and ear cuts to be counted as a double check on the tally, and was in his glory as a surgeon.

While they had two separate crews branding, Cindy rode across from the campsite to pull up alongside Ben and the Swedish tally man.

"Ben, there's another wagon with six men just behind us."

"Who are they?"

"I don't know. But they're just parked there, watching us as if we were a gang of rustlers."

"You stay here. I'm going to check them out."

The wagon was a good mile from their campsite, and he was greeted by a half-dozen frowning faces.

"You lost?" he asked. "This is District Four, and this is my section of it."

"You ain't tellin' us anything we don't know, Foster," said a red-faced paunchy man with a jagged scar on his cheek. "We just come along to save your boys some work."

"Yeah? You're from the Dollar outfit, aren't you?"

"Mighty pleased to know you can recognize a simple brand, Foster."

"Far's I know, you haven't sent anyone to work the roundup."

"That ain't up to us. That's the boss's decision. We just thought we might do a little checkin' up on your work, that's all."

Ben noticed that the driver on the wagon had his Winchester lying across his knees, and the five riders, unlike most men working the roundup, were all armed.

"We've been running across a lot of your beefs,"

Ben said. "More today than yesterday. It would have been nice if Brown thought enough of his investment to send a few of you to work this roundup."

"Hell, Foster, we're just a small outfit. Mr. Brown can't afford to send anyone this year."

"Well, if you think we're up to anything, you can take it up with the Association. This crew's got reps from eight different outfits, and . . ."

"Don't go gettin' feathers up your ass, Foster! We're not accusin' you or anybody else of any mis-brandin'. All we're doing is sticking around to save you the trouble of sendin' our beefs home."

"Yeah, mighty nice of you, isn't it? We do the work of pulling them out of their hidey-holes, do all the branding and separating, then you push them on home."

It was frustrating, but there was nothing that could be done about it. The Dollar was a registered brand on the range, and Association rules demanded that more than twenty five animals carrying a brand from that District were to be sent home with a representative from the owner. Even if the owner didn't contribute to the work of the roundup, his cattle were sent home, or at least in the general direction of home.

Cindy was upset, but she was as powerless as anybody. "The only thing that can be done about it is to have the Association blackball him, Cindy."

"And what happens if he doesn't move his stock out when he's blackballed? Short of killing him, there isn't much the Association can do."

"Oh, I don't know. It could happen that everyone who ships a few hundred head simply has a few of his cows in the load. The brand inspectors will make sure he gets credit for them, but his herd will dwindle pretty fast. I know that's how they got rid of one rancher over in Dakota a couple of years ago. He complained that out of one carload of beefs Jelly Bean Jones shipped, only two of them belonged to Jones, and the rest were his. Since the brand inspector is hired by the Association, all he could do was complain about it, and the inspectors told him he could either manage his own cattle or they'd charge five dollars a head to separate them at the loading pens. All it took was two years, and he was out of business."

Even though the day's catch numbered well over two thousand, most of the men agreed that there were more than a few stragglers. When he came in with nearly a hundred, Kenny had said, "I know there's more back there, Ben, but the ground's so chopped up I just couldn't cover every bit of it."

Cal and Willie agreed it had been the roughest country they'd worked, and there were bound to be beefs stuck back in corners. "Yeah, the ground down there's kinda corrugated, Ben. Ain't no way we're gonna find every one, 'less we go back over it in teams."

"That's what I figured," Ben said. "Tomorrow we'll keep half the crew here to brand, and the rest will go out and scour it inch by inch."

Willie groaned. "I'm being repaid for my sins, sure enough. That corner down there is as bad as any I've seen way over to the headwaters of the Yellowstone."

"I didn't find it that bad," Mike Dwyer said contemptuously. "This country's easy after you've spent a few years in the Cascades."

Dwyer's catch that day was the largest so far, and the crew had been hearing about it all afternoon.

"Yeah," Cal spat, "Ben gave you a dance floor to work today. Try what we had on the other side of the valley."

"He will," Ben agreed. "I've tried to divvy things up so everybody gets the same."

"Doesn't make any difference to me," Dwyer boasted. "You can't find the country that's too rough for me and Sheridan."

The next day, through grueling work and sweat in country that was almost as rough as he'd seen over in the Badlands, Ben nodded with satisfaction as the tally man confirmed the count. "Three hundred seventy-four calves today. Sixty-eight mavericks, including that ancient longhorn bull."

Ben's eyes darted to Clark Terry. "Yeah, and that bull cost us one man. I'm afraid I'm going to have to send Clark back and make sure that arm of his gets set properly." He didn't even worry about the cost of the horse the bull had gored. It was only because they'd been working in teams that Clark wasn't killed by the enraged bull. After charging the horse and knocking the rider to the ground, the bull gored the horse five times, pitching him into the air with his horns, and then turned his attention to the downed rider. Ben and Twice had their rifles out and fired almost at the same instant. They had to roll the dead bull off the boy, and found that his upper arm had been broken, and jagged splinters of bone were sticking through the flesh. They got him back to the camp, and under Fred McCoy's supervision had done the best they could to set it. Both Fred and Clark insisted he'd be all right, but Ben didn't want to take any chances.

"There's a doctor in Powderville. If he shows any signs of fever, we're going to take him there. I've seen too many men crippled for life because there wasn't any doctor around."

While they were finishing supper, Cindy said, "Ben, what's gotten into Mike? He's getting mighty big for his britches lately."

"Some men change completely when they're on roundup. That's one of the reasons I don't like having you along. I sure don't have any idea what's happened to Mike, but as long as he keeps pulling his weight, I'll put up with almost anything."

She wiped her plate with the last of a biscuit, and stared thoughtfully across the valley. "He's been getting pretty chummy with Kenny again, too."

Ben's mind jerked to attention. "I haven't noticed."

"Well, I have. I thought the boy learned his lesson when he got drunk the first time. But since we've been out here, Mike seems to be dragging him off every chance he gets."

Then Ben noticed that Mike and Kenny were sitting off a ways by themselves, and as Mike was talking, Kenny was mending a torn shirt. His face was lit up, and he was paying close attention to every word Mike was saying.

A short while later he asked Muttonhead if he'd noticed anything going on between Mike and Kenny.

"Mostly I don't make it none of my business. Course, I did think it were kinda odd when they done finished their watch last night."

"What happened?"

"Waal, Miss Cindy 'n Cal relieved 'em, but 'stead a comin' in t' git some sleep, they done went down t' pay a visit t' that Dollar bunch back there. They uz gone mebbé half a hour afore they rides back. Shit, middle a the night's a queer time to start gettin' sociable on a roundup."

Ben filed that information into his mind with the rest, and decided it was time to have a talk with Dwyer. Kenny looked aside as Ben walked up.

"Mike, I hear you and Kenny made a call on the Dollar outfit last night."

Dwyer stood up, his dark face glaring. "What the

hell business is it of yours? We haven't missed any work, have we?"

"It's my business to know everything that goes on with my crew while we're on this job."

Kenny stood up, his fists clenching and unclenching. "Who the hell do you think you are, my mother or something?"

"Kid, any more talk like that and you're going to be looking for another job."

Dwyer took a step forward. "Leave the kid alone, Foster. You want to get rough, try me."

Ben didn't hesitate. He whirled and slammed his fist into Dwyer's face, and followed with a left to his chest. Kenny jumped in, swinging a boot that caught Ben in the ribs.

Ben grunted as he felt a rib crack, and the air rushed out of him. Dwyer staggered back, caught his balance and aimed a heavy right to Ben's face, knocking him to the side where he almost lost his balance.

Kenny tried to punch Ben while he was off-guard, but was grabbed by the back of his shirt and pulled off.

Cal Bradley, hanging onto the shirt, said, "You stay the hell out of it, Kenny."

"Lemme go!"

Twice Thompson said, "Boy, you got a lot t' learn."

Kenny struggled to free himself from Cal, and Twice said, "Sorry, kid," and laid a bony fist on the boy's jaw. Kenny slumped to the ground.

Dwyer rushed at Ben while he was still off balance, and they tumbled to the ground. This time, Ben had both arms free, and as Dwyer's rough fingers clamped down on Ben's neck, Ben pounded at Dwyer's ribs.

Slowly he could see things turning pink, then he began feeling dizzy as he fought for air. He clutched at the fingers on his neck, and wondered if he had enough strength to pull them away. He thought it strange to find himself being choked to death and thinking how much it was going to hurt to have to learn how to use wings with a broken rib.

Dwyer had powerful hands and arms, and Ben saw his face begin flashing from orange to red, and through the flickering lights he saw a boot swing, catching Dwyer behind the ear.

The air rushed back into his burning lungs, and he gulped in as much as he could in two breaths as he felt Dwyer's grip loosen. He pushed and rolled himself free, struggling to get to his feet.

"Who kicked him?" he asked, wobbling slightly.

"I did," Cindy said with pride.

"Who asked you to help?"

"Nobody. I just thought it was fair to give him what Kenny gave you."

"Hell, Ben," Cal said, "if I'd known she was gonna try it, I woulda held her back."

Dwyer was beginning to stir, and his hand felt the bloody lump rising behind his ear. Kenny was sitting up, rubbing his bruised jaw.

"Dwyer, pack your things and get out of this camp. Make sure all your stuff is out of the bunkhouse before we get back to the Rafter B."

"It'll be a pleasure."

"You kickin' me out, too?" Kenny asked defiantly.

"No I'm not. You stick around and watch your manners, that's all."

"Shove it," he said, getting to his feet. "I can find a better job."

"Fine. Take your gear and go. But it's a long walk back to the ranch, since you don't have a horse to your name."

Ben thought that might discourage him, but he stood erect and said, "Piss on you, Foster! I've got friends right over there." He pointed to the Dollar crew.

"More talk like that around a lady, and you'll wish you never heard of me, Kenny."

Kenny glanced furtively at Cindy, and then mumbled, "Sorry, Miss Cindy." Then he turned back to Ben. "I quit."

It took ten minutes for Mike and Kenny to pack their things, and with both of them on Sheridan, they rode the short distance north to the Dollar wagon.

"Ben," Fred said, "I think you'd better have a look at Clark."

"Think I'm going to have to take him to Powderville?"

"Yep. He needs something more than I can give him. Hell, I ain't no medicine man, just a blacksmith."

Clark was in agony. The pain-killers they carried in the medicine chest on the chuck wagon had worn off. Even a couple drinks of the rum Earl always kept in the chuck wagon ("strictly for medicinal purposes") had worn off. The boy's face was bathed in sweat. His arm had swollen almost to the thickness of his thigh, and was oozing pus and blood through the poultice and bandages."

"You think you can ride as far as Powderville, Clark?"

"I . . . I hope so, Ben. Sure sorry to be this much trouble."

"Muttonhead, get a couple of horses saddled up."

"We'll make it three," Cindy said. "It'll be easier to keep him in the saddle if he passes out."

Muttonhead and Cindy returned a few minutes later and helped Clark mount up. Twice was ready with three filled canteens, and they were slung on the saddlehorse.

With Ben on one side of Clark and Cindy on the other, they started the ride to Powderville at an easy gait. Every step of the hooves was reflected in the pain on the boy's face, and they stopped frequently to let him rest and bathe his face with some cool water.

"Gosh, I didn't want to trouble anybody."

"Don't worry about it, Clark," Cindy said. "It's not much farther."

He took a swallow of water, and said, "I'm gonna miss havin' Kenny around."

Ben nodded.

"He was kind of like a brother, you know what I mean?"

"Yeah, you two spent a lot of time together. I'm sorry he decided to quit."

"Yeah, but I guess he can make more money workin' with Mike." He winced with pain as they started forward again.

"How does he figure that?" Cindy asked.

"I dunno. He tried to explain it to me, but it didn't make much sense. It's like gettin' a better job takin' care of other people's cattle."

"You mean managing an outfit for someone?"

"I guess that's what you'd call it, Ben."

Ben had his doubts that Mike Dwyer would ever be hired as a manager for an investor, but strange things happen every day. Then he was snapped back to reality when Clark spoke through clenched teeth.

"Yeah, I guess it's about the same. Only not for one company. Taking care of a lot of people's beefs. Kinda like pasturin' them for a year. Sleepin' them somewhere is what he called it."

Ben heard Cindy draw in a sharp breath, and he felt a prickly feeling run up his back. Suddenly, a lot of things were beginning to make sense.

38

For the next two weeks they were so busy Ben and Cindy hardly had a chance to talk to each other. With three men off the crew, he was thankful now that he had Cindy's help, even though he only mentioned it once when they were coming back from taking Clark to Doc Tandy's in Powderville. More often than not, they spent two or three days in one place, which pleased Earl, but not the riders, for it meant that they had rugged country to work. There was a certain amount of pride and satisfaction in knowing that they were pulling in cattle that had been roaming free for years.

"If everybody else is having this kind of luck," Ben said one afternoon, "this ought to set some kind of record."

The big Swede thumbed through his frayed tally books. "Wonder where some of these animals came from? They sure ain't listed with the Montana or Wyoming Associations."

"How about those two old steers with Charlie Goodnight's JA?" Cindy said. "I can't imagine them being this far from home. Texas is a long way down there."

"Probably got mixed up with that last bunch the LU Bar brought up last year," Ben suggested. "They had what, about ten thousand head in that herd?"

The tally man flipped a few pages. "Twelve thousand beefs, and three hundred horses. That ain't countin' the thirty-two thousand Frenchy Wibaux added from Dakota and Oregon. Accordin' to these figures, more than a hundred thousand were brought in last year alone. And that ain't countin' the woolies and their sheep. It's no wonder our grass is gettin' short. There ain't no way you can keep addin' that many grass-eatin' critters every year and have enough feed to go around."

While Ben rode night watch on the herd, he wondered how long it would be before the range opened up in all-out warfare between the cattlemen and the sheepmen. All the signs showed it was coming, and it wasn't anything to look forward to.

He glanced up at the sky. It was certain there would be some rain before the night was over. Just before he'd gone on shift there had been a few drops, but hardly enough to settle the dust. The air was oppressively hot, and he was only too glad to be on watch rather than suffocating under a heavy tarpaulin to keep the mosquitos from eating him alive. The moon was obscured by dense clouds, and he hoped they'd get enough rain to keep the grass in good shape until they finished the roundup. There had been a three-week delay because of a dry Spring, and there had been no rain since. Without good grass in the valleys, it would be difficult to hold the cattle for branding.

The cattle were restless, and from the far side of

the herd he could hear Twice singing hymns to keep
them from getting jittery. Even Midnight was tense,
as though expecting trouble. Ben patted his neck
and muttered some soothing words.

Suddenly the night was shattered by a bolt of
lightning streaking down to earth, and the herd was
instantly on its feet and running, heading down the
valley toward the Dollar wagon. Shouts through the
two campgrounds were drowned out by the thundering hooves as the herd stampeded.

He spurred Midnight forward, awed as always by
the eerie sensation of the silent cattle. All that could
be heard was the clattering of horns and the hooves
thundering across the valley floor. Before they had
gone fifty yards, he could feel the characteristic heat,
almost feverish, that emanated from the stampeding
animals, and for some reason his mind brought up
two things. One was the claim Charlie Goodnight
made that stampeding cattle gave off enough heat
to blister the face of a rider on the lee side of the
herd, and the other was the fact that a steer could
run off fifty pounds of salable meat in a four-mile
stampede. Fifty pounds times a thousand animals
times eight cents a pound was four thousand dollars,
or a hell of a chunk out of the year's profits in a few
minutes. And if they stampeded several times before
getting to market, the cattlemen might wind up making more money cleaning box cars than selling cattle.

Midnight was gaining, and Ben looked across the
herd to see he was ahead of Twice by a hundred
yards or so. Whichever one got ahead of the herd
would attempt to cross in front of them, and the
two riders together would slowly and gradually point
the leaders off to the side, bending the herd back
until they got them running in a wide circle. By then,
the others from the camp would be moving up on
them, and gradually the herd would be worked into

a tighter circle, until they were milling again in a tight bunch.

His mind dragged out something else he'd heard and even seen on occasions, that a stampeding herd would move around anything in its way without slamming into it. Few cowboys ever cared to test that theory, though, and if caught afoot with the herd coming their way, would take refuge behind the chuck wagon, a stout tree or pile of rocks if at all possible. The first time Ben ever saw it, one of the crew had been squatting over a hole in the prairie with his trousers and long johns pulled down around his ankles—hoping the dose of castor oil the cook had given him would take care of his constipation—when the herd, which had been no more than a hundred yards from him, began to stampede straight toward him. He stayed in his squatting position, pulled his arms up over his head and prayed at the top of his voice. When the herd had passed, he was still there, still praying, but his prayers had changed to, "Thanks fer sparin' me, Lord, an' thanks fer curin' the constipaties."

The chuck wagon, however, had been knocked over and trampled. It was in such poor shape the crew kept the iron axles and fittings, and then used the rest of it for firewood.

Midnight put on an extra burst of speed, knowing what was required of him, and moved about fifteen feet ahead of the steers leading the herd, then began easing over to his right. When Ben saw Twice coming up, he and Midnight slowed slightly, allowing the steer behind them to move alongside, then began pushing him gradually to the left. At the right, Twice was now doing the same, and in a few minutes they had successfully pushed the lead animals around so they were almost doubled back on their path.

The five-minute race was tiring the cattle, and

most of the crew had caught up with the tail end
of the herd, working to the right to keep them turning to their left. After another ten minutes, they were
milling in a tight circle, tired and worn, and ready
to calm down again. Give them another hour, and
two or three riders would be able to control them
until morning when they began cutting and branding
again.

"I think we come out okay," Twice said later, building himself a cigarette. "Prob'ly lost a couple dozen
calves. Don't know about them other fellers, though."

They rode to the Dollar wagon, where the men
were standing around taking stock of things.

"Hello the camp!" Ben called from far off.

"Come on in, Foster," came the reply.

"Just seeing if you guys are all right."

The awning over the chuck wagon had disappeared,
snatched away by a horn and then trampled under
the hooves that swirled around it, but the crew had
all come through it, safe under the chuck wagon.

"Yeah, we're okay. Lost a horse that panicked and
stuck his foot in a chuck hole. How about you?"

"Nobody hurt."

Mike Dwyer sneered sarcastically, "I suppose you'd
give a damn if somebody here did get hurt."

"Might surprise you, Dwyer, but I don't like to
see anybody get hurt in a stampede, even if I don't
personally have any use for him."

The red-faced driver of the wagon, whom Ben had
supposed was the boss of the outfit, asked, "Any
chance you'd be willing to sell us a couple of horses?
We're really short now."

"Sure. Just come up to the Rafter B when the
roundup is over. I think we could find a few at a
fair price."

"Foster, we've got two men without ponies now,
and you've got more than you need."

"Think again. We've got a crew doing your work for you. You've got plenty of horses. Just put your extra men in the wagon and let 'em ride."

"Get the hell out of here, Foster!" Dwyer snapped.

As they neared the Rafter B wagon, Twice said, "If there be a good and just God up there, he'll give ol' Mike two things: a Waterbury watch, an' the seven-year itch. That way, when the son of a bitch ain't a-scratchin', he'll be a-windin'!"

When he finally got off watch, Ben unsaddled Midnight at the corral, then walked to the scrubby oak tree away from the main camp, where he had spread out his bedding. He'd finally given up sleeping anywhere near Muttonhead and Twice because of their snoring. He sat down on the grass, pulled off his boots and rolled a last cigarette, hoping the smoke would keep the mosquitos away. He took a few puffs before realizing the mosquitos were enjoying the Bull Durham almost as much as he was, and ground it into the soft earth. He flipped his hat up on the broken limb that served him as a hatstand and gunrack, and reached out to pull the tarp back.

He stopped, staring at his bedding. It wasn't smooth, but was filled with lumps.

His first thought was that Clark and Kenny had pulled another of their pranks on him by filling his blankets with manure, then remembered that neither of the boys had been around all night. Cautiously, he reached up, drew his revolver from the holster and had his thumb on the hammer when he snapped the tarpaulin back.

"Cindy!"

"I was afraid you'd never get here, Ben."

39

"How long are you going to sit there with that thing aimed in my face?"

He didn't know whether he felt foolish aiming his gun at her, or whether he was just plain angry. He slammed the revolver back into the holster, and said, "This is exactly what I was afraid of when you decided to come along."

She propped herself up on one elbow. "You don't have to be afraid of me."

"Damn it, I'm not afraid of you, Cindy. But this just isn't . . . well, it isn't the . . . damn it all, if anyone saw you come over here to wait for me, the talk would be all over the place, and it'd get to your dad, and . . . and that's another thing, when Charlie finds out you . . ."

She reached out and pulled his head down, kissing him hungrily and clutching him tightly to her.

He resisted at first, but gradually succumbed, and allowed himself to return her kisses. His hand found

273

her breast, full and firm under the chambray shirt, and he fumbled with a button.

"Don't you think you ought to get in out of the rain, Ben?"

He hadn't been aware that it had started to rain, but had thought the cool sensation on his back and shoulders was the excitement he was experiencing. Cindy held up a corner of the tarpaulin, and he crawled in beside her.

"Cindy, this is crazy."

"I don't care. I've been going crazy being so close to you and never being alone with you. Ben, can't you see? I'm in love, hopelessly in love with you."

Her hand was rubbing his groin, and he suddenly pushed it away.

"Cindy, there are days I can't think of anything but you, either, but what you're asking for is a lot more than somebody to give you a rubdown."

"Ben, I wasn't completely honest with you. My uncle raped me, not once or twice, but many times before my aunt caught him at it. I got so I didn't resist. And about a year after I got out here, a boy Dad had working for him caught me when I was out riding one day. It was ugly, dirty. Sneak it real fast out in the woods, and not even know what it was all about. I . . . I let him make love to me a second time, and he hurt me so much, that's when I really told myself I didn't ever want any part of loving a man again. I thought there was really something evil about me that every man who looked at me wanted to make love to me. But Ben, it's different with you. Can't you see I want you? I need you, I need the feel of your hands on me, I need you to hold me tight. Ben I want to make love to you so much it hurts. It's not just letting somebody make use of me; now I'm the one who wants it, and you're the only man I've ever known who's made me feel this way."

He rolled to her and kissed her, savoring the feel of her hair in his face. He unbuttoned her blouse, pushed it back and buried his face between her firm breasts while she pulled his head closer, then guided a nipple toward his mouth. His tongue began circling the hardening nipple, and he began sucking, gently at first, then harder as his passion grew to match hers.

While the rain beat down on the tarpaulin covering them, they slipped out of their jeans, and Cindy began stroking Dan's penis with both hands while her tongue flicked in and out of his ear.

Dan's fingers worked down her smooth, hard belly, finding the mound of pubic hair, moist with desire. He had the crazy notion of wanting to light a match to see if it was as red as the hair in his face. She squirmed, pushing herself against his fingers, her legs opening wide.

"Now, Ben, now!" she whispered, and guided him up on top of her.

As he rolled onto her, another trickle of cold water spilled down his back, heightening his excitement. He was rock hard as she guided the head of his strong penis into her, and pushed gently, then withdrew, then thrust home all the way. He paused, savoring the warmth and contentment he hadn't known for years.

"Oh, Ben, darling, don't stop, don't stop."

He began a slow, rhythmic pumping, surprising himself that he still had so much control. Gradually he increased the tempo, and when he heard Cindy gasping, her legs convulsively quivering against his, he allowed himself to let go and timed his orgasm to match hers. Again he saw the night shattered by streaks of lightning, knowing this time it was passion he was experiencing.

He gently rolled to his side, bringing her with him, and left his penis inside her. She stroked his face and kissed him, squeezing his manhood within her.

"Darling, I never had any idea it could be this wonderful. Why did we wait so long?"

"Some things just can't be hurried, Cindy. Any other time would have been too soon."

She kissed him again, hungrily, passionately, while he explored her back, her buttocks, her breasts. Sooner than he expected, he felt himself beginning to rise again.

"Oh, Ben, let's do it again," she whispered, then rolled up on top of him, still keeping his hardening penis clamped inside of her. The tarpaulin slipped off to one side, but neither of them cared.

She pulled her heels up, and began riding up and down as though in stirrups, while Ben's hands massaged her breasts, wiping off the rain that was beating down on them. Her orgasm came faster this time, and she was weak and limp when Ben put his hands under her buttocks and raised her a few inches while he thrust upwards savagely. By the time he had reached a climax, the tarpaulin was completely aside, and the blankets were soaking wet.

They lay exhausted, and he pulled the wet blankets and tarp back over them. As much as he wished it could last forever, he knew it couldn't.

"Cindy, you're going to have to get dressed and go before Earl starts moving around for breakfast."

"I know, but there's tomorrow night, my darling."

"Cindy, I've been wanting to tell you for a long time that I love you, but we can't have it this way. I want it to be after we've stood up and told everybody we love each, and we're married, not sneaking around under a smelly pile of blankets in the rain slappin' mosquitos off each other."

She stiffened, and he felt her push back a little.

"You don't want me to come back?"

"I do, damn it all, I do. But I want to remember

our making love to be something special, something pretty, something that's all bells and whistles and spangles and jangles. I want it to be . . ."

She sat up suddenly, and a river of water sloshed off the tarp onto his chest.

"Spangles and jangles and high button shoes and, most of all, a pretty little frilly dress! Well, Mr. Foster, you can just take your dirty little obsession with frilly clothes to one of the whores in town! That's something I can't bring myself to do."

"Cindy, wait!"

"I did wait, Mr. Foster. I waited. I lowered myself so far to get your attention it was like hitting a mule over the head with a club." She began pulling on her wet clothes. "And now you tell me that it shouldn't be like this. I didn't care how it was going to be, I thought I loved you, and I wanted you, no matter what. I'm just sorry I haven't been able to live up to what you want in a woman."

She stuffed her wet red hair up under her hat. "It just occurred to me that it's possible I could never take Eva's place. Now maybe I'll never know." She disappeared into the rain-drenched night.

When Ben woke after a few hours of troubled sleep, Earl told him she'd ridden back to the ranch about the time he was getting the coffee together.

40

THE summer of 1886 turned out to be one of the hottest, dryest summers anyone could remember. The roundup which had been delayed for weeks because of a lack of spring rains, lasted through six weeks of scorching sun and blistering heat that made many of the Texans wish they'd stayed home. Even the Mexican vaqueros who'd come up for the work agreed that it had been *calientito*, nice and warm. Smaller water holes and streams on higher ground dried up completely, and the herds of cattle that were usually moved back into the higher ground after the roundup stayed in the valleys, grazing closely the grass on what were normally winter ranges. Grass fires, common in late summer and fall, took a disastrous toll of grazing land, and the smoke hung heavy in the air for weeks at a time.

Fred McCoy looked up at the sky and asked, "Geese?"

Ben and Charlie craned their necks. "Yep."

"They're early."

Fred rubbed the flanks of Charlie's mount. "Real thick coat of fur. Charlie, you know what the old-time Cherokee says? When the birds go south in summer and the jackrabbits and deer put on long johns in fall, we're in for a bitch of a winter."

Charlie grinned. "Yeah, sounds like something a Cherokee might say. But your people came from Georgia and Tennessee. Weather's different here on the northern plains."

"Maybe the weather's different, but the animals are the same. They don't think about weather; the great god Asgaya Galunlati takes care of all his little animals, and gives them the clothing they need for the weather. So when little birds go south this early and jackrabbits and horses start wearing wooly britches, it's Asgaya Galunlati's way of saying, 'Hey, man, I'm sending you a real bitch of a winter.' Naturally, you couldn't expect a Sioux to put it that way, but I was talking with Tree Leans West yesterday, and he . . ."

"Who?"

"Tree Leans West, a Sioux scout at Fort McKeogh. You know what he said?" Fred rattled off a sing-song, clicking string of Sioux, and simply grinned when he was finished.

Charlie had spent years listening to Fred McCoy's proud recitation of a dozen different Indian tongues, and wisely kept his mouth shut. Ben had no idea what was coming, and took the bait.

"Translated into English, what does that mean?"

"Heap cold come."

As they rode along the Mizpah that afternoon, Charlie told Ben what he'd learned earlier in town.

"Miguel Sanchez got himself strung up a couple of days ago down in Wyoming. They caught him moving a mixed herd of cows with altered brands and close to a thousand unbranded yearlings back to the Hole-in-the-Wall country. Sanchez and two of his men graced a railroad bridge."

"Who were the others?"

"Sam Groot, used to work for the L Bar L. Nobody knows who the other one was. Oh, I know what you're thinking, Ben, but it wasn't Mike Dwyer or Jack Sully."

"I hope Kenny wakes up in time to see where he's heading. He's really a good kid."

"Was. Damn it, Ben, I liked the boy, too, but when a kid starts stealing cattle from the man who pays him, he's not a good kid any more. He's a thief, pure and simple."

"I'll buy that, Charlie, but I've still got the feeling that he honestly believed there wasn't anything wrong in sleeping a herd. He almost had Clark convinced it was an honest way to make a living."

"You can believe that if you want to, but I still think of him now as a common cattle thief."

"Okay, but I'd like to give anyone the benefit of the doubt. We don't know for sure. We don't even know for sure that Mike Dwyer ever stole so much as one head from anybody."

"There's an awful lot of evidence, Ben."

"Evidence of what kind? He spends more money than he earns as a cowhand. So what? If he'd managed to bank some money he made on even a halfway decent silver strike, he could be drawing it out little by little. Are people going to think I made a fortune rustling if I suddenly take ten thousand dollars out of my bank accounts to set up a string of horses? And Dwyer was seen receiving money from Sanchez and Sully. Who knows why? Sanchez got caught, but does that prove anything about Dwyer? Not a thing. Jack Sully lives on the reservation, and for years nobody's had a scrap of proof that he's stolen cattle. They've tried, but they've never proven anything. Sully laughs at them. And one morning I saw Dwyer talking with a couple of riders from another range. What does that prove? Nothing except that he was talking. We haven't seen him since the day after that stampede, and that doesn't prove anything, either."

"I'd still like to get my hands on him."

Ben grinned and Charlie saw a mischievous gleam in his blue eyes.

"I'd like to get my hands on him, too, Charlie, but I've got better things planned for him if I ever catch him rustling."

"I hope it's rope."

"Better than that. When I was at Mandan in the hide business, there was one old character they suspected of rustling, and when . . ."

They stopped and turned. Cindy was riding Bluebelle hard, the pacing mare covering ground like the wind.

"Ben, Old Four Eyes is at the house. Says he's got some good news for you."

Ben and Cindy exchanged a quick, furtive glance which didn't escape Charlie's notice. "Tell him I'll be there shortly. Ben and I are going to have a look in that little box canyon about two miles down."

Once more her eyes darted to Ben, but she didn't say a word as she wheeled about, nor did her face betray any emotion.

"What's happened to her?" Charlie asked. "You two haven't said much more than a howdy since the roundup finished."

"Maybe it's just that we don't have a lot to say, Charlie."

"Aah, don't try to hand me a lot of crap like that. Maybe what it is, is that you've got a lot to say to each other, but don't know how. I know I haven't been as close to her as a father should be to his only daughter, but I still know her pretty well. However you two manage to knock down the fence that's strung up between your ranges is your business, but I recognize the signs. You're going to be nosing up to the same feed bin for a long time."

"Maybe, Charlie," he replied without enthusiasm.

The canyon they rode into had been one of the best winter pastures on the Rafter B since Charlie Bowen first settled into the country. Stretched out beween steep, sheer cliffs on one side and rugged, deeply-cut and washed hills that were almost perpendicular on the other, the gently-rolling floor covered about three thousand acres. Two streams flowed through it on their way to the Mizpah, joining near the entrance to the canyon, and it was the only place on the Rafter B where Charlie would think of erecting a fence. The barbed wire fence that ran a hundred and fifty yards across the opening had been rolled up and laid aside. Normally, the canyon wouldn't be grazed until after the shovedown and the beef cut in late autumn.

This year, because of the lack of rain and the poor condition of grass in the higher ranges, Charlie was forced to allow his stock to graze here earlier, letting them find it on their own instead of being driven into it.

"Look at that," he commented sadly. "Two of the best spring-fed creeks on the place. One dry, the other just a trickle."

What should have been lush, green grass in the canyon was now dry, parched and scanty. A few hundred head of beefs were grazing near the creek that had some water in it, and Charlie and Ben rode closer.

"Uh, oh," Ben said suddenly, taking his rope from the saddlehorn and racing after a cow. Charlie joined him, and a few minutes later they were looking at the brand on the cow that had been roped and thrown.

"What do you make of it?" Ben asked.

"Son of a bitch! My Rafter B's been redrawn into a Diamond B."

"Sure has. Not too long ago, either. I'd say less than two weeks."

Before going back to the house, they found two more cows and three steers with altered brands.

Roosevelt was bustling with enthusiasm over the results of the roundup.

"By Jove! Over a million head! This roundup will go down in history as being the most memorable of all times. I tell you, Charles, this far exceeded everyone's expectations."

"Sure did," Charlie agreed. "From the figures Granville gave me, the Association's treasury got a pretty good boost, too. Some six thousand mavericks were added to the books."

"Bully for the Association! I can't tell you how deelighted I am with the course of events here. I'm seriously considering enlarging my holdings."

"That's interesting to hear," Charlie said, brightening. "I've been thinking of reducing my own. Let's give it some thought."

"Righto. Charles, what I really wanted to discuss with you was how you feel about having Helena become the capital city when Montana becomes a state."

"Makes more sense than Miles City or Great Falls. I could even see the capital at Butte. Joe Toole isn't as crazy as a lot of people would like to think."

"You're acquainted with Joseph Toole?"

"Sure, known him for years, ever since I first came out here. In fact, Joe financed my first herd for me."

"I didn't realize you were friends, Charles."

"Can't say we're friends, but we know each other pretty well. If he makes it to the governor's seat, he'll be favoring the mining interests while he lets the cattlemen shift for themselves. Even when the railroad came through, he made damned sure it reached the mines. The cattlemen had to adapt to the railroad. Down in Kansas and Texas, the railroads were laid out for the cattlemen first, and the mining corporations built their own spur lines if they wanted to ship ore. Joe Toole's got holdings in some of the biggest copper mines in the country, and do you think that if he's elected governor he's going to use his influence in favor of the cattlemen and the sheepmen? I have to admit that he's right about wanting to seat the state government at Helena. It isn't just because of his mines, though. I could probably name a dozen reasons why it's not a bad idea. It'd be a mistake to put the capital over here at Miles City. Miles City's a cow town, has always been a cow town, and always will be a cow town. Oh, don't think I haven't got a lot of people down on me already because I feel that way. Miles City is the home of the beef industry, but there's a hell of a lot more to Montana than beef."

"Do you think you could convince Granville?"

"If he thinks of it first. Trying to change that old bird's mind is about as easy as breeding steers, but I'll sure give it a try. Now, about those cattle . . ."

41

OCTOBER was cold, and the first snow came in early November. It wasn't much of a snowfall, but it was at least a month early. Unlike most first snows, it never melted.

The fall pushdown and beef cut had been unusually easy work, since there were few of the cattle in the high country. After the snow peppered the ground, the Rafter B crew split up into teams to scour the higher places to make sure the cattle were down on winter grazing land.

Charlie, Ben and Cindy worked a few stubborn beasts out of a gully and sent them packing to join a small bunch along the river, and continued south to the line shack below Twin Tables Butte. Charlie had been leading a pack horse to restock the larder in the shack, and they checked the supplies in the crates that served as a pantry.

Ben looked around, and said, "I think the same builder must have put up every line shack in the

country. Twelve by fourteen foot, logs chinked with
mud. One door, one window, sod roof and plank
floor. Two bunks with Montana feather beds, one table
with a broken leg wrapped in rawhide, a stack of yellow magazines Ben Franklin printed, and a calendar
hanging on the wall that's at least six years old."

"I provide better reading material," Charlie said
proudly. "Look." He pulled back a gunnysack covering a crate, and Ben saw stacks of books, along with
two or three years of Harper's Illustrated Weekly. "I
don't want anybody working for me to have to go
through what I did. First time I spent a winter out in
a line shack, my partner and I each took a couple of
books along. When we finished reading our own, we
swapped. Four times, I think, then we got to reading the labels on the cans. How many periods are
there on the Carnation Condensed Milk label?"

"Oh, Dad, does anybody really know?"

"Seventeen. When you get hungry for something to
read, you read anything that's written. Seventeen
periods. We memorized every label in the place and
made a contest out of it. Only time I lost was when Old
Rat-Nosed Ralph pulled out a can the rats had been
chewing on. Hell, we didn't have anything else to do
for days at a time."

Cindy and Ben stacked the canned goods on the
shelves, and checked the wood box outside. There was
enough wood to get someone started when he was
sent out at the beginning of winter, which was coming all too early this year.

Satisfied that the shack was ready for occupants,
they began moving back toward the ranch. As they
were passing the winter range in the canyon, Ben
asked, "How long since anybody's been in here?"

"Some of the boys were probably here last week.
Why?"

Ben pointed to tracks on the hard ground. "Somebody's been here since last night."

Tracks showed that two riders had gone into the canyon, and they followed them half a mile around the south rim, where they disappeared under the tracks of the cattle. They spread out and searched the ground for any other sign, and after ten minutes Cindy called, "Come here!"

They swung down and examined a cold fire. It didn't take much of a nose to tell it was a recent fire, and all indications were that it had been used to heat branding irons. One branch showed scorched spots where the irons had been rested while being heated.

Charlie took off his gloves, felt the wood, then snapped one of the charred ends.

"It's cold, but I'll bet every cow I have that somebody was working here today. Spread out and see if we can find out where they went. Those tracks came in here, but I couldn't see where they went out."

While they searched the canyon for more tracks, they found two more cows whose Rafter B brands had been changed to the Diamond B.

"Charlie, when we get back, let's not say anything about this to the rest of the crew."

"What are you talking about, Ben? If they've come up with anything, we sure want to know about it."

"Yeah, but they'll tell us if they find anything out of the ordinary. If anybody here is up to anything, let's not go advertising the fact we know what's going on."

"Ben, that's asinine," Cindy said. "There isn't anybody on our crew who'd do anything like this."

"That's what we thought before we found out about Kenny."

"Ben, are you suggesting that Clark . . . ?"

"I don't want to suggest anything about anybody. It

could be Clark, or it could even be Earl. We take it for granted that Earl gets up in the middle of the night to have breakfast ready. Maybe he stayed up all night, who knows? Muttonhead Jenkins is new this year, and I don't know what he's been up to during the three years he was gone. I wouldn't like to think it was him, or anyone else here. Hell, it could even be me, for all you know. You haven't been with me day and night, so you can't discount that. But the less we say about it, the less chance there is that whoever is doing this will find out we're on to him. Charlie, do you remember when we found the first one? The brand was a week or two old, but we found her right here in this pasture. Whoever is sneaking onto your place likes working here. Now, I don't know about you, but I'm getting anxious to take a little ride to-night, and be around here before the sun comes up."

Charlie thought it over, then said, "Fair enough. All three of us'll be here."

The thermometer hovered near zero when three shadowy figures slipped into the dark at four in the morning. Cindy and Charlie had dressed in the dark, and left the house silently, careful not to wake the old dogs curled up in a pile of straw under the steps. Charlie tapped twice on the door of the shanty that served as the foreman's house, and Ben stepped out, grim-faced and silent.

They roped their ponies as noiselessly as possible, saddled them, and led them a good distance from the spread at a walk before mounting, lest they betray their presence by the creaking of saddle leather.

Without a word they rode south along the Mizpah for twenty minutes, then came to a halt. The pale moonlight glistened on the light snow, and their breath hung heavy in the still air.

They walked their horses back into the trees, and

waited. Ben felt himself shivering despite the sheep-skin jacket and extra pair of woolen underwear he had pulled on. After ten minutes, he heard Cindy's teeth chattering, and wished he could hold her close to let her share his warmth.

Another twenty minutes passed, and Charlie said softly, "We'll feel like a bunch of frozen fools if we don't find anybody."

"I'd feel worse than that if we passed up an opportunity," Ben said, rubbing his hands together.

The sky was beginning to turn gray when they heard the sound of two horses coming down the river. Two riders dressed in black were cantering along the river, and cut up the slope across the wide bank toward the opening of the canyon half a mile away.

They let them enter the canyon before mounting, then slowly moved out into the open and started after their quarry. By the time they reached the opening to the canyon, the sky was almost light.

The two riders had gone to the same spot along the south wall, and were already laying a fire.

Charlie held up a hand.

"Let's unroll one strand of wire and stretch it as tight as we can. We can prop it up with a forked stick every forty or fifty yards."

"You don't think you're going to pen them up in there with one wire, do you?" Cindy asked.

Ben chuckled softly. "If they don't know it's there, it just might give them a little surprise."

Ben and Charley each took hold of one end of the pole through the roll of wre, then rode across the opening, paying it out behind them. Cindy followed, and in ten minutes they had jury-rigged the single strand of sharp-pointed wire. It sagged from its own weight, but was an average of four feet off the ground.

"Now," Charlie said, "let's go pay a visit to our guests."

Smoke from the fire was rising high into the still air. One of the men had a steer on his rope and was pulling it to the fire. They were totally unaware of the advance of Ben and the Bowens.

There was a startled shuffling of hooves from the herd, and suddenly they stampeded. The rider bringing the steer in to the fire was caught in the milling herd, and his horse pulled off its feet. Horse and rider disappeared beneath the hooves of the cattle.

The other man made a dash for his horse, and only the racing cattle kept Ben away from him. Charlie and Cindy had to press far back against the steep, rough side of the canyon to escape being caught up in the mad dash of the cattle.

Ben spurred forward, racing to get around the leader of the stampede, and could see the rider on the far side racing for the opening to the canyon.

Ben gritted his teeth, then turned around and managed to keep his horse between the wall and the outer edge of the herd, racing directly toward him. If his luck held, if he didn't get run down by the cattle, he'd make it to the opening before the other rider.

Suddenly the cattle were all behind him, and he had a clear run ahead. He spurred his horse mercilessly, and drew his Winchester from its scabbard.

Once the rider started his run down the dry creek bed, Ben whirled to a stop, hoping to get a clear shot at the oncoming man.

There was no doubt now. It was Mike Dwyer, and he was riding his big, long-legged roan gelding, Sheridan.

But Ben's luck petered out. When he spun around for a clear shot, his horse skidded on a patch of bare rock, and they tumbled to the ground.

Ben jumped to his feet, searching for his rifle. It had landed thirty feet away, and he sprinted for it. When he was halfway to it, Dwyer and Sheridan were on top of him, and Ben saw the horse rear up into the air, his forelegs slashing for the enemy on the ground.

"Damn you Foster!" Dwyer shouted. "We'll take care of you! Go get him, Sheridan!"

The horse plunged forward, and cut Ben off from the rifle. He looked over his shoulder just in time to see Sheridan plunging down, seeking him with his hooves.

He jumped to the side just as a shot rang out and something slammed into the side of his head, turning his world into an inky black void.

42

BEN saw himself sitting stark naked on a small block of ice, the cold wind whistling across his near-frozen body while it sandpapered him with coarse splinters of ice crystals and snow. There was a small, red-headed boy wearing a huge white Stetson standing next to him, pouring hot coffee down the side of his head.

"Ben!" commanded a gruff voice.

He turned, but could see nobody.

"Ben!" The voice reminded him of old Aeschylus, and he turned the other way, almost knocking the boy off his feet. The boy scowled at him, picked up his Stetson hat and jammed it onto his head, then resumed pouring the pot of coffee alongside his ear.

"Ben, are you all right?"

The gruff voice sounded like it was coming from the far end of a long chilly tunnel, and Ben squinted his eyes to see through the snow. His naked body shivered and shook, and he felt rough hands pushing him.

The side of his head burned like hell, and he turned to the boy and said, "Kid, if you don't cut that out, I'm going to belt you one in a minute!"

"Ben!" came the voice again, and now it sounded closer, but no more distinct.

"Dad, he's hurt! Bad!"

Ben turned to look at the boy again. He had a strangely familiar look, and his green eyes and red hair reminded him of someone he'd known a long time ago, and far away.

"He's coming around, gal."

Suddenly Ben came to, staring into the faces of Charlie and Cindy.

"Ben," Cindy cried, "are you all right?"

"Oooh, who's pouring coffee on my head?" He reached up and touched his left temple, and thought he was pounding himself with a hammer. His hand came away bloody.

"What happened?" he asked. He tried to sit up, and felt himself being sucked down through the long, icy tunnel again. He didn't want to repeat that experience, and allowed Cindy to lower him gently to the ground.

"This is going to hurt like hell," Charlie said, "but it'll stop the bleeding." He laid a poultice of warm cow manure on the side of Ben's head and tied it into place with a bandanna. Ben knew he wasn't pulling as hard as it seemed, although he felt like his head was being squeezed in a cider press.

"You're lucky," Cindy said. "I thought Mike's horse killed you when he slashed at you with a hoof."

"Dwyer!" Ben said, and tried to sit up again. Minute by minute his strength was coming back. "I think I can make it here for a couple of minutes. What happened to him? Did he get away?"

"Oh, he's just waiting for you to come around and watch his funeral," Charlie said. "Ain't he a pretty sight?"

Most of the Rafter B crew was there, just inside the opening to the canyon. Muttonhead had a noose around Dwyer's neck, and his hands and feet were securely tied.

"Where'd they come from?"

"Seems to me you ask a hell of a lot of stupid questions," Cindy said, her green eyes flashing. "That happens to be the bunch from the ranch."

"I can see that, but what are they doing here?"

"What the hell does it look like, Foster?" Dwyer spat defiantly. "They're getting ready to murder me."

"The defendant will maintain silence in the courtroom," Earl Howard intoned gravely, and slammed Dwyer in the face with a fourteen inch skillet. He tilted his bowler an inch forward, and wiped his free hand on his white apron.

"We'uns done got us lined up fer breakfuss," Muttonhead said, "an' when yuh didn't show up fer vittles, we done found yuh was gone."

"Seemed mighty odd you'd go out in the middle of the night," Cal said, "but we didn't have no trouble following your tracks."

"Didn't have to folly 'em all the way, neither," Jim Cooper said. "We heard them beefs stampedin' and just follyed our ears."

"Seen that sidewinder tryin' t' run you down, an' didn't dare take a shot at 'im while you was so close. But that ole hunk a Mormon buckskin you slung across there sure s'prised the hell outen his horse."

"Lovely sight," Fred McCoy stated, "lovely. Horse hit the wire and did a triple somersault. Old Mike thought he was a bird, flyin' through the air and flappin' his wings."

Ben shook his head gingerly, decided that wasn't such a good idea, then gently tried to get to his knees.

"Sit still, Ben," Cindy said.

"Yeah," Charlie agreed. "You got a front-row seat for the hanging."

"Murder, you mean," Dwyer said.

"Silence!" intoned Earl, and swung the pan again. The early morning air resounded with a dull clang.

"Dwyer," Charlie said, "we caught you red-handed. All you're going to get is what any cow thief gets, and that's about two feet less rope than it takes for your heels to reach the ground."

"Who was that with you, Dwyer?" Ben asked.

"Go ask him yourself."

"We tried," Cindy said, "but there wasn't enough left of him or his horse to tell us."

"Then you'll never know, will you?"

Earl was getting the pan ready for another swing, but Ben stopped him.

"You find his irons?"

"Yep," Charlie said. "A four-inch straight, a curve, and a blunt end. With a set of running irons like this a good artist can draw just about anything on the side of a cow. That's all the evidence we need. The unwritten law says anybody caught with running irons who's not with a roundup crew is guilty as hell of switching brands."

"I've got a better idea," Ben said. He was able to get to his feet, although for a moment he wished he hadn't.

"Don't bother suggesting we take him to Tom Irvine," Charlie spat. "That'll take too long."

"Yeah," Cal said, "let's get on with the party."

"No, wait," Ben said. "Over at Mandan they took care of one rustler, and ran him out of the country."

"What good would that do?" Charlie demanded. "He'd go somewhere else and be up to his old tricks. I'm tired of talking."

"Hold on, damn it!" Ben shouted at him, and felt

the side of his head throb. "Sooner or later the word's going to get out, and by the time Tom makes a full investigation of what happened, the whole Territory will know you strung up a rustler."

"I'd be glad to have anybody know it!"

"Really? Damn it, Charlie, think what it could do to your future. Sure, plenty of men have strung up rustlers, but name one who's ever been elected to any important office when people find out he took the law into his own hands. Charlie, they wouldn't elect you chairman of the sheep division of the Association if that got out."

"Well, what do you want me to do? Tip my hat to the son of a bitch and let him go?"

"No, we'll just give him a dose of his own medicine. Muttonhead, heat up those irons."

Dwyer blanched. "Foster, you wouldn't!"

"The hell I wouldn't."

"One fahr, comin' up!" Muttonhead and Earl hurriedly gathered an armload of dried limbs and put a match to them. In minutes, the fire was blazing, and the three running irons were shoved in.

"God damn you, Foster! No decent man would do something like this!"

"Tell you what, Dwyer. When we finish, if you think you've gotten a raw deal, just go complain to the sheriff. When he finds out who mistreated you, we'll let him know why. It'll be a pleasure to stand trial for assault, and we'll probably even be fined ten or twenty dollars apiece. But that'll be worth it to watch you hang legally. Or you can get your butt burned and get the hell out of Yellowstone country."

"Damn you!"

"Silence in the courtroom!" Earl swung the skillet again.

"Irons is just about dull cherry, Ben," Cal announced, holding them straight in the air.

"Good. Somebody get the pants off of him."

Willie Wooten and Clark Terry cut Dwyer's belt with a knife, and Fred and Charlie pulled his Levi's down around his boots.

"Better get them stinkin' woolies off 'im," Jim Cooper suggested. "Wouldn't want we should set 'im afire."

"Cindy, go take a walk."

"Oh no I won't, Dad. I'm setting in on this party."

"Damn it gal, can't you see we're undressin' him?"

"Hell, I've seen men without their britches on before, Dad. Go ahead, Clark."

Charlie stared open-mouthed at his daughter while Clark Terry hacked the woolen underwear from Dwyer's backside. Cal and Jim held him down the same way they would a steer; Cal sat on his head while Jim stepped on his leg.

"Rafter B on the right hip!"

Dwyer screamed as the burning iron sizzled into his flesh. Ben deftly traced the Rafter B brand, the stench of Dwyer's frying flesh filling his nostrils.

"What about the other side?" Charlie asked.

"Reckon the Dollar Fifty'd look good."

The irons came out of the fire again, and once more Dwyer let loose a scream as Willie Wooten did the honors.

"Reckon that's 'nuff, Ben?"

"One more thing," Cindy said. "Why not put the Association's vent brand on each shoulder?"

"Damn, gal, you play rough, don't you?" Charlie said, his round face filled with pride.

They stripped Dwyer of his jacket and shirt, cut the underwear the rest of the way off, and neatly traced the MLA brand with the vent bar through it on each shoulder. These were all straight lines, and the work went in a hurry.

"I think that's about got it," Charlie said, his face a mask of pleasure.

"One thing left," Ben said. "He can cover up the brands with a shirt and a pair of pants, but it's harder to cover an ear notch."

"You think like a Cherokee," Fred said with a smile, and deftly cropped Dwyer's right ear, then put two notches in the left. He stood back to admire his handiwork. "Maybe we could turn him into a steer, huh?"

That idea met with almost unanimous consent, but Cindy vetoed it.

"No, that won't be necessary, Fred." She studied Dwyer's naked body. "He can't do any harm with that little thing."

Dwyer groaned.

The men howled with laughter at Cindy's withering insult, and she said, "If court is adjourned, I could use some breakfast. Think you could fix us something at this late an hour, Earl?"

"Now that you mention it, I believe the bacon's still on the fire. Oh well, nobody's perfect."

Clark cut the ropes binding Dwyer's hand and feet, and they mounted up.

"You can't leave me here like this," Dwyer groaned.

"I'll change you to a steer," Fred said, drawing his razor-sharp knife.

"I don't have a horse, damn it!"

"Go steal one. You've had some experience along those lines," Ben said.

Muttonhead dipped the hot irons into the stream, then bundled them onto his saddle.

"Reckon yuh might hafta git 'nuther set a tools."

They were within sight of the spread when Charlie turned in the saddle and said, "What do you mean you've seen men without their britches before? What's been going on behind my back? Damn it, gal, tell me." His voice wasn't harsh, just pleading.

"Let me have breakfast first, Dad, then we can sit down and have a long talk, okay?"

"Well, okay, but . . ."

"Then it'll be my turn," Ben said. "We've got some talking to do ourselves."

"About what?"

"Oh, tearing down a fence or two."

"Fences? Ben Foster, that kick on the head left you crazy. What fences are you talking about?"

Charlie grinned. "Damn it, gal, for once just shut up and listen when Ben tells you something."

She gave Charlie a startled look, then glanced at the resolute look on Ben's face.

"Yes, Dad."

43

It was noon by the time Cindy and Charlie finished their talk, and Charlie hollered out to the cook shack. Earl brought the dinner in, and when the rest of the crew had filed in and taken their places around the table, Charlie announced, "I've got something to tell you. This is the last day Ben Foster will be foreman here."

Cindy looked shocked, but no more so than anyone else crowded into the kitchen.

"Dad, you can't fire him because of . . ."

"Nobody fired me, Cindy. I quit."

"You quit? Why?"

"He quit because I quit," Charlie said. "Old Four Eyes is coming over here this afternoon to make arrangements to buy every head of beef on the place. The Rafter B is going out of the cattle business."

Shocked faces looked at each other in disbelief.

"Nobody's going to be out of work, though. Ben and I have just about wrapped up all the details of turning the Rafter B into the best horse-breeding ranch in the Yellowstone. We'll have all the details worked out pretty soon. In the meantime, I'd like all of you to stay on, and by Spring you can decide whether you want to stick with us or go someplace else. We'll think about a foreman later."

"Y' mean I ain't gonna hafta spend no time up in the line shack this winter?" Jim Cooper asked incredulously.

"That's right. For all we care, you can go down to New Orleans with Earl for the winter, and you'll still draw full pay. Anyone who wants to stick around to look after things will draw double pay. Oh, and you've each got a hundred dollar bonus coming."

This was met with resounding cheers, and Ben and Charlie knew they'd still have a dependable crew when the winter was over.

Fred McCoy smiled broadly. "I think I'll go down to Brownsville. This is going to be a bitch of a winter. This morning I saw one of those big Arctic owls, and it isn't even December. Besides, it'll be good to see my father again. He's gettin' up in years."

Even Charlie dropped his jaw. "Your father? Fred, You're . . . I mean, I didn't think . . ."

The old Indian smiled. "You thought I was so old my father couldn't be on the face of the earth, huh? Us Cherokee are pretty rugged people, Charlie. I was just a young warrior when I fought with Chicken Snake Jackson."

"But, Fred even if you were only ten or twelve, that'd make you eighty-five, eighty-seven now. And your father . . ."

"I've seen eighty-eight snows, Charlie. My father will see his hundred and fourth this year."

"Wow!" Clark Terry said. "I didn't think anybody lived that long."

"Most white men don't," Fred said proudly. 'My

people know that if you live well, you live long. My father works on a big ranch near Brownsville."

"He's still working?"

"Hell yes, he's working," Fred said disgustedly. "How else would he be able to support my grandmother?"

Charlie suggested that maybe a spot of rum would be fitting to toast the occasion, and they finished a long, leisurely meal with what precious little was left of Earl's keg.

"You'll need to get more to finish the fruit cakes, Charlie," he reminded him.

"Seems we run out every year about this time, don't we?"

"It must evaporate," Earl said.

After the rest had left, Cindy asked, "All right, Ben, what is it we need to talk about?"

"Just one thing. After your dad finishes transferring the title to his stock to Roosevelt, we're going to take a trip to St. Paul."

"St. Paul! Why St. Paul, for God's sake? Really, that kick on the head's beginning to get to you."

"You and Charlie and I are going to St. Paul because we need to see someone about some brood mares. And you're going along to spend some time with a good dressmaker, and get fitted for some decent clothes."

"You're out of your mind," she said, glancing at her father and feeling trapped.

"You think so, huh? Well, I'm not. You're going to wash your pretty little neck and learn to wear some stylish dresses, and you're going to learn how to carry a parasol and wear some jewelry and sweet-smelling perfume, because I'm going to marry you, and I've always had my mind set on a frilly woman, that's why."

"Oh, no! You just quit a job, and you expect me to marry you under those terms?"

"Gal, I told you to shut up and listen." Charlie's face was beaming. "You are going to start looking like the pretty woman you are. I don't care if you like it or not, you're going to do it."

"I'm not!"

"The hell you're not!" he boomed. "I made up my mind to get out of the cattle business because for the next couple of years I'm going to be too busy to stick around here and run the ranch. And Ben isn't going to be here, either. He's going to be traveling with me, and I'm going to be shaking every hand and going to every party I can manage to get into, because I've decided I'm going to run for Governor of the State of Montana, and Ben has agreed to be my campaign manager."

"Dad!" she said, her face bright and happy. "You're really going to do it?"

"I'm not going to let Joe Toole just walk in and take that office without a fight. And I'm not going to have people think my campaign manager doesn't have a wife who's every bit as civilized as Nellie Wibaux or Augusta Kohrs, even if I don't have a daughter like that. Now I've got some paper work to take care of before Four Eyes gets here. Why don't you two go take a ride or something?"

She threw her arms around her father, and said, "Dad, I think you were right this morning. Maybe I should have come to you long ago and listened to you."

She kissed him on his bald head, and he grunted, "Yeah, maybe you should've."

"Come on, Cindy," Ben said. "Let's go take a look at that filly you've been wanting for so long. She's yours."

"Oh, Ben, how could you put up with me for so long? I must have driven you up a tree."

"I told you, you purely vexed me."

"And you two are vexing the hell out of me," Charlie shouted from his desk. "Git!"

He looked up with a pleased smile as they walked out into the sunlight.